THE MYSTERY
OF THE
HIDDEN FORTUNE

Totally gripping cozy private detective fiction

Book #1 in the Quentin Cadbury Investigations

Christine McHaines

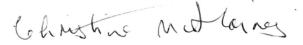

THE BOOK FOLKS

Published by The Book Folks

London, 2023

ISBN 978-1-80462-094-6

www.thebookfolks.com

Prologue

The car slowed and came to a halt a few yards before the barrier. The driver's careful calculation – that embarkation of the last ferry of the day would be less controlled – had been wrong. Border officials had stopped a vehicle in a parallel line and its occupants were getting out. Hemmed in by cars behind and a line of vehicles either side, it was difficult for the driver to manoeuvre his way out without attracting attention. In the seconds it took to decide what to do, a uniformed officer waved him forward. Sweat beaded on his forehead and upper lip as he eased the 1950s Mercedes Benz up to the barrier, praying that he would be allowed to go straight through. The officer put out an arm, indicating for him to pull to the side, and he cursed.

'Please to get out of the car.' The border controller spoke in heavily accented English.

The driver climbed out and stood aside, watching as the officer lifted out a small suitcase from the back seat and handed it to a female colleague. Then, in the light from the terminal and with the aid of a powerful torch, he inspected the interior – prodding and shifting the seats, running his hands along the side panels, opening the glove compartment, removing the mats. After examining the wheel arches and sweeping the beam of the torch along the underside, he opened the boot.

The erratic beat of the driver's heart pounded in his ears and his mouth dried as the official prised up the floor covering of the boot and shone the torch around. He had made this journey often but this was the first time he'd been searched. Border controls here seemed more thorough than in the UK. Or perhaps this wasn't a random search. Perhaps they were looking for something specific.

A tip-off? He kept his expression calm and his manner confident. Inside, his guts gurgled and his stomach seemed to have a mind of its own. Desperate to distract the border controller, he feigned a coughing fit and lurched forward, knocking into the man and sending the torch beam upwards. The fake cough became real, and when he recovered, he saw the boot had been closed. He almost fainted with relief. The specially fitted panel was well camouflaged but it had been a close-run thing.

'Please to come with me,' the border official said, pointing to the terminal building.

The driver followed him inside, where he saw his suitcase being put through a scanner. As though she thought human eyes were better than electronic ones, the female border officer opened the case and searched through it. The male officer led the driver into a small room, where he too was subjected to a search. After answering a barrage of questions, he was allowed to leave.

A faint smile of satisfaction showed on the driver's face as he drove the Mercedes onto the ferry. Yet even after the adrenaline rush subsided, his head swam and his heart beat more erratically than before. When at last the ferry sailed out of the harbour, he wondered if he would ever make this journey again.

Chapter One

April 2005

Quentin Cadbury felt like a sardine, wedged in a can with others of varying shapes and sizes. An animated cheer engulfed him as he stood squashed against the metal barrier, clapping and shouting as swathes of runners came past. His waving hand was one in a sea of arms and his vocal encouragement was lost in the eruption of voices that fractured the warm April air. He turned when, collectively, the watching crowd veered to gaze after the leaders as they pushed on towards the Cutty Sark, the National Maritime Museum's historic ship, before carrying on to Deptford and finally crossing the Thames.

Wave after wave of participants came by, some disappearing with incredible speed, others pacing themselves, a few only walking, all with a mask of determination pasted onto their faces. Nearly at the six-mile marker and some of them hadn't even broken a sweat. Quentin envied their fitness. Next year, he vowed silently, he would be amongst those runners competing in London's prestigious twenty-six-mile marathon, though he'd have to do some serious training first.

In today's crush he almost didn't feel the hand slip into his jacket pocket. He thought at first it was someone being pushed against him, their hand trapped on his hip and unable to move. But the hand did move, and Quentin swivelled his head far enough to see his house keys being drawn from his pocket by chunky fingers.

'Hey!' he cried, trying to twist round and grab hold of the perpetrator.

The hand was jerked away, the keys in its grasp. The crowd behind made a quick getaway impossible, and Quentin gasped in disbelief as the thief shoved the woman next to him roughly aside and vaulted the barrier. In seconds, the stocky male figure had joined the stream of people running past.

Quentin, momentarily paralysed by what had happened, recovered and climbed over the barrier, sprinting ahead while trying to locate the pickpocket. His height was an advantage, and he caught sight of the man, conspicuous in a black anorak amid an ocean of T-shirts and vest tops. For such a thickset person the thief was weaving through the participants surprisingly fast. Quentin was soon panting with exertion. Pure strength of will spurred him on. He was almost on the man when he looked round, spotted Quentin, then tripped on a discarded water bottle. He put his hands out to save himself, dropping the keys as he did so. Quentin spurted forward, his arm outstretched. He bent to scoop up the fallen keys just as another runner teetered sideways, his foot coming down on Quentin's hand. When the foot lifted Quentin swept up the keys with bruised fingers, gasping for breath and grimacing at the stitch in his side. When he straightened up there was no sign of the thief.

While he stood trying to regain his breath, someone in a full Womble costume, carrying a charity fund-raising bucket, shuffled past him. Bloody hell, he thought. Overtaken by a Womble!

After navigating his way to the side of the road he pushed his way through the throng and made his way slowly home. The incident had unsettled him. The marathon was the first big event he'd attended since moving to London and it had been tainted. Bloody pickpockets, he thought angrily, still exhausted by the chase. He was unfit, he realized. It was time he did some regular exercise.

He carried on through the Greenwich streets until he reached his house. Pleased to be home, he unlocked the door, went in, switched on the TV and plumped onto the settee. He'd watch the rest of the marathon in comfort.

Living alone still felt strange to him. He knew he was lucky to be here, in this small but pleasant house, at virtually no cost, lucky to be able to live as he wished, beholden to no one and with no outside pressures. So different from the way he had been living in Oxford with his parents only nine months ago. Turning down the volume on the TV, he fought to remember when his life had changed, what had brought him here to Greenwich. Early last year? Yes, that day he'd overheard the row between his parents. His parents…

* * *

His ears had burned when he'd heard them arguing.

'You're too hard on the boy, Herbert.' His mother's voice was soft but firm, and he imagined her standing in front of his father, small and pale, her mouth set in a stubborn line as it always was when she was defending him.

'Too hard! Not hard enough.' His father's growl came through the doorway. He sounds how he looks, Quentin thought. Like a bear.

The growl grew louder. 'And he's not a boy. He's twenty-four, Rosemary, and what's he achieved? Nothing! Dropped out of university, had umpteen different jobs–'

Rosemary Cadbury's voice rose slightly. 'Oh, let him alone, can't you? Young people often take a few years to settle down these days. It's not like it was in our day, Herbert. Things are different now. Jobs are hard to come by, and he doesn't have to be a lawyer if he doesn't want to. He can turn his hand to anything if he puts his mind to it.'

'He hasn't put his mind to anything yet, has he?' Herbert Cadbury bellowed. 'It's no good looking at me like that, Rosemary. I'm not supporting him anymore. He's old enough to earn his own living like everyone else.'

'But he's not everyone else. He's our son.'

Quentin peered through the gap between the door and the frame. His father's face had turned beetroot and his heavy eyebrows were drawn into a frown as he glowered at his wife. He opened his mouth, then seemed to check himself before closing it again.

'Thank God we've got Shelagh,' he croaked. 'At least she's made something of herself.'

Quentin flinched at the reference to his sister's achievements. He'd always admired Shelagh, loved her, but his father's critical comparisons stung every time.

'I've made my mind up,' his father was saying. 'I'm not spending my retirement bailing Quentin out. Shelagh's asked us to go out there to live, and we're going. You want to see your grandson grow up, don't you?'

'Of course I do, but I'd like to see Quentin settled first. Anyway, he might want to come with us.'

'Come with us? And do what? No. It'll do him good to be on his own. It's time he stood on his own feet.'

'You make him sound like a monster. He's a lovely person with a kind heart.'

His father's snort of disgust made Quentin cringe. 'Kind won't keep him for the rest of his life, will it? He needs money. He can't keep relying on other people.'

Rounding on him, his mother came into view. Her greying hair was streaked across her forehead, and her fingers tugged at the collar on her blouse. 'You're not being fair. It's not as if he never works, and he's very generous when he's got money. He pays his way, when he can.'

'And when he can't, someone else pays for him. I don't know how he does it.'

A smile touched Rosemary's lips, lightening her worried expression. 'Well, he's charming, and good-looking. He's my boy,' she added softly, turning away.

His father banged his fist down on the table. 'For goodness' sake, Rosemary,' he shouted, 'he's a man. And we're going to Australia, so that's the end of it. Now don't start blubbing. It'll be for the best, for us and for him. He'll never learn to support himself if we keep propping him up.'

Quentin's hackles rose as Rosemary suppressed a sob. He'd heard his parents quarrel over him before, but he'd never heard his mother cry. Not like this. Hating to see her so upset, he slammed the door open, strode over and stood between them.

'Don't shout at Mum like that,' he said, putting a protective arm around her and glaring at his father. 'You've made her cry.'

'It's you that's made her cry, not me. I'm just pointing out some home truths. You shouldn't be here listening to this – that's the problem. Get out, get a job and get a life instead of idling your time away at my expense.'

'Just because I don't want to do what you want me to do doesn't mean—' Quentin began, then stopped, seeing the anxiety on his mother's face. As on so many previous occasions, he reined in his anger. 'You know why I left uni…' he muttered.

'Huh!' Herbert Cadbury's face darkened even further. With his shoulders rigid and chest puffed out in military style, he looked as though he might explode. 'Just because your friend died doesn't mean you have to give up living too. A stretch in the army would do you good, harden you up. I've seen people die. You just have to get over it and put it behind you.'

Quentin's anger flared. Get over finding his best friend dead? Curling his hands into balls he swung round towards his father, stopped only by his mother springing between them.

'Quentin, leave it, please,' she begged, tears streaming down her cheeks. 'Don't be so insensitive, Herbert.'

Herbert. Even in his agitated state, Quentin thought how outdated it sounded, like a name from another era. His mother was right. It wasn't worth pursuing and it wouldn't bring Nathan back.

Turning to his mother, he edged her away from his father. 'Don't cry, Mum. You should go and be with Shelagh. I'll come out and visit when I can.'

'Oh Quentin!' Her arms wound around his neck, and he felt her tears on his shoulder. 'I'll worry about you so.'

His anger subsiding, a strange feeling came over Quentin. They were serious about going. His mother had stood up for him, as she always did, but she would go, otherwise she wouldn't be crying like this.

He felt her tremble in his arms. 'How will you manage?' she whispered.

How will I? he thought, alarmed at the idea of fending for himself.

'I'll be fine,' he said, sounding more cheerful than he felt. 'You know me. I always fall on my feet.'

'Quite so,' his father barked, and Quentin thought again that he would have been more at home in the nineteenth century instead of the twenty-first.

'Anyway, my lad, we're not leaving you destitute. You'll have a roof over your head.'

Quentin's heart leapt. They were leaving him the house? He glanced over his mother's shoulder at the mahogany mantelpiece, laden with fine porcelain, and the Regency-style sideboard and chairs that had made this place home for twenty-four years.

'No, we wouldn't leave you homeless.' Rosemary sniffed as she pulled away. 'We'll have to sell this place, of course, but there's your aunt Josie's place in Greenwich.'

'Aunt Josie?' Quentin frowned, remembering his mother's sister who had died the year before. 'I know she left the house to you, Mum, but I thought you were planning to sell it.'

Giving him a watery smile, Rosemary said, 'We were, but now—'

'We're letting you live there for as long as you like,' his father interrupted. 'Rent-free. Not that you deserve it—'

'Herbert!'

'Be quiet, Rosemary. The place is yours to come and go as you please. All you have to do is cover the bills.'

'Oh. That's very generous of you,' Quentin said, relieved that at least he didn't have to go house-hunting. The idea of leaving a quiet Oxford suburb for London filled him with excitement tinged with apprehension.

'You'll be responsible for keeping it up together,' his father went on. 'General maintenance and so forth. I don't expect you to look to us for any repairs. We'll be back every few years to see how you're doing. If we can't make it, I'm sure your uncle Rupert will keep us informed.'

The words reverberated in Quentin's head. *Keep us informed.* Checking up on him from over ten thousand miles away. Quentin had no doubt that Rupert, his father's brother, would see it as his duty to keep an eye on him if he was asked to.

'If you look after the place maybe we'll let you stay there indefinitely, but you've got to earn it…' His father glanced over to where his wife stood staring at him. 'Of course, it's up to your mother,' he blustered. 'It's her property. You'll be answerable to her if anything goes wrong, so it's up to you to keep your nose clean when we're not here to wipe it for you.'

This brought a fresh bout of tears from Quentin's mother. 'Shut up, Herbert.' Turning to Quentin, she said, 'It's a nice little house, plenty big enough for one. You know, Quentin, you've been there enough times.'

'Not for ages,' Quentin said, dredging his memory for the last time he'd been to a family gathering at Aunt Josie's.

He pictured the quiet Greenwich side street with its two-up-two-down terraced houses, just off the main road leading up to the entrance of Greenwich Park. He remembered the house as small but cosy, with a tiny, railed forecourt at the front.

'Well, it hasn't changed much,' his mother said. Casting a defiant glance at his father, she went on, 'It'll suit you down to the ground. Anyway, I've got faith in you, and I'm sure you'll be all right, but I'll miss you so.'

'I'll miss you too,' he said, meaning it. His father's caustic comments echoed in his head. He'll never change, he thought. I pity the poor sods he used to boss about in the army.

For once though, his usual flippancy failed to lift his spirits. They weren't joking, or trying to frighten him into getting a job. They were abandoning him.

Chapter Two

'You're leaving us?' The man sitting across the desk from Quentin looked surprised. His bushy brows drew together, making an unbroken line above his eyes.

In the week since the London marathon Quentin had made the decision to quit his job.

It was the first time he'd given his notice in since moving to Greenwich, but he knew what to say.

'But why?' the man he was speaking to asked. 'We've just offered to fund you if you want to finish your law degree.'

Quentin tried to look apologetic. 'I know, Mr Sackville, and I'm grateful.'

'So why are you leaving? Is it the money?'

Poor old Sackville, Quentin thought. Of course it's the money. Why else does anyone go to work?

'No,' he said, 'it's my Aunt Josie. She's ill, and there's no one else to look after her.'

Hugh Sackville's eyebrows moved up a little, like a caterpillar crawling across his forehead.

'My parents are in Australia,' Quentin went on. 'She's got no children, so it's down to me.'

'Very noble, I'm sure, but you can't throw your chances away on an elderly aunt. Surely there are carers you can get?'

'Oh, I couldn't do that, Mr Sackville. Aunt Josie's my godmother, and she's been very good to me.' Really good, Quentin thought, thinking of the house he now called home.

Trying not to overdo the concerned nephew approach, he said, 'She has good times and bad. When she has a good patch, I can go out, work and everything, but when she's bad—'

'What's wrong with her?'

Quentin was beginning to wish he'd said he'd got another job instead of using Aunt Josie as a reason to leave. He fingered the heart-shaped mole just below his right ear while he considered his answer.

'Arthritis. Rheumatoid arthritis.' It wasn't a lie. Aunt Josie had had rheumatoid arthritis, although she hadn't died from that.

Quentin looked at his boss as a sigh of resignation, or possibly irritation, escaped him. The eyebrows had dropped back into place, losing their caterpillar effect. 'That's a nasty thing. Well, we'll miss your cheerful smile, Quentin.'

A prick of conscience made Quentin shift in his seat. He had a genuine respect for old Sackville, even if he wasn't begging him to stay, but being an assistant in a solicitor's office bored him.

'Thank you, Mr Sackville. I appreciate that. I'll work my notice, but I've got a few days holiday due so I'll be leaving at the end of May.' Just in time for the summer weather, he realized. Ideal for pushing elderly aunts out in their wheelchairs.

'Right. Well, good luck, Quentin. I hope your aunt won't be too much of a burden to you.'

'Thank you, Mr Sackville. It's been a pleasure to work for you.'

The caterpillar appeared again, wriggling on the florid forehead. Hugh Sackville shook Quentin's hand, then turned his attention to a file on his desk, signalling that the conversation was over.

Quentin, hot and uncomfortable, went back to his desk. He'd left many jobs, but that was when he'd had his parents to fall back on. Now he was on his own he had to be more careful. Money, he'd come to realize, didn't grow on trees, but he had enough to see him through the next few months and that's all he needed. He'd worry about the future when it ran out.

He'd decided years ago that working was a mug's game. Make the most of life was his motto, especially after Nathan... How did he know his life wouldn't be cut short like his? He planned to work only when he had to. He wasn't lazy. He cooked, kept house, helped old ladies with their shopping and charmed the pants off everyone he came into contact with.

So, he thought, as he left the office that evening, in three weeks I'll be free again.

* * *

'Oh, Quentin, you're not leaving!' Louise from reception said that evening as he was heading out of the office. 'You can't go. I won't let you. We haven't even been out for that drink you keep promising me.'

It was true, he hadn't taken Louise for a drink. Not because he didn't like her – her bubbly personality often lit up his day – but because he didn't want to mislead her. He was too young to get involved and tied down. At least that's what he told himself.

'I'm sorry, Louise, you are one of the few things I'll miss about this place but I just need a clean break to take care of my aunt,' Quentin said, continuing his lie but feeling horrid now he was spinning the yarn to Louise rather than Mr Sackville. Her eyes broke from his gaze and she grabbed a pencil and started scribbling on a pad.

'My mobile number,' she said pushing it over the counter between them, 'in case you change your mind.'

Quentin smiled at her, took her number, blew her a kiss and, without a word, walked away.

'What an idiot,' he berated himself once he was outside. It was six o'clock on a Friday night and instead of taking Louise out he was going back to an empty house. To settle his thoughts he decided to walk home. It was an hour away, but what else did he have to do tonight?

* * *

As soon as he opened his front door, he knew something was wrong. There was an unfamiliar shape in the dim hallway, and the pungent smell of sardines wafted from the kitchen. Heart thumping, he snapped on the light, half expecting to see a burglar helping himself to his belongings; but it seemed whoever had been there was gone. The layout of the house, two rooms knocked into one with a bathroom and kitchen added on downstairs, and two bedrooms upstairs, made it easy to check the whole house. He groaned at the disarray as he went from room to room, stepping over overturned furniture and books, clothes and papers strewn across the floor.

In the lounge, he was amazed to see the TV and DVD player still in place, apparently untouched, although the cabinet that housed them stood askew, as though someone had searched behind it. His new running machine, bought after the marathon incident, looked as though it had been moved a couple of inches, but whoever had been there had obviously decided it was too bulky and heavy to move any further. Every picture had been taken off the wall, their frames broken and their backs ripped off. Some of the books were open, as though they had been thumbed through or shaken, and Quentin was dismayed to see pages of his detective novels crumpled or torn. One of the three photographs he'd put up lay face-up on the floor, the image distorted by fractured glass, while the others had been taken from their frames and the pictures torn in the process.

'Bloody hell!' he spluttered in the bedroom when he saw drawers on the floor, their contents spilled everywhere.

The duvet, pillows and sheet had been ripped from the mattress, which lay sideways on with one half reaching the floor, showing several long cuts where the foam oozed through. From the doorway of the smaller second bedroom he glanced over to the computer desk in the corner. His laptop was still there, although the stationery box alongside it had been rifled through. Why would a burglar leave a laptop behind? Or the DVD and CD player? Isn't that what kids stole these days?

A noise from downstairs made him start. They were still here! But he'd checked every room and seen no one. Perhaps they'd been hiding and were making their escape through the kitchen. He'd noticed that the back door was open, but he hadn't stopped to close it. Arming himself with the first thing that came to hand – the detachable metal tube from the vacuum cleaner on the landing – he crept down the stairs. Gripping his weapon he took a step towards the kitchen, noticing the lid of the upturned laundry basket too late. In an effort to avoid tripping over it, he stumbled and fell headlong against the wall, the metal tube clattering onto the tiles and rolling against the skirting board. He recovered just in time to see a black and white cat spring from the waste bin to the door and out into the garden.

Rubbing his forehead, Quentin walked into the kitchen. The cat was gone, but a look at the floor told him what it had been after. The contents of the bin were spread across the tiles, and among them was the sardine tin he'd opened yesterday. The cat must have smelt the fish and taken the chance to come through the open door and ransack the bin. A feline opportunist, he thought. But an opportunist hadn't made this mess.

The back door had been forced. He could see splintered wood around the lock, as though a chisel or screwdriver had been driven into it. The place had been targeted; he was sure. But if it had, why hadn't they taken anything? As far as he could see, nothing was missing.

He wondered if other homes in the area had been broken into. Perhaps he should check with his neighbours, ask if they had seen or heard anything. The houses here were terraced in the late nineteenth-, early twentieth-century style, sturdily built in brick. Quentin had rarely heard any sound from the houses either side of him. Gazing through the window into the garden he could see little in the failing light, but he realized how easy it would be for someone to climb the back wall from the alley that ran behind the row of gardens.

A mixture of anger and fear settled on him. How dare anyone come into his house and turn it upside down? What if they *had* still been here? What would he have done? Bashed them with the vacuum tube?

He sighed as he wondered what he should do next. He shouldn't touch anything before he did what he knew he had to do. With a grimace of resignation, he found the phone and pressed the keypad.

'Police? Yes, I want to report a break-in.'

* * *

'You say nothing's been taken?' the female police constable said the next morning. 'No cash?'

'The only cash I had was in my wallet, and there's nothing else missing that I can see,' Quentin admitted. 'But

I might miss something when I start putting things back together.'

'Well, if you do, let us know.'

'Have you finished here then? Is that it?'

A second police officer nodded. 'If nothing's missing there's not much we can do. We've dusted for fingerprints, and there's a footprint in the earth near the back wall, but it looks like a common trainer print, average size. Unless they match anything on our records, or there's a spate of similar break-ins, it's unlikely they'll be found.'

'Have there been other break-ins in the area?' Quentin asked.

The officer shook his head. 'Nothing round here. We'll file a report, but to be honest I don't hold out much hope of catching anyone.'

Typical, Quentin thought. They won't even try. 'What about this mess? They've slashed the armchair and settee, even my mattress. That's criminal damage, isn't it?'

The female police officer looked up from her notebook. 'Yes,' she said. 'So is defacing public property, but no one gets caught for that either.'

'Right.' Enraged, Quentin looked round the room. 'What shall I do about this lot? Can I start clearing it up?'

'You can if you don't want to claim on your insurance,' she answered, closing her notebook. 'It's probably not worth it, unless anything valuable's been broken. At least they haven't put graffiti on the walls, or done anything really awful.'

Quentin flinched. The scene looked awful enough to him, but he knew what she meant. They hadn't put a hammer through the TV or urinated on the carpet.

'You were right to report it though, Mr Cadbury,' her partner said, as though sensing Quentin's anger. 'It'll stay on record, and we'll keep you informed if there are any developments.'

'Right,' Quentin said again. 'OK, thanks. If anything's missing, I'll be in touch.'

When the police officers left, he trawled through the local directory to find a locksmith. He had secured the back door overnight by pushing the washing machine up against it. Then, sinking onto a chair, he gazed about him and wondered where to begin.

Chapter Three

It took the whole of Saturday to get the house in order. Even the contents from the kitchen cupboards had been taken out. The two overhead units were empty, the glasses, mugs and bowls sprawled over the worktop. Food from the lower ones lay in a pile on the floor, including the remaining tins of sardines and two unopened packets of oats that his mother had left there when she'd cleared the place. Aunt Josie must have had a thing about sardines, and he hated porridge. Shoving the boxes carelessly to the back of the cupboard, he stacked the tins in front of them and started on the cutlery.

At six o'clock he replaced the last book on the shelf and heaved a sigh of relief. He was tired, irritable and hungry. He'd done too much in one day, he realized. He should have spread it out more. What on earth were they looking for? Why turn the place over and leave with nothing? And why rip the backs off pictures? It was obvious to him that they were looking for something they thought was here. Money? Jewellery? It would have to be something small or flat to be hidden inside a picture frame. That ruled out kids looking for cash or things they could sell easily. Somehow, that made him feel more uneasy. If things had been stolen, that would be the end of it; but if they thought there was something here and they hadn't found it, they might come back. Perhaps they had found it. Would he ever know?

He was tempted to put in an insurance claim, but decided against it. It would put the premiums up, and the only damage was to the door lock, the pictures and a broken earthenware container in the kitchen. There were the slits in the settee and chair, but they were old anyway. He would buy some throws to cover them. His mattress upset him more – apart from his running machine, it was the only new thing he'd bought since he'd moved here. He would have to put a couple of quilted protectors on it until he got round to getting a new one. Miraculously, the china in the cabinet, another legacy from Aunt Josie, had survived the ransacking with only two breakages.

Satisfied that everything was back in its rightful place, he went to the kitchen to find a can of beer, cursing when he realized there were none left. He stood for a moment, glaring into the fridge as if by some miracle a can would suddenly appear. When this didn't happen, he banged the door shut, cursing again. A mewing sound made him turn to the window. Sitting on the outside windowsill, gazing at him with huge green eyes, was the black and white cat. Frowning, Quentin tried to recall if he'd seen it before. Yes, surely it was the cat from next door, wasn't it? But the owners, whom Quentin had hardly known, had moved out last week, and the house was empty.

Perhaps they left it here, he thought. Or perhaps it found its way back. I bet he saw whoever it was yesterday – pity he can't talk.

The cat mewed again and jumped down from the sill. Seconds later Quentin heard it scratching at the door. 'It's no good mewing at me,' he called. 'Go and raid someone else's bin.'

With no alcohol in the house and his craving for a beer growing, he stumped out to the hall, put on his jacket and headed for the pub. His local was packed so he decided to walk along the river to one he hadn't been to for some time.

It was approaching seven o'clock as he rounded a corner and headed into The Ferryman. He saw Louise before she saw him and thought how nice she looked. The black trousers and top made her seem slimmer and sparkling clips held her hair behind her ears. He watched in surprise as she lifted the hatch and went behind the bar, busying herself as though she was used to the role of barmaid. Realizing he hadn't even changed and probably looked a mess, he ran his hand through his hair. He put on his best smile and approached the bar.

'Quentin!' Louise's eyes widened in surprise. 'What are you doing here?'

'The question is what are you doing here? You have two jobs?' Quentin couldn't believe anyone would want two jobs. He'd have to be in dire need before he even entertained that idea.

'No. This is my mum and dad's pub. They took over last year. I help out to give them a break.'

'I love this place,' said Quentin, 'but I haven't been down here for ages.'

Louise frowned and leaned over the counter. 'Ooh, Quentin, what's happened to your head?'

Quentin touched the bump on his forehead and winced, then grabbed a bar stool and relayed the account of the break-in while she poured him a beer.

'So what about your head? Did the burglar attack you?'

'Well, I had to defend myself, didn't I?' Quentin said, his face muscles straining against a smile. He could hardly admit that he'd simply tripped and been half scared to death by a cat, could he?

'Ooh, l think you're so, like, brave. What about your aunt? She must have been terrified.'

'Well, she takes a lot of painkillers – they make her sleepy. She takes sleeping pills too. She slept through the whole thing.'

'Lucky, and lucky you got there when you did. You probably saved her from some terrible fate. And all that clearing up. I'd have come and helped if you'd called.'

Quentin cringed at her genuine offer of help and the mention of Aunt Josie – one little lie breeds more, he thought.

'That's sweet of you,' he said, 'but I've done it now. Anyway, Aunt Josie couldn't have coped with having anyone in the house today. She wanted an early night and I couldn't face cooking so here I am.'

Louise smiled. 'Well, I haven't eaten yet either. If you give me half an hour, one of the other bar staff will be coming on. Go get that table in the window and I'll come and join you.'

Feeling he could hardly protest, Quentin took his beer and made for the window.

* * *

The meal was typical pub food but Quentin enjoyed every mouthful. Louise seemed happy to be with him, and for the time they were together Quentin was happy to be with her. After the excitement of the burglary, it was good to be out of the house. He was pleased to be in Louise's company, and that she'd insisted dinner was on the house, but secretly relieved that this was a chance encounter rather than a 'proper' date.

Three hours later he stood at the bus stop waiting to see her safely on to her bus home.

'It's been a lovely evening,' he said, slipping an arm round her and kissing her cheek. She looked disappointed, as though she expected more.

'Sorry I can't give you a lift,' he added, thinking of his mother's BMW currently garaged in a rented lock-up, 'but I needed to clear my head and took a long walk here.'

Louise laughed. 'You're so, like, old-fashioned.'

'Oh!' Quentin bridled. Did he seem old-fashioned? 'Sorry. It comes from having older parents and growing up with Jeeves and Wooster.'

'Well, you can give me a proper kiss. I won't melt.' Before he could respond she leaned against him, turned her face up to his and kissed him. And at that minute Quentin found himself wishing he hadn't brought Aunt Josie back to life.

'I'll come with you to see you get home all right,' Quentin offered as the bus appeared.

'No need. I use this bus all the time. It stops at the end of my road. Night.'

'Goodnight, Louise.'

He watched her climb aboard and waved as the bus pulled away, feeling slightly guilty. He'd enjoyed himself tonight but the idea of dating her, dating anyone, didn't sit well with him. Lucky I'm leaving work, he thought as he started walking home. Any more evenings with Louise and I'd have to kill Aunt Josie off.

Chapter Four

Three weeks later Quentin bade his colleagues at the solicitor's office goodbye. He was sorrier to be leaving than he'd thought he would be. He hadn't been there long, and he couldn't help feeling guilty about the presents and the envelope bulging with notes collected from the staff. 'Just a little something to help replace what was damaged in the break-in,' Mr Sackville said.

Louise disappeared before he had a chance to say goodbye. As he passed reception for the last time, he had to admit he was going to miss her smile and was disappointed not to see her there. Still, he thought, it's probably a blessing in disguise. It's easier this way – a clean break.

The thought had barely left his head when Louise more or less pounced on him as he made for the door.

'I can't believe you're leaving without any kind of do,' she said. 'Here, let me help you with those.' She took some of the leaving gifts from him.

Grinning his thanks Quentin said, 'Oh well, I haven't been here long enough for that. To be honest I'm a bit embarrassed about all this.' He raised his arms to indicate the gifts. 'Thanks for giving me a hand – my car's just around the corner. I don't usually bring it to work but I'm glad I did today. It's amazing how much stuff you can accumulate around your desk, and with this lot as well it would have been a pain without the car.'

'Nice,' Louise said as they approached Quentin's BMW.

'It was my mother's,' Quentin replied, suddenly realizing that working as a solicitor's administrative assistant didn't tally with owning a BMW. A 3-Series model, it was already four years old but he loved its sleek silver lines. 'She gave it to me when she left the country but, you know, they're not cheap to run, and anyway there's never anywhere to park round here.' He was lucky, he realized, to have such a good car and somewhere to park it in Greenwich.

'Oh, come on, Quentin, you have to take me for a spin in it,' Louise said.

When Quentin unlocked it, she hopped in and pulled the passenger door closed. Louise was a force to be reckoned with.

'You can't just go back to your aunt on your last day,' she told him when he was in the driving seat. 'I know this amazing curry house.'

And curry it was, which turned into a movie, which turned into the offer of something more.

'Louise, I really like you, but this can't go anywhere,' said Quentin prising his lips from hers.

'I know,' said Louise, rolling her eyes, 'but that's no reason we can't have fun tonight, is it?'

'But I can't invite you to my house,' said Quentin, suddenly annoyed with his long dead Aunt Josie.

'Well, I can't invite you to my parents' house,' said Louise. 'It's late. Isn't there somewhere quiet we could park the car?'

In London? Quentin thought. Not likely.

The brainwave came to him in a flash. The lock-up where he usually kept the BMW – it was a few streets away from his house and definitely quiet at this time of night. 'I know just the place,' he said as they hurried from the cinema to where his car was parked.

Now the possibility was open to him, he couldn't wait to find out if Louise's underwear was as smooth as her dress, and whether her breasts would be quite so uplifted without the support of an underwired bra. His discovery was pleasantly surprising. Her breasts were full but firm in his grasp, and the knickers were silky and easy to remove. The BMW saw more action than it had for years, and Quentin sent a silent prayer of thanks to his absent mother.

'I'll drive you home,' he said afterwards, slipping into the front seat. He switched on the interior light and angled the rear-view mirror, catching a glimpse of Louise, who was still adjusting her clothes. With a satisfied smile he started the engine and jumped out to open the garage door. 'Come on,' he muttered when it didn't budge. It was an up-and-over door, and something seemed to be stopping it from opening out more than a few inches. He moved back to the car and cut the engine.

'What's the matter?' Louise asked, climbing out from the back seat. 'Won't it open?'

'Something's stopping it.'

'There was nothing there when we drove in,' Louise said, pouting.

'Well, there's something there now, and if we can't shift it, we'll be here all night.'

With the zip of her dress only half done up, Louise joined him by the door. 'We'll both push,' she offered.

'Right,' Quentin grunted. 'Come on then. One, two, three!'

The door squeaked and gave another inch.

'Ouch!' yelled Louise. 'That hurt my shoulder.'

'Sorry,' panted Quentin, rubbing at his own shoulder. 'I can't think who would want to put anything in front of a garage door. It's a stupid thing to do.'

'Maybe someone thought it wasn't in use. You said you didn't get the car out much.'

'Yeah. We'll just have to keep trying. If we can get it open far enough, we can crawl out the bottom.'

'But that'll take ages,' Louise wailed. 'I need to get home or my dad will go mental. Isn't there anyone we can ring to come and move whatever it is?'

'Only the garage owner, and I haven't got his number on me.'

'What about Aunt Josie?'

Quentin gave her a withering look. 'Don't be silly. If we can't shift it, Aunt Josie's got no chance.'

'I meant does she know the garage owner's number?'

'Oh, sorry. I can't ring her at this time of night. She's probably taken a sleeping pill. Let's try again.'

The sound of voices drifted through the space under the door and grew louder.

'You sure this lot's all right 'ere, Jack?' said a male voice.

'Yeah, man, it'll be fine,' came the answer in a West Indian accent. 'No one uses this garage, and there's still room for cars to get by. It'll all be gone tomorrow, when the skip comes.'

'Hey!' shouted Quentin. 'Hey, we're trapped in here. Let us out for goodness' sake.'

There was a thud, as though someone had dropped something on the ground.

'Who said that?' said the first voice.

'I did,' yelled Quentin, banging on the door.

'Oh gawd. I thought you said no one used this garage, Jack! Hold on a minute, mate. We'll shift some of this stuff.'

There was a scraping and a grating as things were pulled away from the door. After a while Quentin felt the pressure against it ease, and he was able to swing it upwards a few feet.

'Come on,' he said to Louise. 'You go out first.'

He watched as she knelt down and manoeuvred her way through the gap. Retrieving his keys from the ignition, he followed her through. I didn't think I'd end the night with a limbo dance, he thought as he crawled out. Not exactly an elegant ending to the evening.

Straightening up, he could see his rescuers in the light from the security lamp. The West Indian was a giant of a man, with shoulders like a rugby player with his pads still in place. The other was white, smaller than his companion and wiry looking. Between them was a wheelbarrow full of broken bricks, and in front of them were five or six plastic dustbins, also full of bricks. It must have taken at least twenty minutes for the two men to dump the dustbins by the door – and he and Louise had been oblivious. He'd put the thuds and bumps that had filtered through their ecstasy down to comings and goings in the adjacent garages.

'Sorry, man,' said Jack, the West Indian. 'Is it all right to leave this lot here now? There's a skip coming first thing.'

Brushing dirt from his trousers, Quentin said, 'Not really. I was going to drive my friend home.'

'Are you bringing the car back tonight?' Jack asked, eyeing the bins before switching his gaze to Quentin.

'Yes,' answered Quentin impatiently. 'There's nowhere else to park. There's no space on the road.'

'OK, man, we'll have to move it all back then. We can't leave it anywhere else; it'll block the garages. Come on, Bob.'

A groan escaped the other man. 'I nearly put my friggin' back out getting it all 'ere,' he complained.

'Don't worry, Quentin,' Louise said, pulling at his arm. 'I'll get a taxi.'

The man called Bob brightened. 'Good idea, love,' he said, reaching into his pocket. 'Very good. Here, take this towards the fare.' He thrust a note into Louise's hand.

'Thanks,' Quentin said. 'We'll leave you to it, then.'

Taking out his mobile he rang for a taxi while he led Louise along the alley towards the road. 'Bloody cheek,' he said when he'd finished the call. 'Fancy putting all that rubbish outside someone's garage at midnight.'

He felt a frisson of suspicion, remembering his break-in. Why wait till midnight to move bricks? It would be a good time to break into the garages–

His thoughts stopped as Louise hopped from one foot to the other. 'I need the loo,' she said, 'and I've left something in your car.'

'Nothing important, I hope. Here's the taxi – that was quick.'

Once in the taxi Louise cuddled up to him and he ran his hand down her body over her hips. He gasped when his hand slid smoothly round her buttocks. Too smoothly.

'That's what I left in your car,' she giggled. 'My knickers.'

Chapter Five

Quentin lay in bed that Sunday, revelling in the knowledge that he didn't have to get up for work the next day; or the next, or any day that week. A life of leisure, he gloated, at least until his money ran out.

Throwing back the covers, he padded downstairs to make some tea. A mewing sounded at the back door, and he turned the key in the newly fitted lock and opened it.

'You again!' he murmured as the black and white cat sat looking up at him. 'Why do you keep trying to get in here? Hasn't anyone come back for you?'

The cat mewed and rubbed itself against his legs. It looked thin and scrawny, and he suddenly felt sorry for it. He bent and stroked its back, feeling the bones through the soft fur.

'All right, you win,' Quentin said, letting it over the threshold. 'You look half-starved. Let's see what we can find you to eat.'

Remembering his mother saying that cows' milk wasn't good for cats, he put down a saucer of water while he rummaged through the cupboard. The cat lapped thirstily, then sat quietly until Quentin tipped some sardines onto a plate and put it on the floor. Quentin had never seen a plate of food disappear so quickly.

There was a collar around the cat's neck, with a small tubular pendant hanging from it. Bending down, Quentin held the pendant between his finger and thumb and squinted at the name engraved on it. 'Magpie,' he read. Who calls a cat Magpie? I suppose magpies *are* black and white. 'They steal things too,' he muttered, thinking of when the cat had raided his bin. 'Still, I don't blame you. I expect you were hungry.'

The kettle boiled and he made tea and put some bread in the toaster. The cat sat still, and he forgot it was there until he tripped over it, dropping his toast butter side down.

'Sod it!' He groaned, and glared at Magpie. 'Now look what you've done. You've had your food. Out you go.'

Magpie mewed, then slunk past him into the garden and curled up in a patch of sunlight. Closing the door, Quentin put a fresh slice of bread in the toaster and glanced at the clock. His mother rang from Australia every Sunday, and he wanted to finish his breakfast before then. He wondered whether or not to tell her about the break-in, but decided against it. She would only worry, and with the new double lock on the back door and a security light fitted outside it was unlikely anyone would get in again.

The phone rang just as he was gulping down the last of his tea.

'Hello, Mum,' he said when he picked up the receiver. 'How are you?'

'We're all fine this end,' his mother answered after the momentary time lapse. 'How's it going with you? Did your promotion come through?'

'Yes, it did, thanks. I start my new role next month.'

'Lovely. I knew you could do it, Quentin. You're such a clever boy.'

A flush spread over Quentin's face. Somehow it didn't feel right lying to his mother, but the thought of his father's scathing remarks made him cringe. He knew his mother would get a lecture if they knew the truth: *I told you that boy was work-shy, didn't I? I said he'd never do anything worthwhile.* So he'd kept the pretence of a job going.

When he'd asked all the usual things – how Shelagh, Howard and little Michael were, how Father was coping with the heat – he paused as he heard a scratching at the door. *That cat again,* he thought. *I'll never get rid of it now I've fed it.*

His mother's voice brought him back to the moment. 'Quentin? Are you still there?'

'Yes, Mum. It's just – a cat keeps scratching at the door.'

'A cat? Josie's cat?'

Quentin blinked. 'Aunt Josie? I didn't know she had a cat. No, it belongs to next door, but the people have moved.'

'Is it black and white?'

'Yes, as a matter of fact it is. It's called Magpie, according to its collar.'

'It's Josie's then.' His mother sounded positive. 'We gave it to the man next door when she died.'

No wonder the poor thing kept coming back – it used to live here! Its mistress died, and the new owner abandoned it. Well, thought Quentin, feeling an empathy with Magpie, I know what that feels like.

'I'll keep an eye on it,' he said. 'Thanks for calling, Mum. I'm glad you're all OK over there. Bye for now.'

'Bye, Quentin, dear. Take care.'

Unsettled, Quentin went to the running machine, switched it on and set it on fast. Since he'd started using it he'd found the exercise therapeutic, and it helped him think. He should be used to his parents being on the other side of the world by now, but his mother's calls always made him feel restless.

His mother was a saint, he realized. As well as bringing up two children and keeping house, she'd been active in various charities and belonged to an amateur dramatic group. Of course, she may have engaged in these as a means of being away from an over-bearing husband, but still…

It was her comforting words he missed most. All the things he'd done, all the girls he'd had fun with, even being able to live in this house didn't compensate for a loving word from someone who knew all his faults and still *cared*.

Feeling suddenly alone, he turned off the machine and stood for a while to get his breath back before wandering into the kitchen and looking out to the garden. Magpie had given up his scratching and gone back to sunbathing. Seeing him took Quentin back to the night of the break-in. He'd heard nothing more from the police, so he assumed they had nothing to tell him. Just another statistic, he brooded.

He spent the rest of the day in Greenwich Park, an uphill walk from where he lived, enjoying its green spaces, watching the squirrels darting up and down trees and people milling about or relaxing in the afternoon sun. He made a slow circuit of the paths, vowing to keep up his running until he was fitter.

That night he fed Magpie, then turfed him out again. 'I don't mind feeding you,' he said, 'but you can't stay here.' He almost weakened when the cat gazed up at him with pleading eyes, but he stuck to his resolution, made when he'd achieved his independence. No attachments, no obligations, no ties.

'It's no good getting attached to animals,' his father had told him after he'd promptly removed a West Highland terrier puppy hidden under Quentin's bed when he was twelve years old. 'They break your heart in the end.' Quentin couldn't imagine anything breaking his father's heart. It took a lot to shatter stone.

By the time he went to bed he was feeling better. He poured himself a whisky, bought with the money collected at the solicitor's office, took it upstairs, switched on the radio in the bedroom and settled down for the night. Bliss.

It must have been two o'clock when he awoke, startled. The room was unusually light, and – what was that noise? There it was again – a cat screeching.

'Bloody hell,' he muttered, getting up and lumbering to the window. 'What the–'

He stopped as he caught sight of a shape in the garden – a black figure, silhouetted against the wall in the light of the new security lamp. The figure raised its arm against the brightness, kicked out viciously at something then turned and ran to the end of the garden. The cat's screech carried up to Quentin as he watched the figure scale the back wall and disappear.

For a moment Quentin didn't move. Am I dreaming? he wondered. He knew he wasn't when light spilled from an adjacent window and a voice called, 'Someone shut that cat up!'

Taking the stairs two at a time, he rushed down and opened the back door. He went to where he'd seen the figure go over the wall, climbed up and peered over. There was no one in sight. Back at the house, Magpie limped up to him, blood oozing from one of his ears. Quentin bent to pick him up, but he shrunk away as if frightened of being touched.

'It's all right, boy,' he soothed. 'Come here. Let's take a look at you.' He pushed the door wider and waited as Magpie padded cautiously in, making red paw prints on the tiles. Quentin guessed the intruder had trodden on him in his haste to get to the house. When the cat squealed and the security light snapped on, the intruder had taken fright and run, kicking out at Magpie as he went.

'Bastard,' Quentin muttered. He couldn't stand cruelty. Finding a clean cloth and running it under the tap, he knelt down, held Magpie firmly with one hand and dabbed at the furry ear. Then he did the same with the paw while Magpie wriggled and mewed.

'I think you'll be all right, boy,' he said. 'If it doesn't heal, I'll take you to the vet.'

Pouring water into a dish he set it on the floor. Then, despite his resolution to incur no ties, he rummaged in the cupboard under the stairs, brought out an old coat and placed it next to the water.

'You can stay here,' he said, patting the coat. 'If it hadn't been for you, I might have had another break-in. The thing is, what do they want?'

Chapter Six

A week later a squeal of brakes followed by a metallic crunch sent Quentin running to the front window. Pulling the net curtain across, he peered out. A blue Toyota stood askew in the road; the bumper of a van embedded in its back offside wing.

'Oh-oh,' muttered Quentin, surprised at such a big van being in the little side road. Hurrying outside, he saw it was a removal van. Probably the new occupant of the neighbouring house.

As he walked towards the stricken car, his eyes widened when the driver's door opened and a pair of shapely legs came into view. Swinging her legs onto the road, a woman got out. She looked shaken, and she stared at the van as though she couldn't believe what had happened.

'Are you all right?' Quentin asked, reaching her before the other driver had clambered down from his vehicle.

'I think so,' she answered, placing her hand behind her neck and flexing her head.

The removal man came up to them, concern showing on his face.

'God, I'm sorry. You OK? You stopped so suddenly. I thought number twenty-seven was at the other end of the road.'

'So did I,' the woman said, her voice trembling. 'I came in the other way before. When I saw the number, I braked. I didn't realize you were so close.'

She turned towards her car and gasped. 'That's all I need just when I'm moving in.'

Quentin moved forward and inspected the damage. 'It's not too bad,' he told her. 'You should be able get it fixed all right.'

'Yes,' the van driver agreed. 'Don't worry, my company's insurance will sort it out.'

A second removal man joined them. 'We'll help you push it to the kerb,' he offered.

The woman nodded, her fair hair rippling like a curtain in a breeze. She got back into the car and steered while Quentin and the removal men put their weight behind it and pushed. When she was safely in a parking bay, she got out again and tried to open the rear door, but it wouldn't budge.

'Oh great!' she groaned. She bent down and called through the front door, 'Here, Mozart, out this way.'

A white West Highland terrier jumped out and bounded round the car into the road.

'Mozart!' the woman's voice rose to a scream as the dog ran past Quentin just as a 4x4 came from the other end of the street. Quentin, still on the far side of the car, managed to grab hold of him and scoop him up as the 4x4 skidded to a halt just inches from where he stood.

Completely shaken now, the woman ran to his side and took the dog from him, tears streaming down her cheeks.

'Oh my God, Mozart!' She buried her face in his fur, her shoulders heaving. 'You saved him,' she said, lifting her head. 'Thank you so much. I couldn't bear to lose him.'

'That dog should be on a lead,' shouted the 4x4 driver. 'It nearly caused an accident.'

'You shouldn't have been going so fast,' Quentin shouted back.

The man scowled but said nothing. He waited until the van had been driven into the side of the road, then drove off. 'Bloody dogs, bloody irresponsible owners!' he yelled as he went.

His words brought another gasp from the woman, and Quentin saw fresh tears gathering in her eyes. He took her arm and led her onto the pavement.

'Why don't you come into my house?' he asked. 'I'll make you a cup of tea.'

'We could all do with a cup of tea,' said the second removal man, giving Quentin a hopeful look.

The other man, older and apparently in charge, interrupted. 'No, Mike, not till we've unloaded. Can we have the key, Mrs Merrydrew, and we'll get started.'

Mrs Merrydrew, thought Quentin. What a shame. Still, she must be over thirty. Why wouldn't she be married, especially with her looks.

When she'd handed over the key, the woman allowed Quentin to lead her into his house.

'Have a seat.' Quentin beamed. 'I'll put the kettle on. My name's Quentin, by the way.'

'I'm Wanda.'

'Hello Wanda. And this is Mozart, I presume.' Quentin fondled the dog's ears as it sat by its mistress's feet. Ever since his childhood incident with the banished puppy he'd had a liking for Westies.

Ten minutes later he placed a patterned china cup and saucer beside her. He'd steered clear of the mugs. Wanda definitely looked like a cup and saucer person. He knew he'd made the right choice when she picked up the cup and eyed it appreciatively.

'Spode,' she murmured, sipping from it and replacing it on the saucer.

Inwardly praising Aunt Josie's taste and glad that his mother had let him keep some of her sister's tableware, Quentin smiled at his guest. 'So, isn't your husband or anyone here to help you move in?'

'I'm a widow,' came the answer. 'My husband died a couple of years ago, that's why I'm moving.'

'Oh, I'm so sorry.' Quentin spoke with genuine feeling, yet he saw an unexpected possibility opening up. A pretty widow, with just a dog for company, right on his doorstep.

'Gerry was in antiques,' Wanda was saying. 'I helped in the business, and I could have taken it over. It's not as if I had a family to look after, but I didn't want the hassle.'

That answered the next question that had formed in Quentin's mind. No children.

'So you sold it?' he asked.

'Yes. It took a while, but I got enough to get myself a little house. I like this area, so I snapped the house up as soon as I knew it was on the market. I only saw it once, but I knew it was right for me, so here I am.'

Here you are, Quentin thought, and very nice too. Now the shock of the car crunch and the near miss with her dog had worn off, she looked and sounded even more attractive. Her voice, low-pitched and seductive, reminded

Quentin of a film star from the black-and-white movies his mother used to watch. Her eyes, free from tears, were blue, with fine lines showing at the corners. She was older than she'd first appeared, he realized, probably nearer forty than thirty. Even better. She wouldn't be looking for a serious relationship with a twenty-four-year-old. Would she be looking for any sort of relationship? Not with me, he thought, suddenly chiding himself.

The door moved slightly and Magpie strutted in. His paw had healed and after a week back in his old territory and some TLC from Quentin, his confidence was returning. Back arched and tail flicking, he stopped when he spotted Mozart. A growl from the dog sent him slinking out of the room.

'Mozart!' Wanda looked apologetic. 'I'm sorry – he's all right with cats, normally.'

'Don't worry.' Quentin grinned. 'Magpie's a bit oversensitive. He was my aunt's cat, and when she died he lived next door until the bloke moved out. I've sort of adopted him. He's no trouble, really.'

Wanda nodded and finished her tea. 'Thank you so much. I feel a lot better now.'

'Good. Well, you can call on me anytime if you need anything. I guess we'll be seeing a bit of each other with you only living next door.'

'I expect so, but won't you be working most days?'

Feeling a flush rise from his neck, Quentin said, 'Actually, I'm between jobs at the moment.' He regretted it immediately. He sounded like an out-of-work actor expecting a call from his agent. Yet somehow he felt his usual list of excuses would sound feeble to Wanda. She wasn't like the other girls he'd known. Despite her upset, she had recovered quickly and Quentin could see she was serene and composed.

Wanda sought his gaze and held it, her blue eyes wide and candid. 'And what do you do when you are working?'

'Well, I've got a law degree.' Only a half-lie. He *had* completed half the course. 'I was working at a solicitor's until recently, but...' He searched for words. He couldn't use Aunt Josie. Wanda was too close to home for him to keep up the pretence, and anyway he'd already told her she was dead.

'My aunt died and left me this place, and a little legacy.' Well, Magpie was a legacy of sorts, and then there was the china. 'Quite frankly I was bored with my job—'

Wanda eyed him coolly. 'So you got out while you had the chance. I don't blame you. Unless you're passionate about what you do, you should work to live, not live to work.'

She's becoming more attractive by the minute, Quentin thought. A woman after my own heart.

'I'm not working either,' she said. 'I might take up some voluntary work when I've got the house together. Quite a lot needs doing, but I enjoy a bit of DIY.'

'Let me know if you need a hand,' Quentin answered.

'Thanks.' Glancing round the room Wanda said, 'I take it you're on your own?'

'Oh lord, yes. I can't be doing with someone telling me what to do all the time. I had enough of that from my father,' he said. 'What's funny?' he added when she smiled.

'Nothing,' Wanda said. 'It's just – well, you sound older than you look, that's all.'

'Do I? You mean I sound old-fashioned. I've been told that before.'

'I like it,' Wanda admitted. 'It's refreshing.' She stood up as Mozart yapped. 'Thanks for the tea. I'm pleased I've got a nice neighbour.'

Not as pleased as I am, Quentin thought.

'It's been a pleasure meeting you. And Mozart of course,' he added, stroking the dog again. Mozart yapped and licked his hand. A good sign, Quentin decided, looking back at Wanda. 'I look forward to seeing more of you.'

Her look of amusement told him the innuendo wasn't lost on her. Picking up her dog, she turned and walked out.

Chapter Seven

I suppose I'll have to think about getting another job, Quentin mused when he viewed his bank details. My money will only hold out another month or two.

It was July, two months since he'd left the solicitor's. Although he was trying to stretch his finances to the end of summer, he didn't want them to fall too low. Switching off the computer, he changed into his running shorts, walked to the newsagents, bought a paper and ran to the park. He found an empty bench and sat scanning the employment pages. He wondered why he'd bothered – the situation was the same as it had been yesterday when he'd checked online. There were plenty of jobs, but he didn't fancy any of them.

Since he'd been free during the day, the idea of being tied to a nine-to-five routine horrified him. Evenings would suit him more – bar work perhaps; chit-chat with a few drinks thrown in would serve as his social life. Now his finances were dwindling he couldn't afford many nights out. Since Louise, he'd met several girls in restaurants and bars, but he'd kept it casual, keeping to his no ties or obligations mantra; he wasn't ready to think about settling down, and so far he hadn't met anyone he wanted to settle down with.

Of course, there was Wanda. His new neighbour excited him. She was friendly but cool, with a practised way of keeping him at arm's length. He'd already invited her in for dinner, but she'd been busy that day. 'Another time,' she'd promised. It was just as well. His budget would be stretched considerably if he provided the sort of cuisine he thought she was used to. Definitely not a burger-and-chips woman, he guessed.

After a thirty-minute run he left the park and ran home. When he reached his front gate, Wanda appeared from the other direction weighed down with bags. Quentin hurried to meet her.

'Here, let me take those,' he offered, carrying them to her front door. 'I'll take them in for you.'

'It's all right, I can manage. Just leave them in the hall. It's a nuisance not being able to park outside your own house, but there we are. Thanks for helping, Quentin. It's good of you.'

Quentin eyed the bulging bags enviously. On the top of one he could see fillet steak, as well as mushrooms and fresh cream. Quentin thought of the remains of yesterday's chicken pie lingering unappetisingly in the fridge.

He looked up to see Wanda watching him with what he thought was an approving look. He didn't profess to being a Brad Pitt or Tom Cruise lookalike, but he knew his caramel-coloured eyes, easy smile and toned-up body gave him a certain appeal, especially with the suntan he'd acquired since leaving work.

'I hope you haven't forgotten your offer to invite me to dinner,' Wanda said. 'Just because I couldn't come last time doesn't mean I don't want to come.'

'Oh no, I haven't forgotten. It's just…' – he flushed – 'what do you like?'

'I like most things. What are you having tonight?'

'Not much,' Quentin admitted. 'I need to do some shopping.'

Wanda smiled. 'Well, I've got plenty, as you can see. Why don't you come here for dinner?'

'That's really kind of you. I'd love to,' Quentin blurted, hoping he didn't sound too eager.

'That's settled then. Seven o'clock?'

'Seven's fine. See you then.'

Quentin's heart leapt in anticipation. The gods are with me, he thought. Alleluia!

* * *

At five o'clock Quentin had a shower and debated whether or not to iron his favourite shirt. He decided against it and selected another one. He wanted to play it cool and not look like he was trying too hard. Anyway, they weren't going out… Quentin grew hot at the thought of an intimate evening with Wanda. As if, he thought. But she'd invited him, hadn't she?

Downstairs, Magpie mewed at him. He took yesterday's leftover chicken pie from the fridge, scraped the chicken onto a saucer and threw the pastry in the bin.

'That's all there is, unless you want porridge,' he muttered, remembering the packets he'd found after the break-in. 'Don't worry, I wouldn't inflict that on you.'

He shrugged as Magpie sniffed the meat and turned away. 'Like it or lump it,' he said, stepping back. His heel caught the edge of the cat's drinking bowl and tipped it over, water drenching his socks and seeping under the fridge. 'Blast it!' he yelled at Magpie. 'Now look what you've done.'

Magpie stared at him haughtily before stalking into the lounge. Quentin mopped up the water, knowing he would have to pull the fridge out to get to it all. Resisting the urge to leave it, he took off his socks and manoeuvred the fridge into the middle of the room; then he bent down and soaked up the remaining water with kitchen roll, banging his knuckles against the plug. He looked at the box-like bracket which the plug was screwed to and noticed how far it stuck out. He pushed at it, wondering why the socket wasn't flush with the wall. The whole thing moved under his touch. He bent closer, pushing it from side to side. It's bloody dangerous, he thought. I bet Aunt Josie got some cowboy electrician to put it in. Still, it hasn't blown up yet.

His thoughts stopped. His pushing and pulling had revealed something poking out from behind the bracket. It looked like some sort of material, covered in clear plastic. After turning off the electricity, he pulled at the box-like structure and gasped as it came away from the wall, bringing the electric cabling with it. Reaching past the wires, he grabbed the edge of the plastic and tugged. The bag that emerged became stuck between the socket and the wall, then shot out as Quentin fell backwards, thudding down on the damp floor.

'What on earth?' he murmured, gazing at the bag in his hands.

The bag was of blue linen, similar to the ones used in banks to transport money. It was flat enough to store in the cavity behind the socket, but Quentin could see it wasn't empty. Tearing off the plastic covering, he undid the tie at the neck and peered into it. Then he tipped it upside down and gasped as he watched bundle after bundle of reddish brown fifty-pound notes fall around him.

I've died and gone to heaven, he gloated, opening one of the bundles and fanning out the notes. Whatever was Aunt Josie doing with all this?

Chapter Eight

Quentin spent the next hour counting the money. Fifty thousand pounds. That's a lot of cash, he thought as he stacked the notes into one-thousand-pound piles. So that's what the break-in was about. They must have been after this. But who knew it was here?

A memory came to him: the London Marathon, when a man had tried to steal his keys. He'd thought it had been a random theft, but what if that man had known about the money and was responsible for the break-in?

Whether he was the burglar or not, it didn't answer the question of why the money was there. Surely Aunt Josie hadn't hidden it? A frail old lady with rheumatoid arthritis? But she hadn't always been frail. And her husband, his uncle, John, had been well and active until shortly before his fatal heart attack. Perhaps he'd put it there. It could have been there years, but not that many – the notes were used but still in circulation. Suppose they weren't real? Snatching at one, he held it up to the light. It looked genuine, and he wished he had one to compare it with, but he hadn't seen a fifty-pound note since his father had sold the Regency sideboard.

Gathering up the bundles, he placed them back in the cloth bag. What should he do with it? Maybe he should put it back where he'd found it – after all, the burglar had failed to find it there, and he had only come across it accidentally. Deciding this was a good idea, he returned the bag to its hiding place, then found a screwdriver and tightened the screws to keep the socket more firmly in place. When he'd pushed the fridge back into position, he brushed the dust from his trousers, retrieved his socks and switched the power back on.

Another thought struck him. If the burglar was after the cash, why tear the backs off pictures, in some cases prising off the frames? Suppose it wasn't the cash? He shook his head. It was a puzzle, a puzzle he wanted to solve.

But it'll have to wait, he thought, glancing at his watch as his stomach rumbled. It's time for dinner.

* * *

'More apple pie, Quentin?' Wanda's low voice hummed like Magpie's purr.

'No, thanks. It's delicious, but I'm full.' Full of pie, full of hope, he thought gazing at her. He liked the way her hair was swept to one side and tumbled over one shoulder – the bare shoulder that gleamed beneath the light and contrasted with the black chiffon that covered the rest of her upper body.

An amused smile parted Wanda's red lips. 'I'm glad you liked it. I'll just clear these things away.'

'I'll help wash up,' Quentin said, getting to his feet.

'There's no need, I've got a dishwasher. Just put the plates on the side and leave them.'

Crockery in hand, Quentin followed her to the kitchen, almost tripping over Mozart on the way.

'Out of the way, Mozart,' Wanda commanded. 'You've had your dinner.'

The dog rose obediently, settled himself in a basket in the corner and lay with his head on his paws.

'He's a good little thing,' Quentin said, glad that he hadn't made a fool of himself by falling and breaking the plates. 'Why did you call him Mozart? Is he your favourite composer?'

'Yes, I like classical music, especially Mozart. I like popular music too.'

'And me,' Quentin said, though he preferred modern to classical. 'That was a lovely dinner. I'll have to do the same for you, but it won't be as good as yours.'

Wanda turned and gave him a seductive smile. 'Never mind. There *is* something you can do for me, actually.'

Quentin's heart soared. 'Really?'

'Yes. I was hoping you wouldn't mind looking after Mozart if I'm away at any time.'

His heart bumping back to earth, Quentin said, 'Oh. Yeah, of course. Anything for you.'

'Anything? Well, we'll have to see about that. After all, you haven't known me very long. I might be the Wicked Witch of the West, for all you know.'

'I wouldn't care if you were. The wickeder the better.'

He held her long and searching gaze. She didn't answer, and he wondered if he'd gone too far.

Brushing past him she went to the cabinet that housed the CD player. On top of this stood a photograph of her with a silver-haired, distinguished-looking man. Her husband Gerry, he assumed, the antiques dealer. Looking around, Quentin took in the surroundings. The room was small, not knocked into the next to make one big room as his was, but tastefully decorated, with more than a smattering of attractive furnishings that Quentin took to be antiques. But she's not an antique, he thought, bringing his gaze back to Wanda.

'What music do you like?' she asked. 'I've subjected you to John Barry all through dinner. You can choose now.'

Flicking through the covers, Quentin selected a Leonard Cohen CD and heard Wanda gasp when he handed it to her.

'You know Leonard Cohen? Well, that's a surprise, I must say.'

'My mother – my sister likes Leonard Cohen,' he said, trying to hide his indiscretion.

'Don't worry,' Wanda said, laughing at his discomfort. 'I'm well aware I'm older than you, but you don't have to be old to appreciate things that have been around for a few years.'

You can say that again, Quentin thought. Some things improve with age.

'I'm glad your mother likes Leonard Cohen,' Wanda continued. 'That must be where you get your good taste from.'

They sat side by side on the velvet-covered chaise longue, making small talk and listening to the music. Quentin did a good job of keeping his hands to himself until the song *Dance Me to the End of Love* started playing. They fell silent, listening to lyrics that fired Quentin's emotions and stirred his desire.

> *Let me see your beauty when the witnesses are gone,*
> *Let me feel you moving like they do in Babylon,*
> *Show me slowly what I only know the limits of,*
> *Dance me to the end of love.*

His arm crept along the back of the sofa and rested on Wanda's bare shoulder. Instead of moving away, she turned towards him, her eyes smoky with need. They sat motionless for a moment, their eyes locked; then his mouth was on hers, pushing, sucking, crushing her against him. Her ardour matched his, exceeded his, and he was drawn into a chasm of hitherto unknown pleasure.

When at last he emerged from this erotic dream, his eyes flickered open and he saw Wanda's fair head inches from his own. He rolled towards her, wincing at the stiffness in his back. The pile on the lounge carpet wasn't as soft as a mattress. They hadn't even made it to the bedroom. Smiling at the memory, he slid an arm around Wanda's waist. She stirred, woke up and nestled into him.

'You're a very naughty boy,' she whispered, 'taking advantage of a poor widow like that. It's cold. Why don't we do something conventional and go to bed?'

Following her up the stairs, Quentin's mind drifted back over the events of the day and the cache of money he had found. It's a mystery, he thought. It might solve a lot of problems. But then, so might Wanda.

And as he tumbled into bed and felt her breasts pushing into him and her hand exploring his body for the second time, he couldn't help wondering if Wanda's husband had died on the job. Perhaps she'd worn him out. Well, *he* was too young to wear out yet, and this was one job he didn't mind doing.

Chapter Nine

The following morning he took Wanda breakfast in bed, kissed her bare shoulders and went home.

When he'd showered and dressed, he took out the money and looked at it again. So he hadn't dreamt it. He wondered what to do. His initial elation at finding it had given way to doubt. I needn't work for ages, he thought, but can I spend it? Suppose the notes are marked? The money must have been obtained illegally, or it wouldn't be stashed behind the fridge. Would it? Who's to say Josie or John hadn't drawn it out of the bank and kept it in the house for some reason? But fifty thousand? Unlikely.

Perhaps he should take it to the police, but he didn't want to do that. He hadn't committed a crime and, as far as he knew, nor had anyone else. The money was in *his* house, left there by a family member, therefore it was his by rights. Except it wasn't strictly *his* house; it was his mother's. The house and contents. Useful contents – furniture, crockery and fifty thousand pounds.

Quentin had a twinge of conscience. It was his mother's property, but after all she didn't need the money, neither did his sister, and they would be glad for his good fortune. But suppose it was his aunt and uncle's life savings? Shouldn't he tell his mother? She might tell him to keep it, but he imagined his father's response if he knew about his find. 'I told you that boy comes up smelling of roses,' he would rant. 'He's made an art of wriggling his way out of everything.'

Wriggling or not, finding the money *was* a way out for Quentin. Instead of looking for a job, he'd be able to continue living as he pleased, at least until his hoard ran out. But was it safe to spend it?

There was only one way to find out – use some and see. If he spent a small amount and somehow it was traced back to him, all he needed to say was he'd come by the notes legitimately. He could have been given them for a job he'd done. He wasn't claiming benefits. He was free to earn money any way he chose, and he could have been paid in cash.

'Yep,' he murmured, satisfied with his reasoning. 'That's the answer. Spend a bit, see what happens.'

Now he'd made his decision, his mind was easier, but the mystery of the money remained. It stayed in his head and refused to budge.

Keeping out one of the bundles, he put the rest back in the bag and returned it to the cavity. Peeling off the top note, he thrust it into his pocket.

Nothing for it but to wait and see, he decided. Reaching for his jacket, he shrugged it on and went shopping.

* * *

When he came back, he unloaded his bags and lined his purchases up on the counter, eyeing them as proudly as if they were an award for achieving some great feat.

'Here we are, boy,' he beamed at Magpie. 'A whole stack of sardines just for you. And I got some of this posh stuff in case you fancy a change.'

He dangled a pouch of cat food in front of Magpie, who stretched out a paw towards it. Quentin swung the pouch out of reach. 'Not now – it's not tea-time yet.'

Magpie's tail stuck up in the air and he turned away as if in disgust. Quentin laughed. 'It won't hurt you to wait,' he said, piling the pouches on to the shelf. 'You *do* deserve it though. If I hadn't spilt your water, I never would have found the money.'

With the money still on his mind, he went to his computer and opened his emails. Although he spoke to his family by phone every week, his sister occasionally sent messages, some with pictures of his nephew, Michael, some just for a chat. There was nothing today, but Quentin's hand hovered over the keyboard. If he wanted to discover the origin of the hidden cash, he needed to find out more about Josie and John.

Images of his aunt floated before him; thin, grey, crippled with arthritis in later years. He remembered himself and Shelagh drinking from plastic beakers while his parents and his aunt drank from Spode teacups in this very house, usually at Christmas. He searched his memory for an image of John, but the picture that emerged was grainy. Sharp features, he recalled, but nothing else came to mind, not even his height or colouring. Somehow, John had always managed to avoid family gatherings. Or perhaps he was busy doing – what? Something illegal? Surely no one in his family had been a criminal?

Quentin shook his head. Aunt Josie can't have known. If her husband was up to something, it must have been without her knowledge. She was his mother's sister, for God's sake. But the money had been put there by someone who had access to the house, and John and Josie had lived here for more than twenty years. It hadn't been behind the improvised plug socket for that long. The bag was too clean, the socket box too new.

Clicking the mouse on his sister's email address, he started his message.

> *Hi Shelagh, I didn't get a chance to say much when we spoke last week, so I thought I'd email to catch up. I hope little Michael is recovering from his fall – I fell off the swing when I was a kid, several times if you remember. Is Mum OK? She sounds well enough, but I wonder if she gets homesick. When's the old man going to get up to date and buy a computer? I'm sure Mum would like to keep in touch with everyone here more.*

He paused, wondering how he could get to the real purpose of his message. What could he say? Do you know anything about Uncle John? Was he a criminal? He sat for a while, his forehead wrinkled into a frown. Then he resumed.

> *Someone I work with is researching their family history and it's got me interested, not in ancient stuff, but recent times. I know a bit about Father's side – he was always pushing that down our throats – but I*

*was wondering about Aunt Josie — I mean, I'm living
in her house but I don't really know much about her,
or Uncle John. Can you remember what he did? It
was something to do with cars, wasn't it? Anything
you can remember would be helpful. I'll ask Mum
when I speak to her, but I didn't want to ring her
just for that. That's all for now. Best to Howard.*

Love, Quentin.

After reading it through he clicked on the send button.
He hoped his sister wouldn't wonder why he hadn't waited
and asked their mother direct. Still, Shelagh was a good
sort. She would help if she could, even though they hadn't
seen each other for over three years.

There was a knock at the door, and he went to open it,
it was Wanda; make-up-less but fresh-looking in white
trousers and an apple-green top.

'Hello.' She smiled. 'I don't suppose you've got some
coffee I could borrow, have you?'

Quentin laughed, his heart lifting. 'Come in. I'll make
some.'

She stepped over the threshold, 'I was hoping you
would. I've run out.'

'Oh,' he said, remembering he'd used the last of it for
breakfast. He groaned as he realized he'd forgotten to buy
some filter coffee. 'I've only got instant, I'm afraid.'

'That's all right. I don't mind roughing it.'

Quentin felt a prick of uncertainty. A bit of rough — is
that what she thought of him? Private school, university,
well-spoken, well-mannered? True, she hadn't seen the
BMW, and he only lived in a two-bedroomed terraced
house, but then so did she — and it was in Greenwich.

'I was joking,' she said, as if reading his thoughts.
'Instant's fine. Thanks for a great evening by the way. I did
enjoy it.'

His fears subsided. 'Me too. Thanks for a wonderful meal. I'd like to return your... hospitality – say tonight, or tomorrow?'

Too fast, he thought. I keep forgetting she's a mature woman. I should let *her* call the shots.

'I'm out tonight, and tomorrow,' she said. 'How about Friday or Saturday?'

Disappointment filled Quentin. After last night he hoped Wanda would be as keen as he was to repeat their experience. Their lovemaking had been frantic, almost desperate, and, when he analysed it in the cold light of day, without any love attached to it. Yet he realized, with a little shock, that he didn't see Wanda merely as an outlet for sex. He liked her a lot and he wanted to get to know her better.

'Saturday will be fine,' he agreed, trying to sound nonchalant. 'Or...'

'Or what?'

Quentin hesitated. 'Er, well, there's always lunch.'

Wanda's gaze was cool, but her mouth twitched a little when she answered. 'Tempting. Better not, though. I don't like to eat too much at lunchtime. All I want to do is sleep afterwards so it wipes the rest of the day out.'

She followed Quentin into the lounge and sat down. 'It's nice in here,' she said, glancing round, her gaze lingering on the bureau and the china cabinet.

'My aunt's choice.'

'Quite refined then, your family, by the sound of it.'

For a moment Quentin wondered if she was trying to offset the implication of roughness she'd mentioned earlier, then decided she wasn't.

'They're OK, except for my father. He was a hard taskmaster, still is, though from what I can gather he's mellowed a bit since he's emigrated. Perhaps it's because I'm not there to aggravate him. I never did live up to my initials.'

Wanda drew her eyebrows together. 'Initials?'

'QC. When I decided to read law, my dear father told everyone I'd be Quentin Cadbury, Queen's Counsellor. QC, QC.'

Without a hint of a smile Wanda said, 'That bad, eh?'

'You could say that. Once, when I came home from university, I thought the house had been taken over by a military coup. He wouldn't let anyone talk to me – it took me five hours to find out it wasn't something I'd done, but because my sister wanted to marry an Australian. Not British, don't you know. Still, all is forgiven now she's produced a son and heir, and it turns out that Howard's parents made money from real estate and his grandfather fought in the war, so he redeemed himself.' Unlike me, he added silently.

Wanda nodded sympathetically and looked at a photograph on the cabinet. It was the one taken on Shelagh's wedding day, restored after the break-in. 'Is that your family? You must miss them even if you don't get on with your father.'

'Yeah. I miss Mum a lot, but I never thought I'd miss my sister. When we were kids, she got on my nerves. She was a goodie-goodie, but when I was older I realized it was her way of keeping on the right side of our father. She often used to fight my corner when I was in trouble.'

Wanda's eyebrows lifted. 'Were you in trouble a lot then?'

'Not *real* trouble. I mean, not with the police or anything. But I was a clumsy kid, I broke a lot of things, and I rebelled at school. I think it was because he expected so much of me. It was the only way I could hit back at him. Whatever he wanted me to do, or be, I did the opposite.'

Feeling Wanda's gaze on him, he coloured. Why was he telling her this?

'I'm going on a bit, aren't I?' he said, putting down his cup. 'Sorry.'

'Don't be. Everyone needs to let off steam now and then. I don't suppose your father can help being the way he is – perhaps he treats you the same way he was brought up.'

'Maybe, but that's no excuse. He's just a bully. Don't get me wrong – he never really hurt me physically, though he gave me a good hiding if he thought I deserved it.' Quentin paused. 'It's just – nothing I ever did was good enough, so I stopped trying.'

Wanda nodded. 'I know what you mean. My mother's a bit like that, but it just makes me determined to prove her wrong. She's always telling me how well my brother's done. The trouble is, it makes you a bit – not selfish exactly, but wanting to do things to show that you can. I did *love* Gerry, but I'm not sure I'd have married him if he hadn't been so well set-up. He was quite a bit older than me.'

Quentin stared at her, fascinated. He was enjoying this glimpse into Wanda's life.

As if aware that she'd said too much, a closed look came over her face. 'Well, there we are,' she finished brightly. 'We're two of a kind.'

Two of a kind. Were they? Quentin didn't think so. Whatever the reasons for her being where she was today, she had obviously fared better than him. From her conversation the previous evening he knew she'd worked in her husband's business. She'd kept the accounts, met and entertained his clients. He could imagine her doing that. She would be an asset to anyone's business.

He followed Wanda's gaze to the running machine. 'Clutters the place up a bit, doesn't it? Handy when it's tipping with rain though, and it's good exercise,' he said.

Her interest in running apparently waning, Wanda indicated towards the smallest photo on show. 'Who's that?' she asked. 'Your brother?'

Quentin's spirits, raised since meeting his new neighbour, dipped as he followed her gaze.

'No, there's only me and Shelagh. That's Nathan. A friend.' He looked away, unwilling to expand on this. It still hurt him to think about it.

Wanda said nothing but cast shrewd eyes over him. Feeling she expected him to say more, Quentin volunteered woodenly, 'I was at university with him.'

The pause that followed was heavy with silent anticipation. Then, as if sensing his reluctance to talk about it, Wanda stood up. 'Well, I'd better go,' she said. 'I need to get to the bank, and later I'm meeting a friend and we're off to the theatre. Thanks for the coffee.'

'My pleasure. See you Saturday, if I don't see you before.' He hovered in front of her, searching for something to say that would smooth out the earlier awkwardness. 'It's such nice weather at the moment. Perhaps we could go for a spin in my car one day, have a drink in the country somewhere.'

'That would be lovely. Bye then.' In a swift movement she reached up and kissed his cheek, then whirled out of the room.

He watched her go, wondering why he'd mentioned the car. Not to impress her, like he had with others. Just to let her know there was more than food and sex to their relationship. Did they even have a relationship, he mused, or was last night's frenzy a one-off? Since they'd woken up that morning, she'd given him no clues, no commitment. She'd shown no embarrassment either, issued no demands. Well, that was exactly what he wanted, wasn't it?

'Perfect,' he said, fondling Magpie behind his ear as he came up to him. 'Don't you think so, boy? Fifty grand, a beautiful new neighbour and you for company. What more could I want?'

Chapter Ten

For Saturday's date with Wanda, Quentin risked breaking into another fifty-pound note to buy salmon and a bottle of good wine. That was one thing he'd learned from his father and was grateful for – his liking for fine wines. He could see Wanda approved of his choice and he prayed she would show her appreciation in the best possible way. She did, and although their lovemaking wasn't as frenzied as before, it was still amazing. Afterwards, she acted as though nothing had happened.

'How can you do that?' he asked her the next morning, immediately feeling guilty. He'd acted exactly the same way with lots of girls.

'We're both grown-ups with our own lives,' she told him. 'We don't need explanations or declarations of love. We like each other, and I feel I can talk to you, and you to me. I'd like us to be friends. We both have needs, and if we can fulfil those together that's fine. If you want more then we'll have to call it a day now. OK?'

'Right,' he mumbled, feeling like a schoolboy. 'That's fine by me.'

'Good,' she said as she reached for her clothes. 'Any chance of a cup of tea?'

'Of course, I'll get it.'

When he'd poured tea and made toast Wanda still hadn't come down, so he placed the food on a tray and carried it upstairs. She sat at the chest of drawers that served as a dressing table, her hand inside the third drawer.

'I can't find a brush,' she said as he came up behind her.

'It's in the bathroom.'

'Oh.' She raked her fingers through her tangled hair. 'Not to worry. I'll wait till I get home.'

They sat on the bed crunching toast and sipping tea. 'Not exactly breakfast at The Dorchester, is it?' Quentin said, grinning.

'No, it's nicer than that.' She flashed a smile at him, and Quentin wondered if she'd ever had breakfast at the Dorchester. Probably, he decided. Was that smile a come-on? He took her plate and cup and placed them on the side table. His hopes were dashed as she slid off the bed and stood up.

'I'd better go and let Mozart out. Thanks for a nice evening. I'll see you later in the week.'

Then she was gone, with the thud of her bare feet on the stairs – her lingering perfume and the indentation on the mattress where she had lain the only things to show she had been there at all. Quentin sucked in a deep breath, feeling suddenly bereft. He wanted to call her back but stopped himself. Too much too soon.

Left alone, he went to the front bedroom and switched on his computer, not bothering to shower or dress. He opened his emails and reread Shelagh's message. Apparently, Uncle John had been a car mechanic. He'd worked on the Ford production line in Dagenham for a while, then for a private company as their chief mechanic. Hardly the sort of job where you could *earn* fifty thousand, let alone *save* that amount. Shelagh's next comment sparked his interest.

> *He was away a lot a few years before he died. I asked Mum and she said he used to deliver cars abroad, and sometimes collected them to drive back.*

Perhaps that's why he was often missing from family gatherings, Quentin thought. Hmm… I'll ask Mum about it when she rings.

When the phone rang later that day, he was surprised to hear his father's voice.

'Quentin? Your father here. Your mother's gone down with the flu. Thought I'd better ring in case you wondered why she didn't call. What's this Shelagh told us about a family tree?'

Scrabbling for a credible answer, Quentin said, 'I just thought it would be good hobby, that's all. Everyone seems to be doing it.'

'Do they? Yes, well, it's nice to know you're taking an interest in family matters. Don't know why you're asking about John though. I always thought Josie married beneath her. Could have married a lieutenant colonel, you know, but she turned him down. An intelligent woman like that wasting herself on a car mechanic, letting the family down.'

Quentin gasped, feeling the blood rush to his face. Had he heard right? It was intolerable. It doesn't matter what he was, he wanted to shout. While he fought for words, his father ploughed on.

'How's the job going? You've been there a while now.'

Longer than you've stayed anywhere, Quentin read between the lines. He burned to say he wasn't working, that he didn't need to work but he was doing very nicely thank you. The thought of his mother going through the mill stopped him.

'It's going all right,' he said. 'I–'

'Good, good.' His father cut him off. 'And the house? Everything in order? Rosemary, go back to bed.'

There was a shuffling noise, as though the receiver was being pulled from side to side. Then Quentin heard his mother's voice raised in frustration. 'Leave me be, Herbert. I'm well enough to speak to my son. Quentin? Hello dear. How are you?'

'I'm fine, Mum. You sound dreadful.'

'I feel it, but I didn't want to miss you. Your father's been looking after me – made me stay in bed, brought me hot toddies.'

Quentin grunted, his anger at his father's belligerent attitude mollified. He had to admit that on the rare occasions when his mother hadn't been well his father had always looked after her. It was the only time he showed any feeling, and if nothing else Quentin believed that he genuinely loved her.

'Your father's right about your Aunt Josie, you know. She could have married a lieutenant colonel. She chose John instead – he was much nicer, and very handsome when he was young. He *was* a mechanic – a very good one.'

'Didn't he go away a lot though? What was that all about?'

'Yes, he used to deliver cars, usually classic cars, that had been advertised abroad, Amsterdam and Paris mostly. Sometimes he'd collect one and bring it back for a private buyer. He was the only one his boss trusted to do it. Most of the cars were valuable, and John was a good driver as well as a good mechanic. That's more or less all he did during his last ten years. He must have earned good money then – he and Josie certainly took enough holidays. Lucky she went while she could. The poor thing was almost crippled with arthritis later, and she was heartbroken when he died. She only lasted another year.'

Quentin heard a catch in his mother's voice. He wasn't sure if it was her cold making her voice unsteady, or being reminded of her sister's death.

'OK, Mum, thanks. I'll do what I can with that.'

'You know all about Josie, don't you?'

'Er, yes, I think so,' he said, puzzled. What was there to know? Josie was a housewife, as far as he knew. 'Remind me.'

'She had a good career, you know, before she married John. I'm sure I've told you that before. She was a secretary in the MOD. It was through her I met…' There was a pause, and Quentin could hear her blowing her nose. 'It was through her I met your father.'

It was coming back to Quentin now. Josie was older than his mother, but she'd married late, possibly a factor that contributed to a childless marriage. He remembered his father saying in one of his rants that Josie had been a highflyer who hobnobbed with the top brass. She must have known his father before his mother did.

'I was already married and had Shelagh before she married John,' his mother went on. 'I think–'

A sneeze blasted in Quentin's ear, and he heard his father's voice bellow, 'That's enough, Rosemary. Go back to bed. Have to go now Quentin. Your mother's eyes are streaming.'

Quentin was puzzled as he hung up. All the background details he'd assimilated about his aunt and uncle hadn't brought him any closer to finding out where the money had come from. In order to concentrate his thoughts, he spent half an hour on the running machine, which raised his heart rate and made him break into a sweat but did nothing to solve the puzzle. Sighing, he poured himself a drink, switched on the TV and sank on to the sofa with Magpie curled up beside him. The mystery of the money could wait another day.

Chapter Eleven

'How's the family tree coming along?' Rosemary asked the next time she rang. 'I don't suppose you've had much time, what with work and everything.'

'No.' Having had a week to reflect on things, Quentin was convinced his uncle must have had something to do with the money he'd found. 'I was wondering if you knew what company John worked for,' he said.

'It wasn't really a company, just a garage that specialised in vintage and upmarket cars. The owner, John's boss, was a real East-Ender according to Josie, but he knew his cars.

The garage was in Bromley, down by the football ground somewhere. It had quite a classy clientele. I think Josie said it closed down not long after John died – John's boss owned the business but he rented the property. Apparently the property was sold when the garage closed, and a fast-food place opened there.'

Quentin cursed silently. So he couldn't even contact John's workplace. Where does the previous owner live, he wanted to ask, but didn't. His mother would wonder why he wanted to know – after all, it had nothing to do with the family tree.

'There's no one else on his side, is there?'

'He had an older brother but John wasn't close to him.'

'Did he have any friends or anyone who might know more about him?' he ventured. 'The ancestry website doesn't help much.'

There was a pause, as if she was trying to work out what she should say. 'Not that I know of. What more do you need to know?'

'Nothing, I suppose, for the family tree. Just curious.'

'Well, that's all I can tell you about him, except... as I said before, he was a nice man. I've got all the details from my parents' side. I'll get Shelagh to email them. Anyway, how about you, Quentin? Are you coping all right?'

'Yes, Mum, I'm fine. No problems at all.'

'And how's the cat?'

'He's OK.' Glad for the change of subject, Quentin made small talk about Magpie and expanded the embellishments of his upcoming promotion. He was pleased he couldn't see his mother's face shining with pride when she said, 'Well done, Quentin. I knew I was right to have faith in you.'

Red heat crept up his neck. 'Thanks, Mum. I'd better go now, Magpie's crying for his food.'

'Well, now you've got your promotion you'll be able to save enough to come and visit us. I'm dying to see you again but your father says we can't come home till next year. I'm working on him though.'

'Right, well, I'll see what I can do,' Quentin mumbled, his face growing hotter. 'Bye for now, Mum.'

As the call ended, Quentin wished for the umpteenth time that his mother was still here. He remained unsettled until he reminded himself that if she were here his father would be too. Feeling better, he realized he wasn't pining as much as he had been after she'd first left. At the moment other things took priority – he had a lot to think about, and Wanda helped.

Forcing his mind back to the money, he racked his brain to think of any other way he could find out how John had come by it, if it *was* John who had hidden it. For all he knew, Josie could have led a secret life. After all, she had worked for the MOD.

He pictured the mild-mannered woman he'd known and shook his head. No, he decided, whether Josie knew or not, it must have been his uncle who'd got the money somehow. Either way, it had to be one or both of them, and he had to start somewhere, so he'd start with John.

He was still absorbed in this when the doorbell rang. Roused from his thoughts, he was pleased when he opened the door and saw Wanda.

'Come in,' he said, stepping back to let her pass. A tingle of excitement went through him as she brushed past, her figure accentuated in a white, Lycra top and tight trousers. The heady scent of her perfume filled the air and she sat down without waiting to be asked, a sign that their friendship had reached a level of familiarity.

'Tea, coffee or something stronger?' he asked, hoping she would stay for the evening, though he hadn't even thought about a meal.

'Nothing, thanks.' She gave him a sultry look from beneath her lashes. 'Actually, I wondered if you'd like to take me out tonight. My friend's let me down, and I don't

59

want to waste the tickets. Something tells me you wouldn't mind sitting through Puccini.'

'Opera? I like opera, though I've only ever seen Carmen live. I'd be delighted to take you. What time?'

'We'd need to leave by about six-thirty. We'll take the tube, it'll be easier.'

'Fine.' Quentin wondered whether he should suggest going earlier so they could get a meal first, but he hesitated. His bank balance was low, he only had about thirty pounds cash and he was reluctant to use too much of his secret stash until he was sure there would be no comeback.

As if reading his mind, Wanda said, 'I've just had lunch, so I won't want to eat before I go. I don't usually like take-away food, but that Indian along the main road's quite nice. We could pick some up on the way back if you like?'

'That'll be great,' agreed Quentin.

Standing, Wanda made to leave. 'That's settled then. Will you knock for me?'

'Yes, but—' He stopped. He shouldn't ask about her unreliable friend, not after what she'd said about being free agents and making no commitments, but he really wanted to know if it was another man.

'But what?'

'Nothing. That'll be lovely. I'm looking forward to it.'

She eyed him coolly for a while. 'He's an old friend of my husband's. I've known him for years. When Gerry was ill, he promised him he'd keep an eye out for me.'

'Sorry,' said Quentin, flushing. 'None of my business.'

'No. Well, anyway, he's got the flu, so he can't come. Right, I'll see you later.'

'OK. Bye, Wanda.'

He closed the door after her, furious with himself. They'd agreed to keep their affair casual and here he was, acting like a schoolboy again. No pressure, no expectations. That's what he'd always wanted from a relationship and that's the way it should be now. After all,

Wanda was older than him. It was ridiculous to think it could turn into something permanent.

'I'm going soft in the head,' he told Magpie, squeezing gelatinous chicken from the pouch onto a plate. 'What do you think, boy?'

Magpie mewed, rubbed himself against his leg and devoured the food in record time. Quentin laughed. 'You really don't care who feeds you, do you, as long as you get fed? You and me both, boy.'

Chapter Twelve

Quentin enjoyed *Madama Butterfly* more than he'd thought he would. He already knew the arias, and liked them more in the context of the story. Wanda held his arm as they walked to and from the theatre, but made no attempt to snuggle up or lean against him during the performance. On the homeward tube she sat opposite him, talking enthusiastically about the show.

After collecting a vegetable korma and chicken biryani from the Indian take-away, they made their way home. The Greenwich streets seemed unusually quiet, and Wanda's heels click-clacked on the pavement, echoing in the night air.

'Yours or mine?' Wanda asked.

'Mine's nearer,' Quentin laughed, pushing open his front gate and gesturing her in.

Once inside they plated up the curry and sat on the settee, trays balanced on their knees, spicy aroma filling the air. When they'd eaten and cleared the dishes away, Quentin filled the kettle.

'Will you stay for coffee?' he asked, hoping she would understand the coded message.

'Would you like me to?' Her voice whispered in his ear as she came up behind him.

Turning and slipping his arms round her waist, he said, 'You know I would.'

Eyes smouldering, she leaned back and looked at him. 'You've talked me into it, but I should go and let Mozart out first. Make the coffee. I'll be ten minutes.'

Loosening his hold, Quentin watched as she walked along the hallway and through the front door, leaving it slightly ajar. With a triumphant smile he turned and poured hot water into the cafetière. There was something to be said for living in a terraced house. Although he'd been brought up in suburban elegance, he found his present situation very convenient. Just a few steps to Wanda's, or a hop over the garden wall.

There was a sudden draught and a noise from the hallway. 'That was quick,' he called, setting the cafetière on a tray.

He turned, anticipation rising like mercury on a warm day. His heart pounded and he gasped as a black-clad figure charged at him. Before he could move, the figure was on him, one huge hand around his throat, the other slamming into his ribcage, then into his stomach. He cried out, tearing at the hand that was choking him. But his adversary was strong. With his free hand he caught hold of one of Quentin's arms and forced him against the wall, pinning the other arm to the wall so that he couldn't move. Winded, Quentin gulped for air.

'Where is it?' the man's voice hissed through the balaclava, his grip tightening on Quentin's throat.

'W-what?' choked Quentin, struggling to break free.

A vicious headbutt jerked Quentin's head back against the wall. Stars danced before his eyes and Quentin stopped struggling.

'Don't give me all that bull. You know what. The last lot, the one he got before he snuffed it. Where is it?'

'I... I don't know what you mean—'

Another headbutt. 'Now listen, sonny, I know the old woman was your aunt, and she must have known about it. There's no way she'd have departed this life without telling someone where it was. I've turned the place upside down, but there's nothing here that I can see, so you must have found it. Now, it don't belong to you, so where is it?'

'What?' Quentin managed to force the word through his constricted windpipe.

'Maybe this'll jog yer memory,' the man grunted, pushing his weight against Quentin and removing his fingers from his throat in a swift movement. Suddenly Quentin felt a blade against his neck. 'I'll give yer ten seconds—'

At that moment, the front door swung open and Wanda appeared. Quentin's attacker turned to see what he was looking at, one giant hand still pinning him to the wall while the other held the knife at his throat.

Quentin heard him swear and then hiss in his ear, 'I ain't finished with you, sonny. I'll be back when you've had time to refresh yer memory. And no police, or I might have to pay a visit to yer friend.' Then he relinquished his hold and sprang away.

Gasping for air, Quentin tried to shout a warning to Wanda, who was starting to edge back towards the door. The man reached her, pushed her roughly against the wall and sped past her into the street.

For a moment it seemed as though time was suspended. Quentin stood, his hands still on his neck, staring at Wanda, who stood open-mouthed staring back. Then pain shot through him where he had been punched, his arms slipping to his stomach as he doubled over and fell to his knees. He heard Wanda rush towards him, felt her hands on his shoulders.

'Quentin! Are you all right? Shall I call an ambulance?'

Struggling to his feet, Quentin shook his head. 'I think I'm OK,' he murmured, leaning on Wanda as she led him into the lounge.

Collapsing into a chair, he drew a sharp breath when she lifted his shirt and prodded him.

'You might have a cracked rib,' she said. 'You should have an X-ray.'

'Just bruised, I expect. I didn't see him until he was on top of me. I thought it was you.'

Wanda lowered her eyes. 'I shouldn't have left the door open. He must have seen me go out – he must have been waiting outside or' – she shivered – 'or hiding in the forecourt, behind the bins.'

She sat for a moment, staring straight ahead. She looks like I feel, Quentin thought, noticing her white face. Then she shook herself and said quietly. 'We ought to call the police.'

'Yeah, we should, but… he said no police.'

There was a pause, as though she was trying to think what to say. 'You're not going to report it?'

Quentin hesitated. It was the sensible thing to do, but something was holding him back. 'Let's have a coffee and think about it,' he said.

Wanda gazed at him, her blue eyes wide. She said nothing, but rose and went to the kitchen. Quentin slumped back in the armchair, his head buzzing. Someone knew the money was here, and they wanted it pretty badly.

'Here.' Wanda pushed a cup into his hand, and the smell of coffee helped to revive him.

He drank it gratefully, feeling its warmth as it travelled down his throat. 'Nice,' he said, tasting the whisky she'd added. 'Thanks.'

Putting her cup on the side table, Wanda settled into the opposite chair and looked at him. 'Right. So someone attacks you, threatens you with a knife. Any idea why?'

Quentin winced as he changed position. What could he say? Should he confide in Wanda? He'd never even told her about the first break-in because he hadn't wanted to frighten her when she'd just moved in. But that wouldn't worry her as much as what she'd witnessed tonight, so there was no reason not to mention it now. It wasn't what had happened that was stopping him, he realized, but why.

He glanced over to where she sat tapping her fingers on the arm of the chair. Sighing, he made his decision.

'Not long before you moved next door I had a break-in. The place was gone over but nothing was taken. I reported it to the police but no joy so far. Later on, someone tried to get in again, but whoever it was set Magpie screeching and the guy made a run for it.'

Wanda nodded. 'Any idea what they're looking for?'

Quentin hesitated, unsure whether to tell her about the money. Suppose she told him to go to the police anyway, and what would she think of someone who found fifty grand and kept it for himself?

'No,' he said at last, 'but whatever it was they ripped the backs off pictures looking for it.'

'I still don't understand why you won't go to the police. You said you did the first time, and this time it's much more serious.'

'Because of my family.'

'Your family? Why do you think it's got anything to do with your family?'

Quentin hesitated. 'Well, the house belonged to my aunt and uncle, and it's been targeted twice.'

'You mean – you think someone's got a grudge against them? Someone who thinks they're still alive?'

Quentin shook his head. 'This bloke knew they were dead. He said so.'

'What exactly did he say?'

'He said there was something in the house that didn't belong to me, that my uncle had left it here.'

Wanda gave him an enquiring look. 'Anything else?'

'No. You came in then.'

'So…' Wanda paused. 'Do you think your uncle might have been involved in dodgy dealings? Is that what you're afraid of?'

When Quentin didn't answer, Wanda went on, 'Even if he was, your aunt and uncle are dead. Going to the police won't hurt them, will it?'

'No,' Quentin said, his mouth tight. 'But it might hurt my mum. I don't want her name dragged through the mud.'

'But your mum's in Australia,' Wanda said, leaning forward. 'It's nothing to do with her.'

'Josie was Mum's sister,' Quentin snapped. 'If anything untoward comes to light, she could be called back for questioning. I can't believe Josie did anything wrong, and I'm not burdening Mum with this if I don't have to. I'd rather sort it out myself.'

Wanda pursed her lips. 'I see your point, but you've been attacked, injured. If they're so desperate to get whatever they want, they're not going to give up. They could really hurt you next time. Or me.'

Quentin pursed his lips. He shouldn't put Wanda in danger. The intruder knew where she lived – suppose he attacked her as he'd threatened?

'Yeah,' he murmured. 'Of course. Sorry. All right, call the police. They didn't do much last time though.'

Wanda didn't move. Instead, she shifted in her seat, chewing at her bottom lip as though trying to decide something.

'Well, we could try and sort it out ourselves,' she said at last, with a sideways look at him. 'If we work together.'

'But you just said–'

'I know, and that stands, all of it. We both know what we *should* do. That doesn't mean we have to do it that way.'

Baffled by her change of attitude, Quentin stared at her. 'What are you suggesting? We form our own detective agency?'

'Nothing so dramatic,' Wanda said, laughing. 'We just do bit of sleuthing off our own backs, that's all, and two heads are better than one. That should suit you, shouldn't it? I notice you have a lot of crime novels on your bookshelves.'

'Reading about it is not the same as doing it,' Quentin countered, 'but still…'

Wanda took up his train of thought. 'We could try, at least. We'll go through everything we know so far, make a search of the house, that sort of thing.'

Unease crept over Quentin, adding to his discomfort. If the man who'd attacked him was after the money he'd already found, it would be counterproductive to search the house. Unless there was more hidden somewhere; or something else…

'If there was anything here I'd have found it by now,' he said. 'It's a small house. There aren't many places to hide things. I'll have a burglar alarm fitted. You should too, and we'll turn them on every time we go out.'

'Em, well, I suppose that's sensible.'

'Sensible! I'd say it was essential.' Quentin winced again as he shifted in the chair.

'I still think you should go for an X-ray,' Wanda said. 'You don't have to tell them anything. You can just say you fell down the stairs or something.'

'I'll go tomorrow if it's too bad. At the moment I just want to sleep.'

Wanda nodded. 'Yes, let's get a good night's sleep, then we can start piecing things together. I'll get you some painkillers.'

Rummaging in her bag, she brought out a packet of Ibuprofen, popped two out and fetched some water. 'I'll stay if you like?' she offered.

Quentin shook his head. 'No, I'll be all right. Unless…' He stopped. Perhaps Wanda was frightened to be on her own. 'Unless you'd rather stay? I don't think he'll come back, if that's what you're worried about.'

'Oh no, I was just thinking of you.'

'Thanks, but there's no need. It'll be sore for a few days, but I'll live.'

'I hope so. Well, ring me if you need to.'

After Wanda had gone, he bolted the door and went back to the lounge. Walking pulled at his stomach muscles, and he grimaced at the thought of climbing the stairs. He was glad now that the bathroom was downstairs, and after he'd been in there he lay on the settee, using a cushion for a pillow and the throw as a blanket. He managed to doze off but woke when pain shot through him as he turned over. Arms folded across his damaged ribs, he walked gingerly to the kitchen, located and swallowed another painkiller and managed to get to his bedroom, where he crawled gratefully into bed.

Sleep evaded him as thoughts spun round his head. Fifty thousand pounds. A serious amount of money. Where had it come from, and why were the backs ripped off his pictures? That thug clearly wasn't hunting for bundles of cash. He tried to imagine John associating with the likes of his attacker. Surely his uncle hadn't been a thief? If he had been, could Aunt Josie have known about it? She was so like his mother – articulate, cultured, rational; yet his mother had married his father, whereas Josie had traded the stiff upper lip and boorish bureaucracy for... what? Excitement? Love?

That's another story, he thought. The question is, was the intruder after the money?

Chapter Thirteen

The shrill of the telephone woke him. Moving carefully, he picked up the bedside phone.

'How are you feeling?' Wanda's voice chirped in his ear.

'OK, I think.'

'Good. I'll come in and get you some breakfast.'

Blinking the sleep from his eyes, Quentin glanced at the clock: 8.10 a.m.

'Give me time to get downstairs and open the door.'

'No rush. Go careful.'

Sitting on the stairs and lowering himself down one at a time was more comfortable than walking. At the bottom he hauled himself up and shuffled to the door just as Wanda's voice called, 'Are you there?'

Releasing the catch and drawing back the bolt, he stood aside to let her in. She had obviously been awake for a while – she looked alert and fresh, with her hair still wet from the shower.

'I brought eggs,' she said, holding out a carrier bag, 'and bacon. Why don't you go and get in the shower while I cook? Or have a soak in the bath – that might do you more good.'

In the bath Quentin brooded over his situation. Wanda had suggested they search the house. He would have to tell her about the money. It was pointless searching for something he'd already found – unless… The suspicion that had been niggling at him arose again. Suppose they weren't after the money? Suppose it was something else? Something just as valuable, more valuable; something white that could be divided up and packed into small, flat packets, more easily hidden. An unwelcome image flashed in front of him and he knew he had to find out. He had to make sure there was nothing else here, that it was just the money they wanted. He recalled what his assailant had said: *where is it, the last lot, the one he got before he snuffed it.* The last lot. Did that mean the last lot of money? Now he thought about it, it didn't sound like it. So he would search the house, check every nook and cranny, every unlikely place he could think of, though it might be a hard task if the burglar hadn't found it. By his own admission his attacker had turned the place upside down.

After his bath and a shave he felt better. The smell of frying bacon made him hungry, and he emerged from the bathroom expecting to see Wanda at the stove. The frying pan was off the hob, the food keeping warm under a lid. Padding through the kitchen in bare feet, he went into the lounge in search of his slippers. He stopped in the doorway, surprised to see Wanda in front of the bureau. The lid was open and she was rummaging through the contents. When she heard his intake of breath, she whirled round and flashed him a smile.

'Thought I'd make a start,' she said easily. 'We should make a search. You never know, there could be something here. It can wait till after breakfast, now you're ready.'

'Oh.' Quentin had been about to tell her about the money, but something stopped him.

'We did agree, didn't we, last night?' Wanda continued. 'That we'd try to solve this mystery together? The quicker we start, the better. Come on, I need to get the eggs on, or the bacon will go hard.'

Breakfast and painkillers improved Quentin's mood. Wanda was right – it was a mystery, but a problem shared was a problem halved, and he felt vaguely optimistic as she settled into the chair opposite with a pen and a writing pad balanced on her Lycra-clad knees. Her white top clung to her breasts and the thought of delights to come lifted his spirits even more.

'So, let's start by recording everything we know,' Wanda said.

Business before pleasure then, Quentin thought, wishing he could switch off his feelings as easily as she seemed to. He shifted in his seat and winced. Oh well, perhaps it was for the best.

'We don't know much,' he admitted. 'I've been broken into but nothing was taken. I've been attacked by someone who thinks I know where something is, but we don't know what.'

Wanda took the lid off the pen. 'Let's start at the beginning. How long was it after your aunt died that you moved in here?'

'At least eighteen or nineteen months. She died the year before my parents emigrated, and John died a year before her.' Quentin frowned. 'Why? You mean, why didn't whoever it is try to get whatever they want before? I did wonder about that. Perhaps they only just found out it was here. Wait a minute though.' He tapped his fingers on his knee as a memory took shape. 'Did I tell you that someone tried to take my keys, at the London Marathon? I thought it was just a random pick-pocket attempt, but what if the attacker was him? If he'd got my keys without me noticing, he could have got in then and looked for what he wanted in broad daylight without arousing suspicion.'

Wanda nodded. 'Yes, he could have.'

'I suppose my aunt and uncle might have known nothing about it,' Quentin ventured. 'It could have been a visitor – a friend or someone who hid the stuff here.' He felt himself grow hot as he said this. It was possible that someone could have hidden something in the house, but only someone who lived here could have hidden the money – they had to know about the cavity and adapt the socket fixing.

Wanda cut through his thoughts. 'Did they have many visitors?'

'What? No, not that I know of. But...'

'But what?'

'Well, I remember Mum saying that in the last years of his life, and before Aunt Josie got too ill, they had a lot of holidays. I suppose someone could have stayed here while they were away.'

'I'll put that down as a possibility. Stuff could have been hidden over three years ago.'

'But why wait this long to try and get it back?'

Wanda pursed her lips. 'Perhaps they couldn't come and get it.'

'You mean, if they were ill, or abroad or–'

'Or in prison,' Wanda finished.

Prison. Was that it? The culprit had been caught on some offence and banged up for three years?

'It could be that,' Quentin said. 'Thinking about it, it's probably the most likely explanation. No one would wait that long if they didn't have to, would they?'

'I shouldn't think so.'

'So,' Quentin went on, 'what we need to find out are the names of people who have been released from prison recently, receivers or dealers in illegal or stolen goods, I mean. How do we go about that without involving the police?'

Wanda looked up from the pad and gazed at him. 'My friend – the one I was supposed to go out with last night – he's got contacts in the prison service. I could ask him.'

Alarm bells rang in Quentin's head. 'Won't he want to know why? We'll have to tell him what's happened.'

'He owes me a favour. He'll do it if he can, if only for Gerry's sake.'

Quentin fingered the mole by his ear, wondering what else her friend did for Gerry's sake. Jealousy rose inside him and he pushed it away. It was untimely and unwelcome, and he had no right to assume things about Wanda.

'What's his name, this guy?'

'Colin.'

'Right. Well, I don't know.'

Wanda raised an eyebrow. 'We've got to start somewhere. Or would you rather keep searching until we've found something?'

'It would help if we knew what we were looking for.'

There was a silence. We're going round in circles, Quentin thought as Magpie came in and rubbed himself against his legs. 'Sorry, boy,' he murmured. 'You haven't had your breakfast, have you?'

'I'll do it.' Wanda stood up and disappeared into the kitchen.

While she was gone Quentin tried to make sense of the situation. Were they being stupid, trying to deal with this on their own? Things could get dangerous, and if they got into trouble they'd only have themselves to blame.

'Have you had any ideas?' Wanda asked, coming back in.

'Not really, except I think I'll search the internet and find a security company. The sooner we get an alarm the better.'

'Hmm. Actually, I was thinking perhaps I should have a key, in case I need to get in here in a hurry. I mean, if I hear a kerfuffle, I could let myself in and frighten an intruder off, or check everything's all right if you're not here.'

Quentin stared at her. 'I hope you wouldn't come barging in if you thought someone was here. That would be asking for trouble, wouldn't it? Just call the police if that happens.'

'You could be killed by the time they arrive,' Wanda pointed out. 'When someone broke into Gerry's shop, they took two hours to get there. I couldn't sleep easy in my bed if I heard something and left you to get your head caved in.'

Mollified, Quentin said, 'That's sweet of you, but the same applies the other way round. He said he might pay you a visit.' He saw Wanda flinch and remembered he hadn't mentioned that to her at the time. He added hastily, 'But I'm sure he only said that to frighten me. He's got no axe to grind with you.'

Wanda's expression confused him. She looked unnerved, understandably, but there was something else, something he couldn't put his finger on. She opened her mouth as if to speak, then closed it again.

'All right,' she said at last. 'Get an alarm, but that will take a while. I'll get duplicates of my keys cut for you today, and I'll take yours and get a set cut for me. OK?'

Quentin nodded. 'Yes, but that won't work if the bolt's on the front door.'

'It won't be bolted if you're not here, will it? If you are here when someone breaks in, I'll come in the same way they do. How are your bruises?'

'I'll live. I'll be moving a bit slowly for a few days, and running is definitely out, but I'm all right.'

'Good. Well, I'll go and get these keys cut, then I'll go and see Colin.'

'I thought you said he had the flu.'

'He has, but I'm sure he'll see me. I won't catch anything. I've got a natural immunity, according to my mother. I'll pick you up some more painkillers, and I'll be back later to cook dinner.'

Brightening at the thought of a cosy evening with Wanda, Quentin settled back in the chair. He closed his eyes and tried to forget the events of last night. Filling his mind with images of Wanda, he recalled their first meal together, the wild night that followed, and smiled. He felt her caress, heard her voice, silky and sexy as she whispered encouragement into his ear. Something silky and soft brushed against his hand. He jumped and his eyes flew open, expecting to see Wanda nestling against him.

'Magpie! You gave me a start.'

'Meow!' Magpie curled up on his lap and started purring.

Quentin relaxed, trying to recall his daydream, but an idea kept gnawing at him. He tried to push it aside, to overlay it with nicer thoughts, but it persisted. Why was Wanda really going through his bureau? He hadn't thought she was the type to rifle through someone else's things without asking. She was too much of a lady – wasn't she? What was she up to?

'Nothing,' he said aloud. Pushing Magpie off his knees, he eased himself up. With the speed of an acrobat the cat twisted in mid-air, landed on his feet and stared haughtily at him. For once, Quentin ignored his how-dare-you-disturb-me look as he puzzled over Wanda's actions, his thoughts darkening as he forced himself to face the reality of the situation.

What did Wanda see in him, really? She was mature, experienced, sexy, beautiful, desirable... She could have any man she chose. Why him? Because he'd saved her dog's life? A contributory factor, perhaps, initially. Because she found him attractive? Or because, as she'd admitted, she had needs and it was convenient? Maybe she had a soft spot for younger men. Or was it something different, something he didn't want to think about?

Why was Wanda as reluctant to involve the police as he was? She had played it cool – she had urged him to call them, but then completely changed her mind. She hadn't seemed keen on the burglar alarm suggestion either, and had been quick to suggest she should have a key.

He shook his head, which was beginning to ache as much as his ribs. Someone knew there was something hidden in this house. Whether it was the money or something else, they knew it was here. Did Wanda know what it was?

Deciding that whisky didn't mix with painkillers, he shuffled into the kitchen and poured himself a glass of water. Magpie followed, and sat at his feet as though forgiving him for interrupting his sleep.

'What do you think then, boy? Are we being taken for a ride?'

'Meow.'

'Is that all you can say? Well, we need to know, don't we? And I suppose there's only one way to find out.'

Chapter Fourteen

'Quentin?'

Surprised that his mother was calling midweek, Quentin answered, 'Mum? Everything all right?'

'Yes, dear. Why wouldn't it be?'

'It's just – you don't normally call in the week, that's all.'

'No, well... I was feeling a bit homesick. Your father's joined this ex-servicemen's club and Shelagh, Howard and Michael are away for a few days. Course, I'm glad your father's getting out of the house.'

I bet you are, Quentin thought. Was he making life difficult for her? His mother had always coped with his belligerence, but in England she'd had friends and activities to fall back on.

'Anyway,' she was saying, 'I just wanted to hear your voice, make sure you're all right.'

'I'm fine, Mum, don't worry.'

'What time is it there? I don't want to make you late for work.'

'It's OK, I've got plenty of time. So, you're missing old Blighty then, eh? Bet you don't miss the rain.' He imagined his mother's rueful smile.

'No, but I miss you, Quentin. When do you think you'll be able to come and see us? I could send you the money for your fare.'

Was that it? Had she suggested they paid his fare? He could hear his father's impatient reply – 'For goodness sake, Rosemary, we haven't been gone five minutes, and Quentin's working now. Let him stand on his own feet and pay for himself.'

'No, no, Mum, it's not the money, it's work. It's difficult to get time off at the moment. They're short staffed.'

He thought he heard a sniffle from his mother. 'Well, if you don't come soon, I'll just have to come over there.'

Cringing at the thought of his parents discovering his unemployment and uncovering his lies, he said hastily, 'Don't be silly, Mum. If you come home because you're homesick you might find it harder to go back, then how would Shelagh and little Michael feel? Just a few months, and things will be easier at work. Then I'll ask for some leave and come over. I'd love to come.'

'Would you?'

'Of course I would. I'm looking forward to seeing you, and Shelagh.'

His mother's tone lifted a little. 'Oh good. I was beginning to wonder if you really wanted to come.'

'What, and miss all that sunshine? You must be kidding.'

'So you haven't got yourself a girlfriend yet then? No one special, I mean? Don't let that stop you coming – you can bring her with you.'

'Not exactly. There is someone, but she's more a friend.'

'Oh. Well, as long as you're not lonely. I feel as though I've deserted you.'

Quentin paused before answering. There had been times when he'd felt deserted.

'It's all right,' he said. 'It's only natural you'd want to be with Shelagh and Michael. Anyway, I'm a big boy now.'

He heard her sigh. 'I know. I expect I'm being silly. Well, I'd better let you go. I'll speak to you again on Sunday.'

'OK, Mum. Thanks for ringing. Oh, Mum? I was wondering, you know when John and Josie went on holiday, where did they go?'

'France mainly, as far as I know. Sometimes Spain. His boss had a place there. Why?'

Floundering for a few seconds, Quentin blurted, 'Just curious. I was thinking about the family tree and I remember you saying they had a lot of holidays.'

'They did. They never seemed short of money, though I don't think John earned that much. John wouldn't let Josie go short, though, he always looked after her. Bought her some nice jewellery too, a lovely necklace and earrings, which I've got now, though I never did find the bracelet that went with them.'

'Sounds like a good bloke. What was his boss's name, do you know?'

The line crackled in the ensuing silence. For a moment Quentin thought she'd put the phone down. Then, she said, 'He was a good man. I can't remember the boss's name. I'd better go, Quentin. Your father will be back soon. I feel better now I've spoken to you.'

'Great talking to you, Mum. We'll speak at the weekend, but I'll call before that if you like.'

There was another pause, longer than the normal time delay between countries. 'Tuesdays and Thursdays are best.'

Quentin heard the underlying message – that's when your father isn't here. 'All right, Mum, I'll remember. Bye for now.'

'Bye, Quentin dear.'

The phone clicked in his ear and he put it down thoughtfully. Had something upset his mother or was she just missing home? He wished she were here. So... John and Josie had holidayed in Europe. Well, why wouldn't they, with fifty thousand quid to back them up?

* * *

By Wednesday, with the aid of anti-inflammatories, Quentin's pain had eased, and as long as he was careful he was able to carry on as normal. After days of being cooped up, he was desperate to get some fresh air and decided to drive out of town. Wanda had a hair appointment so couldn't go with him. He drove to Arundel, where his late grandparents had lived, grateful that the BMW was an automatic and he didn't have to strain his muscles changing gear. When he got there, he marvelled afresh at the majestic towers of the castle and imposing lines of the great church outlined against the blue of the summer sky.

He found the pub he recalled, The Black Rabbit on the river, bought a Coca-Cola and sat outside, his thoughts turning to what he had deliberately been avoiding all morning. Wanda.

What did he know about her really? Mystery was part of her attraction, he realized, but he had enough mystery in his life now. She said she'd spoken to Colin, the friend who had contacts in the prison service, and was waiting for him to get back to her. I've got to find out what her angle is, he mused. It's cards-on-the-table time.

When a pretty barmaid came to collect empty glasses, he snatched up an abandoned beer glass. 'Let me help you with that,' he said, forgetting his recent beating. He stood up swiftly and pain stabbed at him. He lost his balance, knocking the tray and sending the glasses crashing to the ground.

'I'm so sorry,' he gasped, straightening up. The glass he still clutched in his hand was in one piece, but the remains of its contents had splashed over his trousers and dripped into his shoe. The barmaid seemed annoyed, then grinned as she looked down at his legs.

'I think you've come off worse,' she said.

After he'd helped pick up the glass and sponged the beer from his trousers with damp tissue, he felt more uncomfortable than ever. Hoping he didn't look as though he'd wet himself, he went back to the car.

He'd only driven a short way when he made a snap decision to go to Bromley to see if he could find the place where his uncle had worked. Someone in the area might remember the garage and the name of the owner. Down by the football ground, his mother had said. A good starting point.

By the time he got there his trousers had dried and he drove around the surrounding area, looking for a fast-food restaurant that could once have been a garage. He carried on until he saw a restaurant alongside a concrete car park. Not one of the fast-food chains, he noticed, but styled like one. He pulled into it, left the car and went inside.

'Sorry,' said the manager when Quentin questioned him. 'I've no idea about the previous owner. I only rent this place, and it's all dealt with through an agency.'

After he'd taken the name of the agency, Quentin made enquiries at neighbouring properties. The only information he gained was that the garage had closed down suddenly. Back in the car he rang the agency. The person he spoke to had only dealt with the present owner, whose name she refused to give, quoting the data protection act.

Bugger it, he thought. At this rate we'll never find out anything.

* * *

When he got home, he fed Magpie, had a shower and changed ready for dinner with Wanda. As he reached into the wardrobe he frowned. Surely his suede jacket had been on the other side this morning? He glanced round the room to see if there was anything else out of place. There wasn't, but he had the distinct feeling someone had been through his things. There was no sign of forced entry, so that meant one thing: whoever it was had a key. And only one other person had a key.

His heart felt leaden. Wanda knew something, something she wasn't telling him. How did she know, and why wasn't she telling him? Was she behind the whole business?

'No,' he muttered, 'please don't let it be Wanda. Why on earth did I let her persuade me to give her a key?'

Reaching for his aftershave and splashing some on, he continued, 'But she gave me a key to hers, didn't she, so...'

He stopped, not knowing how to go on. 'Sod it,' he said, thumping the handrail as he went downstairs. 'I'll have it out with her and be done with it. Do you hear that, boy?'

Magpie eyed him solemnly.

Quentin eyed him back. 'I don't care what you think. I'm going to ask her – tonight.'

* * *

'You smell nice,' Wanda purred, pouring Quentin another glass of wine.

'So do you,' he murmured, unable to tear his gaze from her creamy throat and the tantalising swell of her breasts under the gossamer blouse.

Since his arrival at her house before dinner, she'd been teasing him with her come-hither looks and gentle banter, inflaming his desire.

God, she's so sexy, was all he could think as he ate his way through three courses and sipped the accompanying wine. His heart beat fast when her hand brushed his, faster when the toe of her shoe traced the seam of his trousers up to his thigh.

'Time for some Leonard Cohen,' she said, going over to the CD player, pressing a button and turning to him. With a seductive smile she opened her arms and he walked into them, all thoughts of confrontation banished. What the hell, he thought as his head bent to hers. What the hell.

Chapter Fifteen

A persistent noise shattered Quentin's dream.

'Wassat?' he murmured sleepily when Wanda sprang out of bed and rushed downstairs.

The noise continued, and Quentin sat up as he realized it was Mozart barking. He rubbed his eyes and peered at the luminous bedside clock: 5.03 a.m. Then came the sound of glass shattering, muffled as though coming through a closed door. A scream from Wanda made him leap up and run downstairs, cursing as his still tender ribs sent pains shooting through him.

'What is it?' he shouted, seeing Wanda silhouetted against the kitchen window, her arm raised towards it.

'A man,' she choked. 'There was a man in your garden. I saw him over the wall – the security light came on, he threw something through your bathroom window and ran off.'

Making for the front door, Quentin grabbed the nearest coat and threw it on. Snatching up his keys from the hall stand he flew into the tiny forecourt, through the gate, and stood before his own house in the early morning half-light, wrestling with the key as it stuck in the lock.

'Come on, damn you,' he muttered, then heaved a sigh as the lock clicked and the door swung open. Switching on the light he saw Magpie cowering against the bottom stair. 'All right, boy,' he said, hurrying past him. He could feel the draught coming from the gap where the bathroom window had been. In the bath, something brown and solid showed beneath the cascade of broken glass. Wrapping his hand in a towel, he scraped away the glass and picked up the brick. There was a piece of paper tied around it.

Quentin stared in disbelief. A brick through the window – surely that sort of thing only happened in films. He whirled round as he heard footsteps and Wanda appeared, looking fraught. Her worried expression lifted and she grinned when she looked at Quentin.

'What's so funny?' he spat, irritated that she could smile at such a time. They would have to clear this mess up – she wouldn't think it was funny then. Catching sight of himself in the mirror, he relaxed and grimaced, the corners of his mouth twitching.

'I suppose I do look a bit of a sight,' he admitted, drawing the front of her red coat together over his nakedness. He caught her eye, and she dissolved into nervous, almost hysterical laughter. Soon, he was laughing with her, each intake of breath pulling at his stomach muscles.

'Is that a note?' she gasped when they'd recovered.

Pulling the paper from under the string, Quentin's eyes widened as he read aloud,

> *You've got until 1400 Saturday, 13 August. Have the goods ready by then, or my friend will visit you again, and you'll have more than a broken window, so will your delectable neighbour. Don't even think about leaving, and of course, no police.*

'My friend,' he repeated, handing the note to Wanda. 'I assume that means the bloke who duffed me up. *He* obviously didn't write this. It's too articulate for him. So, our visitor wasn't the brains, just the brawn. And my delectable neighbour. That's you, I take it.'

Wanda shuddered. 'They must be here,' she whispered, staring into space, 'they must be. We've got to find them.'

'Find what?'

No answer. 'Wanda? Find what? You know, don't you?'

A tear trickled down her cheek, and she wrapped her arms around herself. 'I thought I could do it,' she said, her teeth chattering, 'but now I'm scared. Quentin, I'm scared.'

Quentin held her close, marvelling at the change from laughter to tears and sophisticated woman to vulnerable child. He hadn't seen her quivering like this since the day Mozart had nearly been killed. He felt suddenly protective, the difference in their ages melting away.

'It's all right,' he soothed. 'It'll be all right. Go back to yours. I'll just get something up at this window, then I'll come in and make you a cup of tea.'

'But,' she blubbed, nodding towards the gaping window.

'It won't matter,' he told her. 'They've delivered their message. They won't come back again.'

'All right.' She sniffed as she walked away. 'Don't be long.'

Bastards, Quentin thought as he fastened a piece of cardboard to the window frame. Still, one thing had been resolved. Whatever it was that Wanda knew, she would have to tell him now.

* * *

Back at Wanda's he dressed and made tea.

'So,' he said as he watched Wanda gulp her tea, her hands still shaking. 'Tell me.'

He waited until she'd put her cup down and settled back in her chair. She pushed a lock of blonde hair behind her ear and squared her shoulders, looking more like the Wanda he knew.

'Well?' he prompted.

Averting her eyes she began. 'I haven't been totally honest with you, Quentin, and I'm sorry.'

You and me both, Quentin thought.

'Not long before my husband died, I found out he wasn't just an antiques dealer. He... he dealt in something else, that is, he acquired certain things and passed them on.'

Quentin's gaze shifted to the photograph of Gerry, trying to imagine this distinguished-looking man having anything to do with illegal dealings. He couldn't. 'You mean he dealt in illegal goods – he was a fence?'

Swallowing hard, Wanda nodded. 'Yes, that's what it boils down to. When I found out, he laughed it off, said I wasn't to worry or get involved, that nothing bad would happen. I was stupid, naïve, not to realize that he couldn't have made all his money through antiques. The shop was never that busy. But I did the accounts, and they seemed OK. Mind you, *he* recorded the figures initially. I just worked with what he gave me.'

'What sort of things did he handle?' Quentin held his breath as he waited for her answer.

'Only one thing. He didn't trouble himself with trivia.' Wanda looked at him, her eyes wide. Then drawing a deep breath, she said, 'Diamonds.'

'Diamonds!' Despite his amazement, he felt a quiver of relief. It wasn't drugs. Not those destructive substances that made a mockery of self-control, reduced people to impotent creatures desperate to get their next fix at any cost. The familiar image rose before him, and he pushed it away.

Wanda continued, 'The thing is, Gerry was expecting a consignment, but it never came. He knew it had arrived in the country because he had a call to confirm it.'

'A call – from whom?'

'I didn't know who it was then, not till much later. Anyway, the caller was your uncle.'

'My uncle?'

'Yes. He wasn't well but said he would get the goods over to Gerry as soon as he felt better. But he never delivered them.'

'Of course he didn't,' Quentin blurted out. 'He had a heart attack.'

'Yes, well, whoever set the job up leaned on Gerry to get the diamonds, threatened him. The only reason he didn't carry out his threat was because he got had up – I can't remember the details. Anyway, he went to prison, so the pressure was off for a bit. It played on Gerry's mind though, and when he was ill with cancer, he told me he needed to get these diamonds before this guy was released.'

'So why didn't he?'

Wanda cast him an impatient look. 'Gerry wasn't a thug. He knew your aunt still lived here, and that she wasn't well. He wouldn't have dreamed of approaching her or breaking in. Anyway, he was ill himself by then.'

'Right. So Gerry knew who set the job up then? I mean, how did he know he went to prison?'

Wanda shrugged. 'He didn't say, and he didn't give any names. When he died, I went through his effects and found a notebook with some initials and phone numbers in. I had no luck with any of them except one, which I traced to your uncle. I should have gone to the police then, but I didn't want to expose Gerry if I didn't have to. Not long after that, I got a note – printed, like that one round the brick. It said if I didn't want to end up like Gerry, I'd better find that consignment and hand it over.'

Quentin gasped. 'End up like Gerry? You mean they killed him?'

'No, no. Why would they kill him before he'd got the diamonds? No, he died of cancer. They just meant if *I* didn't want to end up dead like him.'

'But that's a threat – to kill you.'

'I know. They said if I went to the police, they'd kill me. So I didn't.'

'You decided to try and find the diamonds yourself?'

Wanda sighed. 'Yes.'

'And that's why you moved next door? And why…' Quentin gulped as the next thought came to him. 'That's why you came on to me – to get into my house and at the diamonds.'

'No! Well, yes, initially, but once I got to know you, that wasn't the reason. I really like you, Quentin, honestly I do.'

'Honestly!' Quentin barked. 'I wouldn't think honesty had anything to do with it.'

'I admit I didn't tell you the whole truth,' Wanda said, 'but trying to find the diamonds wasn't the reason I carried on seeing you.'

'No? What was the reason then?'

'Because I wanted to. We have a mutual attraction and enjoy each other's company. There's nothing wrong with that, is there? Anyway, I've got a feeling there's something *you* haven't told *me*. You were too quick to agree not to involve the police.'

Quentin stiffened, guilt swamping him. He hadn't told her about the money. Even when she'd witnessed his attack, and been threatened herself, he hadn't told her that at the time he'd thought they were after the money. But why should he tell her? She had used him, lied to him. Yet something told him she wasn't lying now, and she stood to lose as much as him if the diamonds weren't found.

As he gazed at her, an image of his slashed pictures came to him. That knife-crazy burglar had ripped the backs from his pictures, which now made sense if he was looking for diamonds taped into the frames. The thought of that knife being held against his throat made him shiver. What if Wanda had been in the house? What if she'd got in the way? Her beautiful face... It didn't bear thinking about.

'I found some money,' he said at last. 'Quite a stash, hidden in the house. I thought that's what the break-ins were about. I had no idea where it came from, but if my uncle was smuggling diamonds, I suppose he might have sold some and made money that way. Anyway, I've kept hold of it. I need the money, but I'm frightened to splash it around in case it's hot. It could be traced.'

Wanda raised a well-shaped eyebrow, and Quentin waited for the who's-not-been-honest-now comment. Instead, she said, 'Have you spent any of it?'

'A little. Steak dinners and fine wines for beautiful neighbours don't come cheap you know, but no comeback so far.'

Wanda flushed. 'Right,' she said. 'What if you gave it to the guy who attacked you? That might be enough to make him leave you alone.'

Quentin considered this. 'I could try that, I suppose, but I don't think it would work. I'm guessing diamonds would be worth more than fifty grand, and what's to stop him taking the money and still coming back for the diamonds he thinks are here? He might even think I've found them and sold them for some fantastic amount. He'll want a lot more than fifty grand then, and if I say there's no more money, he'll think I've spent it or kept it for myself.'

'OK. So what now?' Wanda asked. 'We've got until Saturday, 13 August, that's ten days.'

'Yeah, and the time was written 1400, not two o'clock. Do you reckon he's got military connections?'

Wanda shrugged. 'Who knows? Are we going to carry on trying to sort things out ourselves, or should we go to the police and ask for protection?'

Quentin slumped back in his chair. 'I don't know. What do you think?'

'I say we give it a bit longer. It would be best to find the diamonds, get these people off our backs.'

'What if we find them? They haven't told us how to contact them.'

'I'm sure they'll contact us when they need to. Like I said, I just want to hand the diamonds over and forget about the whole thing. I mean, I'd like to see them behind bars, but it would drag on for months, maybe years. All that publicity…'

'Yeah.' Quentin shivered. He imagined the newspaper headlines – Man found dead in Greenwich.

'Quentin.' Wanda's voice broke into his thoughts. 'Did you hear me? I said, where should we start looking? We need to get on with it. This is getting scary.'

'You're right. OK, let's have some breakfast, then we'll get cracking.'

While Wanda cooked breakfast, Quentin went home for a shower. If he was going to spend the day searching the house, he needed to be alert, but he also wanted to check something without Wanda being there. Going straight to the kitchen, he pulled out the fridge, knelt down and removed the plastic panel, one thought uppermost in his mind: John had hidden the money here – could the diamonds be here too?

Chapter Sixteen

His heart beating fast, Quentin put a hand into the cavity and felt around. Nothing. His hand touched solid brick at every turn, concrete on the bottom. The cavity was just big enough to take the bag. To be sure he hadn't missed anything, he fetched a torch and shone it in the hole, but there was nothing but dust and cobwebs.

He pushed the money bag back. He wasn't sure why he still felt the need to hide it. The burglar was looking for diamonds probably worth much more than his stash, but, if there was another break-in and it was found, it wouldn't be left behind. And Wanda was going to be poking around. Did that matter now she knew about the money? She hadn't asked how much, or where it was, and he hadn't felt the urge to tell her. He'd make sure *he* searched the kitchen.

The fridge squeaked on the floor when he pushed it back into position, and his hands lingered on the handle. A thought struck him. He hadn't bought this, he'd inherited it with the house. Remembering a scene from a film he'd seen, he opened the door, drew out the ice tray and placed it in a bowl. Then he unplugged it so the freezer compartment would defrost. If the diamonds were frozen into the ice round the edges or in the ice tray, they would be revealed when it melted.

Was there anywhere else where diamonds might be hidden? He glanced at the washing machine. No, that had come from his parents, along with the cooker and the microwave. That only left the cupboards, and he'd been through them.

'Bloody hell!' he groaned to Magpie. 'This is ridiculous!'

Magpie mewed as if agreeing with him. 'Fat lot of good you are,' Quentin told him, and with a last look round the kitchen, he headed to Wanda's for breakfast.

* * *

After hours of painstakingly searching each room, both Quentin and Wanda were beginning to think they were wasting their time. It was four in the afternoon before Quentin ventured into the loft, squeezing through the narrow hatch that seemed to have been designed for a much smaller person. The musty smell of disuse filled his nostrils. He hadn't been up here before. Any of his meagre possessions not on show were stowed in the cupboard in the second bedroom. The loft floor had been partially boarded, and he perched on the chipboard with his legs dangling through the opening.

'Pass me that torch,' he called to Wanda, leaning down to take it. When he switched it on, he swung its light around, seeing nothing but bare bricks and wooden beams. Cobwebs hung like tapestries from the rafters, and the remains of a bird's nest was tucked into a corner. He could see a pinprick of daylight behind it, from under the eaves where they'd gained access. Pulling up his legs he shuffled nearer and shone the torch on it. It was empty except for some pieces of eggshell and a large spider, which scuttled out and disappeared. He flicked the light to the other side. Nothing. He was about to come down when something bright caught his eye. He turned the torch on it again. There. Whatever it was, it glittered from beside one of the beams that formed the floor of the loft. Shuffling to the end of the boarded area, he leaned towards it. His heart missed a beat as his fingers closed round something round, rough and shiny. Either this was the biggest diamond ever known or…

Staring at the thing in his hand, his hopes slid away. Small, round, covered in silver sparkles, it glittered up at him mockingly. A Christmas decoration. Quentin felt the laughter bubbling inside him. A Christmas bauble! As if it could have been a diamond. But just think if it had been…

Throwing it down in disgust, he picked up the torch and sidled towards the hatchway. 'Total waste of time,' he breathed, then stopped as he spotted something else. Nestled in some paper clippings, the edge of a piece of card was visible. From what he could see Quentin guessed it was a photograph, and he leaned across and pulled it out. It *was* a photo, curled at the edges and filmed with dust. Blowing away the particles that clung to it, he guessed from the colour and the clothes of the two people it showed that it was taken some time in the seventies or early eighties. He pushed it into his pocket, intending to look at it properly later. Going part way down the ladder, he felt for the cover to close the hatch. Instead, his hand came down hard on the Christmas bauble and he felt a sharp pain as it shattered under his palm.

'Sod it!' he muttered, seeing the blood drip from his hand. 'Half an hour clearing broken glass from the bathroom without a scratch, then stabbed by a bloody bauble!'

* * *

'We've searched the house from top to bottom,' Wanda said when they took a break for tea. 'Well, not quite the bottom. What about under the floorboards?'

Quentin groaned. He was tired, his ribs ached and the thought of lifting carpets and prising up floorboards filled him with dread.

'Not today,' he answered. 'The kitchen and bathroom are concrete and if my uncle had to hide the diamonds in a hurry, he wouldn't have had time to take up carpets and floorboards, plus it would be a difficult thing to do if he was ill and without Aunt Josie knowing.'

'*Did* he hide them in a hurry?'

'Well, we know it was after he brought them back and before he died. If he wasn't feeling well – I don't know, perhaps he had a premonition. Maybe he didn't want Aunt Josie to find them, to get involved. Whatever the reason, he felt he had to hide them until he could offload them to Gerry.'

He saw Wanda wince. 'Sorry,' he added. 'That was thoughtless of me.'

'That's OK,' Wanda said in between sips of tea. She sighed. 'They may not be in the house at all. They could be buried in the garden.'

'That would be difficult, seeing as it's all patio. There're only a few tubs. I'll empty those tomorrow, just to be sure.'

Going to the kitchen window, Wanda gazed out. 'There's no shed,' she said frowning. 'Everyone's got a shed. Why haven't you?'

Quentin shrugged. 'How do I know? It probably blew down in a gale or something and wasn't replaced.' Thank goodness, he thought. That's one less place to search.

He liked his garden. Small and easy to keep, with no grass to cut and only the border by the back wall to weed, it was a far cry from the showcase garden he'd grown up with in Oxford.

Magpie wandered in and sat at his feet. 'All right, boy. I know you want your dinner. Talking of dinner, what are we doing tonight? Have you got anything planned?'

Wanda pulled a face. 'I was supposed to be meeting a girlfriend for a drink, but I think I'll phone and cancel. I can't be bothered to cook though. Shall we eat out? Or perhaps we shouldn't go out. Still, they've given us ten days.'

'That's what's worrying me,' Quentin said. 'It doesn't make sense. How do they know we won't do a disappearing act?' He thought of the warning in the note: *Don't even think about leaving.*

He saw alarm on Wanda's face. 'You mean – you think they'll be watching us? Watching the house?'

To Quentin's mind it was the only scenario open to whoever had written the note, but he didn't want to say this. 'Who knows? It doesn't matter. We have a choice, three actually. Stay and try to find the diamonds, go to the police or cut and run. We've already ruled out the police for the moment, and if we want to find out what's going on we'll have to stay here. We have to carry on as normal. We'll go out, set the alarm. They won't break in again, though. They've done their search – they're making us do the work for them now. Yes, we'll eat out. Good idea.'

'OK, but early. I'm exhausted.'

Quentin nodded. 'You go and get ready. I'll hop in the shower and call for you at six.'

When she'd gone, Quentin hauled himself up, fed Magpie and undressed ready to shower. As he stepped out of his jeans, he felt something rustle in the pocket. Remembering the photograph, he drew it out. The colours had faded and the white edging had yellowed, but otherwise it was clear enough. The picture was of a man and a woman, arms around each other. The man was smiling, and the woman was gazing at him with a look so full of love Quentin could almost feel it. John and Josie when they were young, he thought.

After placing the photo in the bureau, he showered and put on fresh clothes. Apart from being hungry, he felt better, but decided Wanda was right. An early dinner, a glass of wine, and straight to bed. Alone.

Chapter Seventeen

The next morning Quentin checked the ice tray and freezer compartment in the fridge. There were no diamonds, and when he emptied the garden tubs he found nothing but soil, roots and worms. He muttered to himself as he refilled the last of the tubs.

'This is a bloody fiasco. I don't believe there's any diamonds here at all.'

'Morning. You putting bulbs in there?'

Quentin looked up to see the man from next door peering over the fence. 'Er, yes.' He floundered. He hadn't got to know any neighbours apart from Wanda, but he'd seen this man in the garden a few times.

'Daffodils,' he said, quoting the first flower that came into his mind.

'Good idea,' the man agreed. 'Plant daffs round the edges and you'll have colour in the spring before those roses flower. Pretty, those rock roses.'

Quentin had no idea that the plant he'd just shoved carelessly back into its container was a rock rose. It could have been a variety of dandelion for all he knew, but he nodded and said, 'Yes.'

'Your security light's a bit sensitive,' the man carried on. 'I thought I saw it come on the other night – well, early in the morning. Thought I heard something too – sounded like glass breaking – but I couldn't see anything when I looked out. Everything all right? Not another break-in, I hope.'

Remembering the police questioning the neighbours after the initial break-in, Quentin glanced towards the house. The bathroom window couldn't be seen from this angle, because Wanda's house looked on to that side. Searching for something to say, his gaze fell on some empty wine bottles outside the back door.

'No,' he said. 'It was… it was my cat. I left him out last night and he knocked some bottles over.'

The man's disapproval of cats showed in his disparaging look. 'Let's hope he doesn't make a habit of it. My name's Jim, by the way, and my missus is Carol.'

Brushing the soil from his fingers, Quentin strode across and held out his hand.

'Quentin,' he said, hoping he could draw the conversation to a close and not have to answer any more questions. 'I'd better go in – I've left something on the stove.'

Before the other man could reply Quentin released his hand and hurried indoors.

'That was close, boy,' he said as Magpie padded up to him. 'Lucky I thought of blaming you.'

Magpie gave him a how-dare-you-take-my-name-in-vain look and walked away. 'No need to get the hump.' Quentin grinned. 'You don't know when you're well-off. You'd still be homeless if it wasn't for me.'

He washed his hands and then rummaged in the cupboard for his new breakfast cereal. 'Crunchy granola with nuts,' he read, pouring some into a bowl. He was halfway through it when he chewed on something hard and felt a crack. 'Bloody hell!' he groaned when he realized he'd lost a filling. 'And I've swallowed it!'

Scraping the remainder of the food into the bin, he rang for a dental appointment.

* * *

When he saw Wanda later that morning he asked her about her so-called friend, Colin. 'Hasn't he come back to you yet? And hasn't he asked why you want to know who's been released from prison recently?'

'I told you, he was a friend of Gerry's.'

'But Gerry was... Is he bent then, this Colin?'

'No. He knew Gerry dabbled a bit, but he never got involved. They went to school together, and apparently Gerry saved his life once. He fell into a lake and couldn't swim. Colin's brother is in the prison service.'

'Right. So has he come up with anything?'

'Not yet,' Wanda groaned. 'He's supposed to be calling me tonight or tomorrow. It's awful, this waiting around.'

'I know. What can we do? We've been over the place with a fine-tooth comb. There's nowhere else to look.'

'Perhaps they're not here at all,' Wanda suggested. 'Your uncle could have passed them on to someone else, or hidden them somewhere else.'

'How could he? He was ill, and we're not talking about dodgy TVs or nicked computers here. You can't just give someone thousands of pounds worth of smuggled diamonds, and anyway he'd have wanted his payment. If he could have got them out of the house, he'd have given them to Gerry.'

'Hmm, I guess so. What's wrong?'

Having managed to secure an emergency dental appointment for that afternoon, Quentin told Wanda about his broken tooth. Her suggestion that a day's break would do them both good was welcome. They could approach it tomorrow with fresh eyes, as well as hopefully getting some information from Colin.

* * *

At three-fifteen Quentin lay back in a leather chair, breathing in antiseptic air and staring at the ceiling while the dentist probed the gum around his broken tooth.

'Hmm,' he said after what seemed like an extensive exploration of Quentin's mouth, 'Quite a big filling you lost there. What time's my next appointment, Ellen?'

'Three fifty-five,' the nurse answered.

'Good. That means I can do it now, Mr Cadbury, save you coming back another day.'

'Really?' Quentin eyed the row of instruments lined up on the trolley. 'Right, OK then.'

'Good decision. Always best to do things straight away. A stitch in time, you know.'

Quentin didn't know. All he could think of as he waited for the anaesthetic to take effect was the following few days and where he'd be on August 13th. It suddenly seemed ridiculous, hilarious even, that he should be worrying about a broken tooth when he could end up with it being pushed down his throat.

'Open wide, Mr Cadbury.'

Blinking, Quentin forced his mind back to the present. He opened his mouth and gripped the arms of the chair, a childhood habit he couldn't kick even though he knew he wouldn't feel any pain. No pain, not today. But next week?

His grip on the chair arms tightened and his teeth clamped down hard on the dentist's finger. 'Orry,' he spluttered open-mouthed when he realized what he was doing. Ignoring the man's glare, he tried to focus on keeping still. I must be mad, he thought, putting myself through this, letting some bloke poke a metal rod into my cavities. Cavities! That's it! Perhaps that's what Uncle John did with the diamonds – swallowed them in desperation! We'll have to get an exhumation order – Ouch!

A sharp scratch went deep as a finger was yanked out of his mouth and the probing instrument scraped the inside of his cheek, making him release the chair arms and fling his hands upwards. As he did so, his fist caught the dentist in the face and knocked him off balance, sending him sprawling sideways. Clutching at the nearby trolley and tipping it over with a crash, the dentist fell awkwardly on top of it. He let out a surprised cry.

'Oh God, I'm tho thorry,' Quentin lisped through swollen lips. 'Are you all wight? You were hurting me.'

The nurse shot Quentin a look of disbelief. 'You bit Mr Milsom's finger again,' she said, helping the man to his feet. 'He didn't hurt you deliberately.'

'Thorry. Got a lot on my mind at the moment.'

Recovering his composure Mr Milsom said stiffly, 'Mr Cadbury, I can't continue to treat you if you go on like this.'

'Ith's all wight, it won't happen again.'

'It certainly won't. I've got a bite block here. It'll keep your mouth open.'

Hot with embarrassment, Quentin said, 'Yeth, carry on.'

He lay back and allowed the bite block to be put between his teeth. While the dentist worked in silence, the nurse scurried around picking up the spilt instruments and placing them in the sterilizer. When he got up to go, he gave them both a lopsided smile.

'Thorry about the trouble,' he said, 'and I'll pay for any damage. Thankth for thitting me in.'

As he left the surgery he couldn't help smiling at the memory of the dentist's face as he lay sprawled on the floor. If only he could have floored his attacker that easily, he might not have suffered bruised ribs. The thought of his ongoing dilemma sobered him, and the grin disappeared completely when he reached the car and gazed in the mirror.

'What a sight,' he muttered, fingering his swollen face and running his tongue over the scratch on the inside of his cheek. Get a grip, Quentin, he thought. Where's the good-looking, smooth-talking, confident man you used to be? You can't let some manky criminals get to you like this. Think of something. Think of something and get on with it.

He sat brooding for a while, then banged his fist down on the steering wheel. He got on with starting the car, but by the time he reached home he still hadn't thought of anything.

Chapter Eighteen

That evening Quentin sat at Wanda's dining table, chewing a piece of quiche on one side of his mouth. 'It's not that funny,' he said between mouthfuls, hearing Wanda's scornful laugh. 'People swallow things all the time to avoid detection – secret codes, drugs.'

'To avoid detection, yes. Not just to hide something from their wives. The only people who knew about the diamonds were Gerry and whoever was behind the whole thing. He didn't need to hide the goods from them – if they'd turned up, he'd have just handed them over.'

'Unless he got greedy, like I said before, and decided to try and sell the diamonds to somebody else for a higher price. Even so, I don't suppose he would swallow them, especially not as many as John must have brought back. Silly idea.'

There was a knock on the door and Wanda jumped up. 'That's Colin,' she said. 'I know his knock.'

I know his knock. Jealousy stabbed through Quentin and he stiffened. He relaxed a little when a thin, balding man with dark-rimmed glasses came into the room, dressed in casual trousers and a short-sleeved shirt, a jacket over his arm. He'd been worrying about nothing. Wanda couldn't possibly fancy this guy. He caught a whiff of musky aftershave as the older man drew nearer.

'This is Colin, Quentin,' Wanda said.

Holding out his hand, Quentin said, 'Pleased to meet you.'

Ignoring his outstretched arm, Colin nodded and said, 'So you're Wanda's neighbour.'

Embarrassed, Quentin let his arm fall to his side. 'Er, yes.'

'He's a friend, too, Colin.'

'A very young friend. I'm not sure Gerry would approve.'

'Colin!'

At Wanda's cry Colin turned to her. 'Sorry. It's just – you know, I promised to keep an eye out for you.'

'Keep an eye out *for* me, not keep an eye *on* me!'

Quentin could see that Colin would like to keep more than his eyes on Wanda, but he let it pass. They'd obviously known each other a long time.

'All right, point made. Sorry,' Colin said.

'Scotch?' Wanda asked Colin, as if trying to relieve the tension.

'Just a small one, please, love.'

'Quentin?'

'No, thanks,' Quentin said, though he knew Wanda had only bought the whisky for him. He watched with amusement while Wanda poured whisky into a tumbler and handed it to Colin. He saw the other man's gaze follow Wanda's every move. He fancies the pants off her, he thought.

'So, what have you got for us?' Wanda asked when Colin had settled into an armchair.

'Us?' Colin eyed Quentin, the suspicious look returning. 'I thought I was doing a favour for *you*.'

Quentin stood up. 'I'll go,' he said, 'then you can talk.'

Wanda waved him back. 'No, Quentin, stay. What I asked you to do, Colin, was for me *and* Quentin. We both need help.'

Colin frowned. 'What's it got to do with him? You said it was to do with Gerry.'

'It is.'

Startled, Quentin stared at Wanda. Just how much had she told Colin?

'Don't look so worried, Quentin. We can trust Colin.'

Quentin said nothing. If Colin had information that could help them, he had no choice but to trust him.

'You knew, or at least suspected, about Gerry's dealings,' Wanda was saying to Colin. 'Not long before he died, he was threatened because something he was expecting didn't arrive. I never knew who threatened him – Gerry didn't tell me anything about it until just before he died, but he said I should try and find what they wanted in case they came after me. When I went through Gerry's papers, I found out he got things from a man who used to live next door, where Quentin lives now. The goods weren't named, just the date, initials and a phone number. The thing is, Quentin's house was broken into and they've tried to get in again since. Whatever Gerry was expecting, they think it's in that house. We've had the place upside down. There's nothing there.'

'We think whoever it is has been in prison.' Quentin took up the story. 'That's the most likely reason for things to go quiet for so long.'

Colin gave a low whistle. 'So that's why you want to know who's been released from prison recently. I'm surprised Gerry didn't mention it to me if he thought they might come after *you*, Wanda.'

'He wouldn't have wanted to involve you,' Wanda told him. 'You were a good friend. He knew you turned a blind eye to his under-the-counter dealings, but he didn't want to lose your friendship by telling you exactly what he did. He didn't tell anyone, not even me–'

'But surely,' Colin interrupted, 'if he said you should find the goods, he should have told you who'd threatened him.'

Wanda looked away. Whether she loved her late husband or not she obviously found it hard to talk about his death. 'He was very ill,' she said, her voice quavering. 'I think he was torn between telling me and not wanting me to know more than I needed to. I don't know who the goods went to once he had them – *he* might not have known, not their true identity anyway. Isn't that how these things work, contact with as few people as possible? The less you know, the less you can give away. He... he didn't want to implicate me. He thought it would be dangerous.'

'Well, it is dangerous, bloody dangerous,' Colin snapped. 'Oh well, it's no good worrying about what he did or didn't say. What are these goods, anyway?'

A few seconds ticked by. Quentin exchanged glances with Wanda. Would she tell him?

'We don't know,' Wanda said, looking directly at Colin. 'That's what makes it so hard.'

Colin looked incredulous. 'He said you needed to find them but didn't say what they were?'

'He tried, but I couldn't make out what he was saying. He was drifting in and out of consciousness by the time he told me about it. But if you've found out if any recently released prisoners were handling stolen or smuggled goods like I asked, that might give us a start.'

'Right. Well, here's the list of names I promised you. James has made some notes – dates they were convicted etc – if that's any good.'

'James?' Quentin asked.

'My brother. He's in the prison service. I hope it helps, but I don't like it. You should go to the police.'

'We will if we can't sort it out,' Wanda said, taking the list from him. 'I expect we'll end up going to them, and I know it's the sensible thing to do, but if we could only get these criminals off our backs without involving them it would be so much easier. I don't want to drag Gerry's name through the mud if I don't have to. He was a good husband to me.'

Colin looked uncomfortable. 'Yeah, well, I'd be dead if it weren't for him... Still, he wouldn't want us to take risks, especially not you.'

'No, and we won't, will we, Quentin?' Glancing at the paper in her hand, she continued, 'There are no addresses.'

'James wouldn't give addresses. He reckons he's put his job on the line giving us this much, and he says he can't do any more.'

'But,' Quentin said, disappointment setting in, 'whatever prison they were in bears no relation to their home address, does it? You can be sent anywhere in the country.'

Colin shrugged. 'Now you've got the names you can try the internet or the electoral roll. You can write to the courts, James said, but they won't necessarily tell you. Your best bet is the local newspapers. The trial would have been covered there, and they often give the defendant's address.'

'Local papers? How can we do that if we don't know where they lived?' Wanda asked.

'Surely they wouldn't be too far away,' Quentin said. 'After all, Gerry was involved and Gerry lived here. I bet the guy we're looking for is a Londoner. That still leaves a lot of newspapers to trawl through.'

Wanda groaned. 'Looks like we've got our work cut out. We'd better get on with it then. Thanks for your help, Colin.'

'What else can I do? I can't leave you to face this on your own. I promised Gerry–'

'It's all right, Colin, you've already kept your promise. You don't have to do anything else; you've got Emma to think of. How is she?'

Quentin jerked his head up. Emma? Colin was married? But didn't Wanda go out with him sometimes? He stole a surreptitious glance at her, which told him nothing.

Colin grinned. 'As cheeky as ever. Can I have this and can I have that. She thinks I'm a bottomless pit. That's daughters for you. Still, I can't refuse, can I, now it's only me and her.'

Daughters. Quentin relaxed, but his jealousy returned when he noticed that Colin looked a lot better when he smiled.

'There is something you can do, Colin,' he said, trying to focus on the situation.

Wanda shot him a warning look, as if she was worried he would contradict something she'd said.

'Anything,' Colin said, taking off his glasses and polishing them with the hem of his shirt.

'It's just...' Quentin paused and looked at Colin.

'Go on.'

'Can we rely on you as a back-up? If anything goes wrong, I mean? We will go to the police when the time is right, but... in an emergency, can we call on you to get help, or go to the police for us?'

Colin pursed his lips. 'If you think that's necessary, then it must be dangerous. Why put yourselves at risk? Go to the police now.'

'They'd take too long, Colin,' Wanda told him. 'We want to get this thing off our backs. We've only got ten days – well, nine now.'

'What do you mean, nine days?'

Colin listened while Wanda explained about the note. When she'd finished, he sat back, frowning. 'Why on earth would they give you that long? That's more or less giving you carte blanche to disappear or... or do anything, really.'

'That's what we thought,' Quentin admitted. 'But now I've had time to think about it I'm guessing it doesn't matter to them how long they give us as long as they get what they want. After all, they've waited three years, and even if I left, I'd have to come back to my house at some point, unless I did a complete disappearing act.'

'I'd have to do that, too,' Wanda said. 'I don't see why we should be driven out of our homes when we've done nothing wrong.'

'You could get police protection,' Colin pointed out.

'Not indefinitely,' Wanda said. 'We won't take unnecessary risks, honestly, and if there's anything else you can do, we'll let you know. All right?'

'Fair enough, but I still don't like it. If anything happens to you...' Colin looked directly at Quentin when he said this, a warning look in his eyes.

'I'll keep her safe,' Quentin assured him, though he wasn't sure he could.

'You'd better. Well, I'll be off. Call any time, Wanda, love, night or day.'

Wanda planted a kiss on his cheek. 'I will, and thanks again, Colin.'

'Phew!' said Quentin when he'd gone. 'What a marathon. Did I pass inspection, do you think?'

Wanda laughed. 'Colin's all right. He'd do anything for me.'

'That's obvious,' Quentin muttered. And not just because your husband saved his life, he added to himself. 'What does he do, anyway?'

'He was a quantity surveyor, but they offered him a good redundancy package and he took it.'

'No wife, I take it?'

Wanda shook her head. 'He was divorced ages ago. She led him a merry dance and then pushed off to work in Greece. I think he realized quite quickly that he's better off without her. Emma goes over to see her sometimes but she was sixteen when it happened and she chose to stay with Colin. He thinks the world of her.'

As if deciding she'd revealed enough about Colin's matrimonial status, Wanda snatched up the piece of paper he'd left and straightened it out.

'Eric Thomson, John Browning, Richard Simpson, Tom Weekes, Jason Miller, Dennis Moore, Sam Jenkinson,' she read aloud. 'All released from prison recently, all convicted of receiving stolen goods.'

Quentin peered over her shoulder. 'Simpson and Weekes only served eight months,' he said, 'so we can count them out. Browning, third offence, served two years. Thomson and Miller, sentenced to eighteen months. Moore and Jenkinson served three years, convicted of handling stolen goods in the London area. Those dates fit.'

'Hmm. It doesn't say what the goods were, though. We need to find out more about them.'

'Yeah,' Quentin agreed. 'Thanks for not telling Colin about my connection, by the way. I mean not saying that the person who lived next door was my uncle.'

'Why rock the boat? We'll keep it on a need-to-know basis, at the moment anyway.'

'Is that why you didn't tell Colin about the diamonds?'

'Yes,' Wanda admitted. 'The less he knows, the less he'll be implicated. I should hate to get him into trouble. He probably thinks the goods are rare antiques – that was Gerry's business after all. If he knew diamonds were involved, he'd realize how big this thing is and then he *would* go to the police.'

Reading the last two names on the list again Quentin had a thought. 'Hmm. Receiving stolen goods. Wouldn't diamonds be in a category of their own? I mean it's not like handling the usual stuff, is it?'

'No, but I asked him to list anyone involved with stolen or smuggled goods. That covers pretty much everything, and our man could have been handling other things as well as diamonds.'

'Right. Well, we can look these two up on the internet, can't we?'

Wanda groaned. 'I hate looking things up on the internet. It takes forever.'

'You should change your service provider,' Quentin suggested. 'Lead me to your computer, and I'll have that drink you offered me now. It could be a long night.'

Chapter Nineteen

'I've had a thought,' Wanda said in Quentin's house the next day.

Quentin handed her a cup of coffee and proffered a packet of biscuits. 'Sounds ominous. Go on.'

'Well, we've been looking for diamonds as we know them, you know, small, shiny things. What if they're uncut?'

'Uncut?'

'Yes. They'd be easier to smuggle. Lots of people wouldn't realize what they were.'

'True, but unlikely. Uncle John went to Amsterdam and Paris, so the odds are he smuggled them from there. He's far more likely to have brought in gems that can be used straight away, plus Britain's not known for diamond cutting.'

Wanda pushed her hair back from her forehead. 'Hmm. I suppose you're right. Well, it doesn't matter what state they're in – unless they're bricked up in the wall, they're not here. Where did you find the money?'

'At the back of the fridge,' Quentin said, still unwilling to tell her about the cavity. 'I've checked all the walls and found nothing. It's not as if this place has plasterboard walls – these old houses are pretty solid. There's no evidence of bricks being removed or replaced that I can see.'

'Oh,' said Wanda gloomily. 'I can't think anymore. The internet didn't help. Perhaps we'd better get to the library and start looking through the old papers.'

'Which library and which papers? Could be anywhere in London.'

'I know. We'll start local. It's a long shot, but we've got to do something. You start here, in Greenwich. I'll go over to Woolwich. The library's not far from Gerry's old shop.'

The shop. Quentin cleared his throat. 'Em... I suppose there's no chance the diamonds are at the shop, is there? I mean, could Gerry have, you know...'

'Could Gerry have what? You think John gave him the diamonds and he decided to keep them instead of passing them on? What would he do with them? He was an antiques dealer, not a diamond merchant. He'd been threatened. He was worried, and he wouldn't lie to me when he was dying. What would be the point?'

'Yeah, sorry. Just a thought. What about your friend Colin?'

'What about him?'

Quentin hesitated to put his thoughts into words he might regret. 'Well, you said he knew about Gerry's dealings. Suppose he knows more than he lets on.'

Wanda's eyes blazed. 'If you're suggesting Colin's got anything to do with this, you're wrong.'

'All right, calm down. It was just an idea.'

'It's not Colin.'

'How can you be so sure?'

'I just know, that's all. He'd never do anything to hurt me.'

'Why? Because he fancies you?'

A flush stained Wanda's cheeks, but she glared at Quentin defiantly. 'Yes. He's been in love with me for years, but he never told me until after Gerry died, and no, we're not having an affair.'

It was Quentin's turn to flush. 'Sorry, I didn't mean to pry. It just seems... well, unlikely that he didn't know what was going on, that's all.'

Raising an eyebrow, Wanda said quietly, 'As unlikely as *me* not knowing what was going on?'

Quentin felt the air between them crackle. He stared at her, his mind in turmoil. Is that what he meant? 'Look,' he said at last, 'this thing's making us both edgy. We're clutching at straws, trying to think of something to shed light on things, saying anything that comes into our heads.'

Wanda backed away from him. 'Exactly, and we know what's in *your* head, don't we? Colin and Gerry were working together, or Colin found out what Gerry was expecting and decided to get the diamonds for himself. Or perhaps me and Colin are in it together.'

'I didn't mean that at all.'

'I don't care what you meant. And my friendship with Colin is none of your business. For goodness' sake stop being a petulant little boy and grow up.'

She swung round and stalked out, her shoulders shaking. Quentin stared after her, stunned at her outburst. A petulant little boy? She was upset. Of course she was, but *petulant*?

Perhaps she had a point. What right did he have to make assumptions about her relationship with Colin? Yet after all they'd been through together in the last few weeks, the way they'd talked openly and frankly, and their physical closeness, he felt he'd earned the right to know everything about her. He was sleeping with her, for God's sake. Didn't that give him rights?

He believed her when she'd said she and Colin weren't having an affair. The way Colin had acted when he'd met him at Wanda's bore that out. But that didn't mean they hadn't been lovers in the past.

Wanda and Colin, lovers. The thought sickened him, and he curled his fists into balls. What was it she'd said that day when they'd gone to the opera? *We both have needs and if we can fulfil those together that's fine. If you want more, we'll have to call it a day.*

Did she still feel like that? He'd agreed to it then, but as he gazed at the space where she had been and breathed in her lingering scent, he knew he couldn't agree to it now. He wanted more.

Chapter Twenty

Trying to get away from thoughts of Wanda and focus on more pressing matters, Quentin sat tapping his fingers on his knee. If things didn't get sorted out soon, his feelings for Wanda might be irrelevant.

He checked the internet for Dennis Moore and Sam Jenkinson, the two names on Colin's list that seemed the most likely to be involved with the diamonds – nothing. According to Colin's brother, they'd both been imprisoned for handling stolen goods at the relevant time and released not long before someone had tried to steal Quentin's keys in April.

Another thought struck him. What about John's boss, the garage owner? Had he been in on the smuggling? Or could John have managed to collect the diamonds abroad and unload them *before* delivering the car to the garage? It was possible. It was also possible that the garage owner had set the whole thing up. There was no way he could find out. John was dead, Gerry was dead. Silent witnesses, he thought grimly. He'd learned nothing about the garage owner when he'd visited Bromley. He frowned, recalling what his mother had told him. John's boss had moved to Spain not long after John had died. That ruled him out then. He couldn't have been banged up for handling stolen goods if he'd been in Spain.

Magpie came in and rubbed against his legs.

'Hello, boy. If only you could talk. I bet *you* know what was going on. Another silent witness. Not much help, are you? You'll probably still be here when I've been beaten to a pulp. It serves me right – I should have gone to the police ages ago instead of trying to do their job for them.

Oh well, back to Moore and Jenkinson. Looks like the only way to trace them is the hard way.'

Sighing, he put on his jacket and went out. At the gate he hesitated, wondering whether to knock on Wanda's door. Deciding to leave her to cool off, he made his way to the library.

* * *

Four fruitless hours later, he went home, grabbed a sandwich then walked to the park to try to clear his head. He strode as fast as his recovering ribs would allow, deep in thought and almost oblivious of his surroundings.

'Hello, Quentin. I thought it was you.'

The voice sounded vaguely familiar. Quentin looked at the girl striving to keep up with him. Her face was red from running and he stared at her for a few unknowing moments before recognition swept over him. He slowed down, then stopped and turned to face her.

'Louise! What a surprise. What's this, jogging now?'

Nodding, Louise put her hand on his arm to steady herself. 'Yes,' she panted, pushing a strand of hair from her eyes. 'I'm trying to keep fit. My mum and dad are in the Observatory, so I thought I'd run here for a change.'

Quentin glanced up to the famous Observatory, with its rise and fall red orb, from where Greenwich Mean Time and the Meridian Line had standardised time and established longitude all over the world.

'How are you, Quentin?' Louise asked. 'We still miss you at the office.'

'Really? That's nice. I'm fine, thanks.'

'Good. How's your aunt? Is she any better?'

'Eh? Oh, Aunt Josie. Well, she's… she's…' Quentin floundered. Should he keep Aunt Josie alive? Yes. If he killed her off Louise would expect him to be free to get involved with her again. 'She's about the same,' he lied. 'You know, good days and bad days.'

Louise gave a sympathetic click of her tongue. 'Poor you. It must be exhausting.'

'Well, it keeps me busy.'

Louise raised her arm and waved at someone behind Quentin.

'My parents. I'll have to go – we need to go home and pack. We're off to Spain tomorrow. My uncle's got a place there. Bye, Quentin.' She whirled around and ran from him as quickly as she'd appeared.

'Bye, Louise,' Quentin called after her. He needn't have worried about keeping Aunt Josie alive. Louise seemed far more interested in Spain than seeing him again. Feeling somewhat crushed, he wondered if he'd ever be able to judge a woman's true feelings for him and chalked it up as another reason for not getting close to anyone.

Seconds later he wasn't thinking about Louise's feelings or her jogging or if she would tell people at the office she'd seen him. He was recalling something she'd said, something he couldn't stop thinking about. Her uncle had a place in Spain.

It niggled at his memory. Someone had said that. Who was it? His mother! John had sometimes gone to Spain – because his boss had a place there.

* * *

'Is that significant then? Why shouldn't his boss have a place in Spain?' Wanda asked later, her earlier outburst seemingly forgotten.

Quentin shrugged and sat down on Wanda's chaise longue. 'I don't know. I know John's boss went to Spain when the garage closed but I've only just remembered that he had a house there before that. It just seems odd, a boss inviting an employee to use his holiday home.'

'Does it?'

'Well, why would he unless they had something going between them?'

Chewing on her bottom lip, Wanda looked as though she was weighing up this information. 'But didn't your aunt go with him?'

'Yeah, but she needn't have known anything. He could have said his boss was rewarding his good work instead of giving him a bonus.'

'Perhaps he was. It doesn't sound sinister to me.'

'No? Oh well, maybe it isn't, but I think I'll ring Mum and ask if she remembers anything else.'

'Won't she wonder why you keep asking questions? Who is this Louise anyway?'

Quentin felt a blush rise to his face. 'A girl I used to work with. She was in the park, jogging.'

'Was she? You sure she wasn't looking out for you?'

'No, why would she be? She doesn't know where I live.'

'Does anyone know where you live, apart from burglars?' There was a note of sarcasm in Wanda's voice. 'I've noticed you never have any visitors. Haven't you got any friends?'

'Not that I want to come calling. I don't particularly want everyone to know my business.'

'What business? That you're not working, you mean? Don't look so worried, Quentin, I won't give your game away. Anyway, that's the least of our problems at the moment.'

'Too right.' Quentin sighed. 'Did you find anything at the library?'

'No. We could be wasting our time, and we haven't got much to waste.'

Wanda sounded tetchy and looked tired. There were dark shadows under her eyes and her skin was pale. Deciding against offering to share his pizza and asking if he could spend the night with her, Quentin went home and phoned his mother.

'Quentin! You're early. I wasn't expecting your call till tomorrow.'

'Sorry, Mum, I wanted to ask you something and I forgot about the time difference. Shall I call back later?'

'No, it's all right. Anything wrong?'

'No, just–' He stopped. Just what? His mother was going to think he was obsessed with John at this rate. 'I know I've asked you before, but John's boss at the garage – have you remembered his name?'

'I might have known, but I can't remember it now. I remember he sent a huge wreath to John's funeral, though he didn't come to it. Why?'

'Was his name Moore or Jenkinson?'

Quentin could almost hear her thinking. 'I don't think so. I think it was something common, like Smith or Brown.'

Smith or Brown. Or Jones. Or anything under the sun. 'It doesn't matter, Mum. I'm not getting far with this family tree that's all.'

'I don't see how knowing John's boss's name would help. Surely all you need is his date of birth, who he married and the date he died.'

'I'm doing a little biography of each person if I can, you know, things of interest to the family, that sort of thing.'

There was a pause before she answered. 'I see. If I think of anything else I'll let you know. Are you sure you're OK? Nothing on your mind?'

'No, course not.'

'Any other news from your end? How's your girlfriend?'

Caught off guard, Quentin blurted, 'Girlfriend?'

'Didn't you say you were seeing someone? I thought you did.'

'Did I? Yes, she's fine thanks, and don't worry, she won't stop me coming over to see you.'

'I hope not. Actually, Quentin, I was thinking of…' There was a pause. 'I'd better go. Your father will be wanting his breakfast. Lovely to hear your voice.'

'And yours. Take care. Bye now.'

'Bye, Quentin.'

'Smith or Brown,' Quentin groaned as he hung up. 'It could be Rumpelstiltskin for all anyone knows.'

A thought came to him and he jerked himself upright. John's boss had sent a wreath to the funeral. If he checked with the florist or the funeral director, they might have a record of everyone who had sent flowers. He could check all the florists in Bromley, and all the funeral directors in Greenwich. If he tried now, he'd catch them before closing time.

He spent the next hour on the phone and managed to track down the company that had handled his uncle's funeral.

'I wonder if you could help me,' he said when the call was answered. 'I'm trying to contact one of my late uncle's friends, but I can't remember his surname. I know he sent a wreath to the funeral, and I wondered if you kept records.'

'Yes, we do keep records of people who sent flowers,' the female assistant told him. 'What was the deceased's name and date of death?'

When he'd given the information, Quentin waited until the assistant had checked and then listened to the names as she read them out. He recognized some as family members, but none of the others meant anything to him. They were mainly from couples, except for one simply given as Bob.

'Thank you,' he said when she'd finished. 'You've been most helpful.' Not strictly true, but "it costs nothing to be polite" was Quentin's mantra.

He learned nothing from the florists. Most of them didn't keep records that far back. Also, he realized, because the garage was in Bromley it didn't mean the garage owner lived there. He could have ordered the wreath from anywhere.

He stroked Magpie's ear as he came up to him. The phrase "getting nowhere fast" played repeatedly in his head, and he groaned. What did it matter? He was probably wrong about the garage owner anyway.

Discouraged, he unwrapped a pizza and put it in the oven. Then, seeking compensation for the day's disappointments, he poured himself a glass of whisky.

Chapter Twenty-one

'I think traipsing round libraries is a no-no,' Quentin said the next day. 'We could try the courts, but that would take just as long. We'd better come up with something else, and quickly.'

'I've been going through Gerry's notebook in case I missed anything,' Wanda said. 'But it's all gobbledegook.'

'Would you mind if I looked? You know, a fresh pair of eyes.'

Wanda shrugged and pushed a blue-covered book into his hand. 'Help yourself.'

Opening the book, Quentin saw the pages were divided into columns showing dates, amounts and initials. JD appeared frequently, with an amount shown in the outgoings column. JD. John Davidson – Uncle John. So, the amounts shown were what Gerry paid John for handing over the goods. Another set of initials was RS, alongside an amount shown under incomings. Payment to Gerry when he passed on the goods? RS – could be any number of people.

There was a phone number shown against his uncle's initials, but nothing against RS. Sighing, Quentin asked, 'Is this all there was?'

'All of any interest. There're the accounts for the business, but they don't show anything. He didn't keep a diary. I kept any dates on a calendar – doctor, dentist and stuff. This seems be the only written record of any other dealings.'

'Did you check his computer?'

Wanda grimaced. 'Gerry was old-school. He never used a computer, didn't know how, didn't want to know. I took the figures from the accounts and filed our tax returns, but he never touched a computer.'

Stumped, Quentin stared into space. 'We're getting nowhere,' he said eventually.

'Why don't we have a brainstorming session,' Wanda suggested. 'Go home and write down anything and everything that comes into your head. I'll do the same. Then we'll get together, compare notes and see what else we can think of. That works sometimes.'

'Yeah.' Quentin was beginning to think his brain would explode if it was subjected to any more storming. Unable to think of a helpful alternative, he went home, found a writing pad and pen and collapsed into an armchair. When he looked at the paper an hour later it was still blank.

'Bugger it,' he muttered.

He looked longingly at the running machine. His ribs and stomach were mending but he didn't want to aggravate any lingering inflammation. Deciding not to risk it, he hauled himself up, poured a whisky and drank it before sitting down again. He wanted to pour a second, but stopped himself. His brain seemed paralysed. We must do something, he thought desperately. Must do something…

He awoke with a jolt when Magpie jumped onto his lap. 'God, boy, you frightened me. Bloody hell, is it really seven o'clock?'

Looking from the clock to the blank pad that had fallen onto the floor, he wondered how he'd been able to fall asleep when he was supposed to be finding an answer to their predicament.

After splashing his face and drinking some coffee he felt better. He scooped up the notepad and jotted down as

117

much as he could, including the initials in Gerry's notebook. 'RS', he muttered. Why did that ring a bell? Wasn't there someone with those initials on Colin's list?

With his notes in his pocket and his keys in his hand, he went to Wanda's, elated that he may have found a lead at last. He was about to knock when he heard a noise from inside. It was a man's voice followed by a woman's cry. Wanda's cry. Turning to the window he saw the blind was drawn, but the light inside made shadows showing silhouettes of a man and a woman very close together. Quentin caught his breath. Wanda was being attacked! His first instinct was to knock furiously at the door to frighten the attacker off, but he fought against it. Better to use Wanda's key to let himself in and creep up on the man.

He cast about for a weapon and spotted an old TV aerial by the dustbin. Scooping it up, he gripped it tightly in one hand while he opened the door with the other. Dim light and the soft strains of a classical symphony engulfed him as he went inside. Moving as quietly and quickly as he could he turned immediately into the more brightly lit front room where he'd seen the shadows. All he could see of Wanda was a sliver of her right-hand side, the rest of her being blocked out by the figure in front of her. The back view of a man filling his vision was enough for Quentin. He didn't hesitate. He leapt forward, bringing the TV aerial down on the man's skull. The man teetered, then slumped sideways, letting out a long moan.

'Oh!' Wanda clutched at the man's arms as if to stop him falling. When he hit the ground, she straightened up and glared at Quentin. 'Quentin! What the devil do you think you're doing?'

'Well, of all the ungrateful…' He looked down as his victim squirmed on the floor. A faint smell of musky aftershave floated up to him. 'Oh my God! Colin!'

'Yes,' said Wanda testily. 'Colin. He came to see if he could help. He was worried about me.'

'I saw his shadow on the blind and I thought you were being attacked. It looked like it.'

Wanda's expression softened. 'Thanks for the thought, but as you can see, I wasn't. Well, don't just stand there, help him up.'

Quentin put down the aerial and pushed an arm under Colin's. Colin staggered to his feet and Wanda guided him to a chair. 'Get a flannel and some water,' she ordered. 'He's bleeding.'

He's a bleeding nuisance, Quentin thought. Why did he have to stand so close to ask if you needed help?

His thoughts ran on as he filled a bowl with warm water in the kitchen. Colin must have been kissing her, or trying to kiss her. He was sure he'd heard Wanda cry out – perhaps she'd been trying to rebuff him. Or was it a cry of encouragement?

He found a clean flannel and took it to Wanda with the bowl. 'Sorry, mate,' he said. 'I thought someone was hurting Wanda. I was only trying to help her. Are you all right or shall I take you to casualty?'

'Don't know,' Colin mumbled. 'Give me a minute.'

Removing Colin's glasses, Wanda dabbed at his head with the flannel. 'Get him some sweet tea, Quentin,' she said. 'And put some brandy in it.'

Grimacing, Quentin did as he was told. This is ridiculous, he thought. Why should I feel guilty for protecting Wanda? How was I supposed to know Colin was here, doing God knows what?

And for a fleeting moment, he was glad he'd mistaken Colin for an attacker.

* * *

'He'll be all right,' Wanda said from Quentin's doorstep when she returned from the hospital at eleven o'clock. 'They've cleaned it and stitched it and I've taken him home.'

'Right. Coming in?'

'Just for a minute.'

She stepped inside and Quentin hovered for a moment. What could he say? He waited until they were in the lounge before speaking. 'I'm really sorry. I just saw this shadow on the blind and it looked like he was... What *was* he doing?'

Wanda looked at him but said nothing.

'Right. None of my business.'

Leaning forward, Wanda put her hand on his arm. 'You've no need to be jealous of Colin.'

'I'm not jealous. Yes, I am. I can't help it.'

'He came to see if I was all right. OK, so he tried to kiss me. We're old... friends.'

Quentin stiffened. 'Friends?'

'He tries it on from time to time.'

'Huh! I knew it.'

'And I'm perfectly capable of handling him without any outside help, thank you. Anyway, his intentions are good. He... he wants to marry me.'

Quentin's thoughts raced. Colin wanted to marry her. Well, why wouldn't he?

He couldn't think of a single thing to say so he plumped for, 'What did he say at the hospital? About the gash on his head?'

Wanda's mouth curved into a half-smile. 'He said he cracked it on some scaffolding.'

'That's decent of him,' Quentin muttered. He suddenly felt exhausted, drained of any positive thoughts. 'I think I need some sleep,' he said, forgetting his afternoon nap. 'We'll do our brainstorming in the morning.'

'We'll have to,' Wanda reminded him. 'Only seven days left, now.'

As he closed the door behind her, Quentin's heart thumped. Seven days. They'd spent the last three scrabbling around, chasing their tails, wasting their time and getting nowhere. As he lay in bed trying to sleep, he felt he was swimming out of his depth, striking towards the shore but drifting further away. Help, he wanted to cry, help me, I'm drowning.

But there was no one to hear.

* * *

That night he awoke in a sweat. It was a nightmare, he realized, a dream he hadn't had since coming to Greenwich. He was banging on a door, harder and harder, but it didn't open. 'Nathan,' he called. 'Let me in.'

Then the door was opened, he didn't know how or by whom. It was opened and he could see inside. Nathan's girlfriend appeared from somewhere, her face white with shock and her eyes black with smudged mascara. 'We're too late,' she said.

'No,' he breathed, all his senses screaming in denial. He pushed past her, his arms flailing wildly as if to bat away the image he dreaded seeing. And there was Nathan, his closest friend, lying on the bed, his unseeing eyes staring hopelessly into nothingness.

'Nathan!' he shouted, grabbing his friend by the shoulders and heaving him into his arms. 'Nathan, please, no.'

But there was no reply, no response from the only real friend and confidante he'd ever had. No jerk of a limb, no flicker of an eyelid. It was like holding a rag doll.

He slapped Nathan violently on the back, shook him as though he could shake breath into his lungs. But Quentin knew, with uncanny certainty, that life would not flow back into Nathan's body.

Cocaine had claimed him, and Quentin sat helplessly by his side until they took him away.

Chapter Twenty-two

The next morning, he was up early, a new determination settling on him. A few more days to focus on the situation, then if nothing happened, it was the police. In the furore of last night he hadn't checked the names on Colin's list. A job for today, he told himself.

He went over all the events in his head, wondering repeatedly why they'd given him until next Saturday to find the diamonds and how he was supposed to hand them over even if he found them. He assumed whoever had written the note had their reasons and would make contact when it suited them.

The sound of car doors being slammed disturbed his thoughts. Not many cars stopped on the yellow lines, unless they were unloading.

'Sod off,' he murmured, annoyed at having his thoughts interrupted.

A knock came at the door, and he sighed and went to answer it. Wanda's up early too, he thought, raking his hand through his hair. Another knock came. 'All right, all right,' he muttered, and pulled open the door. He gasped, and gripped the edge of the door for support.

'Father! Mum! How can you be here? I only spoke to you the other day!'

'Last-minute decision,' Rosemary Cadbury said. 'Your father's been invited to a reunion dinner. We thought we'd surprise you.'

'Going to keep us on the doorstep?' his father growled. 'Been on a plane for nineteen hours.'

'Sorry, I'm just so surprised to see you,' Quentin said, recovering. 'Come in.'

He shook his father's hand, then hugged his mother. She looked thinner than he remembered and despite her Australian tan, dark circles showed under her eyes.

'What about this lot?' His father pointed to two large suitcases and a holdall.

'Bring them in. Here, I'll take them.' He hauled the cases into the hall, his mind in turmoil. His parents here, now of all times.

'You sounded strange on the phone, Quentin. I thought I'd come straight here and make sure you were all right.'

'Why didn't you say you were coming? I'd have made arrangements—'

'No need,' his father told him. 'We'll be staying at your Uncle Rupert's. Just called in en route to see how you're doing.'

'How long are you here for?' Quentin asked, dreading their reply. It was wonderful to see his mother, but now, amid all this diamond business?

'Two weeks,' his mother said. 'We'll stay at Rupert's, but of course we'll come and see you, and perhaps we can go out next weekend, when you're not working.'

His father glanced at his watch. 'Expect you'll be off to work in a minute. We won't hold you up, but your mother insisted on coming straight here.'

'It doesn't matter if I'm in a bit late,' Quentin said, his heart still thumping. 'I can make up the time another day. Let me make you some breakfast.'

'Just tea, dear,' his mother said. 'We ate on the plane.'

'That was at five o'clock, Rosemary,' snorted his father. 'Toast would be nice, my boy.'

My boy. Quentin felt he was back in the family home, his father laying down the law with an iron fist. His father's insistence on calling him my boy had started in Quentin's childhood, at the same time he'd insisted on being called Father. Ridiculous, was Quentin's opinion, but sheer bloody-mindedness made him determined to stick to it until his father capitulated.

He made tea and toast and carried it in on a tray. As he set it down there was another knock at the door. He rushed to open it, putting his finger to his lips when he saw Wanda. 'You can't come in now,' he whispered. 'I'll explain later.' She looked mystified but nodded and walked away.

'Who was that, dear?'

'The postman,' Quentin lied. 'He had a package but then realized it was for next door.'

He heard his father harrumph. 'Typical! No one knows what they're doing these days. Need a good spell in the army, that'd sort them out. Bring back National Service, I say.'

'Hush, Herbert. We've got no right to criticize. We don't even live here anymore.'

'No, thank goodness. Old country's going to the dogs. What's that contraption in the corner?'

'A running machine,' Quentin told him. 'I'm trying to keep fit.'

His father harrumphed again, and to avoid a lecture on the benefits of hard work and square bashing he asked swiftly, 'When's your reunion, Father?'

'Saturday. Be good to see all my old comrades again.'

Saturday. The day the ten days were up. He'd have to put off seeing them until at least after then.

'Right. Well, why don't you give me a ring on Sunday? We'll make arrangements to meet and you can tell me all about it. It's quite a journey from Sydney. Where did you stop?'

'Los Angeles,' Rosemary said. 'But we didn't have much time between flights, did we, Herbert? It is exhausting, I must admit. I can't sleep on a plane.'

'You look tired, both of you.' Quentin's mind went round in circles. How could he expect his parents to leave when they'd come to see him after such a long journey? But how could he ask them to stay?

'You're welcome to stay here and rest,' he said. 'I can get off to work so you'll have the place to yourselves. Or I could ring in, see if I could take the day off?'

His father shook his head, as if the idea of taking an unscheduled day off was preposterous. 'No need, my boy. Can't be playing fast and loose with a good job. We'll get off to Rupert's and catch up with you later. Phoned Rupert from the airport. He's coming to pick us up.'

'Oh. That's good of him. Right, well, if you're sure,' Quentin said, relieved. He didn't relish the thought of repeating what he'd told his parents to his father's brother. Rupert, he recalled, was as pedantic and petty as his father, though not so overbearing. It must be a Cadbury family trait. Thank goodness he hadn't inherited it. Turning to his mother he continued, 'Thanks for coming to see me. You stay here and rest until Rupert comes, then you'll feel more refreshed.'

'Thank you, Quentin,' his mother said. 'Rupert said he'd be here about ten, depending on traffic.'

'It must have taken you a while to get from Heathrow,' Quentin said. 'It would have been quicker to go straight to Rupert's, wouldn't it?'

'Got the Heathrow Express then a taxi. Couldn't be doing with the underground with the luggage. Anyway, it's easy enough for Rupert to come down from Chelmsford,' his father said, as though he would expect nothing else from a family member.

'Right. Well, how's Shelagh? Does she get homesick?'

'She doesn't seem to,' Rosemary answered. Not like me, he read in her eyes.

'We've got a good life out there already,' his father blustered. 'Doing well.'

Quentin had to admit that despite looking tired his father did look as though he was doing well. His usually florid face looked more brown than red, and though he was a big man he was upright without a hint of fat.

'Howard's got a good job, earns a bit,' his father went on, looking around the room. Quentin waited for some caustic remark, but nothing came.

'Perhaps I'd better be going,' Quentin said, glancing at the clock.

'Yes, dear, you get off. I'm all right now I've seen you. Give us time to get over the journey, get your father's reunion over, then we can spend some time together.'

'That'll be great, Mum. I'll go and get ready.'

After he'd washed and shaved Quentin fished his suit out of the wardrobe. His parents would expect him to dress smartly for work. When he was ready, they said their goodbyes and Quentin walked along the road to the corner. He hovered for a moment, wondering what to do. He didn't want to go home and find his parents still there – there was too much to do to worry about entertaining them at the moment. He didn't want to hang around the street corner all morning either, but he needed to know when Uncle Rupert turned up. And there was only one way he could do that.

Chapter Twenty-three

After a furtive look along the street to ensure no car pulled up outside his house, Quentin ran back to Wanda's, hoping neither of his parents would spot him through the window. With a peremptory knock he used her key and stepped inside, closing the door quickly behind him.

Apparently hearing him come in, Wanda emerged from the kitchen. 'What's up?' she asked when he had caught his breath and taken a seat in the front room.

'My parents, they've just arrived out of the blue. I had no idea they were even in the country.'

'You're not pleased to see them, then?' Wanda said, raising an eyebrow.

'Not now, with all this going on. I don't know what to tell them.'

'Hmm, awkward. Are they staying with you?'

'No, thank goodness. They're staying with my uncle in Chelmsford. He's coming to pick them up, about ten hopefully. Can I stay and watch from the window? I'll see him arrive and see them all leave, then I can go back.'

'Yes, of course, but why are you here? Why aren't you with them?'

Quentin lowered his eyes. Now he'd have to admit to lying to his parents. 'I had to go out. They think... They think I've still got a job.'

'You haven't told them you're not working?' Wanda sounded amazed.

'I will, just not yet. I'll sort it out later, when we've got this business under our belts. Anyway, I'm not seeing them again till Sunday so we'll be all right till then.'

Wanda nodded. 'Make yourself some breakfast if you like. I'm just going up to get my handbag.'

In her absence Quentin sat brooding, his gaze fixed through the window as though a chariot might appear and carry his parents away. He felt bad at having to leave them after only an hour when they had broken their journey to see him. He wondered how long he could keep up his non-existent employment, whether he should or, if not, how he could come clean with the least possible impact on his relationship with them. His head was swimming with everything he had to think about.

When Wanda came downstairs, she put her head round the door. 'Do you want something to eat?'

'No thanks. I had toast earlier.'

She disappeared and returned with two cups of coffee. For several silent minutes they sipped their drinks, Quentin's tension palpable.

'So, what's the real reason you don't work?' Wanda asked suddenly. There was no judgement in her voice. 'I mean, I know working to live is better than living to work, but there's more to it than that, isn't there? You've had girlfriends, but not kept one, and you don't seem to have any friends. Don't you like people?'

Quentin felt his face burning. 'I like people, yes, and I've had lots of friends, but I don't like getting too attached. They either let you down or expect too much of you. It's easier not to give them a chance to have any expectations.'

'*I* don't expect anything of you, except your help in getting out of the mess we're in.'

'You're different.'

Wanda leaned forward. 'Really? How, exactly?'

Quentin shook his head, confusion filling him. Why was Wanda different? Because she was independent and didn't demand his undivided attention, didn't expect him to marry her, start a family, take responsibility for her? At the start, yes. But now?

'Never mind,' Wanda said, not giving him a chance to answer. 'What about the boy in the photo on your cabinet? The one you were at university with? He must have been a close friend, or you wouldn't have a photo of him.'

There was a small silence. Quentin's heart hammered, his breath shortening.

'Nathan's dead,' he said at last.

A chink of china sounded as Wanda put her cup down. 'I'm so sorry, Quentin. That must have been hard for you. And it's none of my business.'

'Yeah, well… That's what I mean – what's the point of slogging yourself to death doing what people think you should when you could drop dead any minute without doing anything you wanted to do? I knew Nathan from college. He was the only real friend I ever had, the only one who understood how I felt about my father, how he always made me feel inferior. Nathan was the brightest student in our year, but he didn't want to study law. He was pressurised by his parents – well, his father mainly, who threatened to stop supporting him if he didn't carry on. He was a judge, believe it or not. Some judge. Couldn't even judge his own son's character. Nathan was – sensitive. Call it weak if you like. He should have defied him, but he couldn't. He couldn't hack it, so he turned to drugs. I tried to stop him, pleaded, but it was no good. He couldn't stop. Then one night, either by design or accident, he died of an overdose.'

Wanda looked at him for a long moment. 'I shouldn't have asked,' she said, 'but I'm glad you told me. Good friends are hard to come by.'

Quentin's mouth tightened. 'They still leave you, though, don't they? Even my own family left me.'

For a few seconds Wanda was quiet, still looking at him as if considering the right thing to say. Then, as though deciding it was not the time to pursue the subject, she pulled herself upright and sighed. 'Right,' she said, 'back to our more immediate problem. Have you come up with anything?'

'Yes,' Quentin answered, glad of the change of subject. 'Well, possibly. Where's Colin's list?'

When Wanda had fetched the list Quentin ran his fingers down the page. 'Richard Simpson,' he said triumphantly.

'RS,' Wanda said, noticing the connection immediately. 'Gerry's notebook. I should have realized.'

Quentin's triumph faded. 'And we've been hung up on Moore and Jenkinson.'

'That's all we had to go on. Anyway there's millions of people with those initials, and thousands with the same name.'

'So where do we start?' Quentin asked. 'The internet?'

'It's pretty random but we need to check – it's the only name that means anything so far. I can ask Colin if James can find out anything about Richard Simpson as well. He might.'

'All right,' Quentin said. 'I'll have a search when my parents have gone.'

'OK.' Wanda hesitated. 'Er…'

'What? Well go on.'

'I've sort of had an idea.'

'Sort of? Either you…' Quentin broke off as a car pulled up outside. He turned to the window and nudged a strip of the vertical blind aside, saw the driver peer at the number on the gate and drive forward a few feet. 'Uncle Rupert,' he breathed. 'Good. They'll be gone soon.'

'He'll probably want a cuppa before he drives back,' Wanda pointed out.

'He'll have to park up the road then, if he doesn't want to get a ticket.'

Quentin watched and waited, hoping his uncle would leave the car on the single yellow line and persuade his parents to go quickly, rather than re-park. His patience was rewarded when, five minutes later, his uncle reappeared hauling a suitcase. His father followed with another, and then his mother with the holdall. He watched while they loaded the car, feeling a stab of guilt as he saw his mother's thin frame climb in. Dear Mum. It was wonderful that he had been the first thing on her mind after landing. Despite the bad timing, her visit had given him a boost, and he knew she would always love him no matter what.

His emotions had been stirred, but he was still glad his parents were going. 'Phew!' he said, turning back to Wanda as the car drove off. 'What a relief. I couldn't cope with them at the moment. So then, Wanda, what's this idea you've had?'

Wanda looked uncertain. 'It doesn't seem as good now as it did when I first thought about it.'

'Any idea's better than none. What is it?'

'You won't like it.'

Exasperated, Quentin snapped, 'Wanda, just tell me.'

'Well, we've wasted enough time running around trying to find out who these people are. We can't go to them, so couldn't we get them to come to us?'

'Come to us? How?'

Wanda pulled a face. 'I don't know, really. I thought some sort of publicity – something that would make them contact us before the ten days are up. We could set a trap for them.'

'You mean lure them here and grab them? Suppose more than one turns up? What will we do with them anyway? They're hardly likely to say, "It's a fair cop guv'nor, and we'll leave you alone now".'

'They could tell us who's the brains behind it.'

'How are we going to make them do that? Torture?'

Impatience showed on Wanda's face. 'Blackmail. We say we won't give them up to the police if they tell us what we want to know. After all, it's obvious your uncle and Gerry weren't working alone. I shouldn't think any of the top people will come. They'll send one of their minions.'

Quentin mulled this over. 'You mean flush them out?' he said eventually. 'And then what? If we caught one of them, or found out who the top man is, we couldn't prove anything without the diamonds. They'd deny everything. Even if they admitted to the break-ins, they could just say they were after other goods – money, jewellery and things. Anyway, how could we lure them here, or anywhere for that matter? Put an advert in *The Times* – we've got the diamonds, come and get them? Or something more subtle – would the person who contacted Mr Cadbury please meet him under the clock at Waterloo, where he'll gain something to his advantage?'

Wanda shook her head. 'I don't know, but anything's better than doing nothing. We're running out of time.'

Quentin rubbed his forehead. Five days before the deadline given in the note, and still no answers and no diamonds. And now his parents were here. As if he didn't have enough to think about without worrying that they would find out he wasn't working, that his so-called girlfriend was a mature woman and that he was under threat from diamond smugglers. His father would probably give him his marching orders. Fortunately, the house was his mother's, and he knew she wouldn't make him leave. But she would be disappointed, not because he wasn't working, but for lying to her.

'Well, isn't it?' Wanda demanded, obviously tired of waiting for a response. 'Or are we going to sit here and twiddle our thumbs waiting for Saturday?'

Quentin flinched. 'You're right, we should do something. If only we could wrap this up before–' Before I see my parents again, he added silently. 'Perhaps the advert idea isn't so stupid. Next time they contact us we could say we've found the diamonds and arrange to hand them over–'

'And we could nab them!' Wanda interrupted.

They stared at each other, the idea hanging between them. Then they both laughed.

'It's a silly idea,' Wanda admitted. 'I sound like I'm in one of those TV crime programmes. As if we could actually catch them. I mean, when they realize there are no diamonds they'll probably kill us.'

'Not if there's only one of them. We could overcome them.'

'Really? Have you forgotten what they did to you last time?'

'We were taken by surprise then. We'll be prepared this time.'

'Yes,' Wanda said. 'A stake-out!'

'Now you *do* sound like a TV programme.' Quentin grinned. 'Are you sure you weren't a burglar in a former life?'

Wanda's expression froze, and Quentin could feel the air between them spark.

'Why did you say that? I could just as easily have been a policewoman.'

'Only joking,' Quentin said, surprised at her reaction.

'You'd better be,' Wanda replied testily. 'Just because my husband wasn't a saint, it doesn't make *me* a criminal. We're supposed to be on the same side here.'

'Of course we are. It was just a figure of speech. Come on, Wanda, don't look like that. We haven't got time to argue.'

Her shoulders sagging, Wanda nodded. 'Yes, well... Where were we?'

'Trying to work something out and not succeeding. We're too tense, too close to the problem, that's the trouble. We need a distraction.'

'We haven't got time for a distraction. You've just said so. Of course we're tense. We could be dead in a few days.'

'I'm sure it won't come to that,' Quentin assured her, hoping he sounded more convinced than he felt. He fell silent. He could feel Wanda's anxiety as much as his own.

As if by telepathy she edged forward on her seat. 'Perhaps we *do* need a distraction,' she whispered. 'It might relax us and we'd be able to think more clearly.'

She rose and held out her hand. Quentin took it and stood up to face her.

No time? What the hell, he thought as her arms snaked around his neck. Some things you just have to make time for.

Chapter Twenty-four

Later, while Wanda was in the bathroom, Quentin retrieved his discarded clothes and got dressed. A delightful distraction, but it hadn't solved anything. He sat on the edge of Wanda's bed, his mind going over the facts they had so far.

Wanda had rung Colin, who'd said he'd approach his brother about Richard Simpson, though Colin had thought James might not agree to it. A slim chance, Quentin thought.

'What about the car?' he said, fresh excitement rising. 'What happened to the car?'

'What car?' Wanda asked, appearing in the doorway, her satin dressing gown wrapped around her.

'The car Uncle John brought back. You said Gerry had a call from John to say he had the goods, but he wasn't well enough to take them to him. If he wasn't well enough to hand the diamonds over, he probably wouldn't have driven the car to the garage. He'd have come straight home, so what happened to the car?'

Wanda shrugged. 'Perhaps he put it in his lock-up — you said he rented one, didn't you, the one where your car is now? Or he could have left it on the street. Where was *his* car while he was abroad?'

Quentin frowned. 'Probably left it on the forecourt at work.'

'And anyway,' Wanda went on, 'didn't you say he sometimes *took* classic cars from here to the continent? That would mean he'd have to bring the diamonds back a different way.'

Quentin was stumped. He hadn't thought of that. 'But surely he wouldn't risk carrying the stones on him? All the time they were in the car he could say he didn't know they were there. But if they were found on him...'

Wanda combed her fingers through her tousled hair. 'He might have hired a car to come back with,' she suggested. 'It could have been waiting for him, with the diamonds already hidden inside. A bent worker in the hire company, or an arrangement with someone in on the plan.'

'Hmm. Maybe. So now we don't know whether he came back in a hired car on that last journey, or in a car he was sent to collect.'

The brick wall Quentin felt he was beating his head against seemed to get thicker.

'So what's your point?' Wanda said impatiently. 'You think he could have left the diamonds in the car?'

'I did think that, but they wouldn't be there now,' Quentin said, dismissing the idea. 'Whoever was waiting for them would have thought of that. I don't think John would risk leaving them there. Anyway, they can't have been in the car or they wouldn't still be looking for them. I think I'll check the lock-up though,' he added. 'Not that there are many places to hide anything. It's all bare walls and a concrete floor. Still, I'll check, just in case.'

Wanda stood up, the dressing gown falling open as she did so. Quentin feasted his eyes on her voluptuous curves and put a hand out towards her.

'Down boy,' she said in the same tone she used for Mozart. 'Once can make you relax. Twice will knock you out for the rest of the day. Off you go and let me get dressed in peace.'

Women, Quentin thought as he let himself out and made his way to the lock-up garage. Or to be precise, Wanda. He felt out of his depth with her, like he was struggling against a strong current. He hoped the current would ease one day, just as he hoped the tide would turn against whoever was trying to get the diamonds. For the first time, he regretted ever moving into his aunt's house, regretted not finishing his law degree and "making something of himself," as his father would have put it. He could have had his own house by now, or at least been able to afford to rent somewhere different.

He reached the lock-up, unlocked it and swung the door up. Squeezing by the BMW, he looked around. Perched about two inches above Quentin's head was a shelf that ran along one wall. Underneath hung a battery charger and a hook supporting a tow rope. On the metal shelf was a torch, a petrol can, a tin of oil, a bottle of screen wash and a cleaning sponge. Running his hand along the shelf he moved each item, shaking everything except the sponge. The slurp of liquid sounded on each shake, with no tell-tale signs of anything being hidden inside. There was nothing else except a layer of dirt.

'That's that then,' he muttered, wiping his grubby fingers on the sponge. Reassured that the diamonds weren't in the garage, he locked up and strode home, his mind full of questions and doubts.

Logging into his computer, he typed in "Richard Simpson" and was inundated with hits. He tried to narrow the search down by adding words and phrases he thought might be relevant, including news reports of convictions for handling stolen goods, but got nowhere.

'Sod it all!' he said aloud as he plodded downstairs and entered the kitchen.

Magpie lay curled up in a patch of sunlight, his black and white fur gleaming. He sat up and looked at Quentin disdainfully, as if shocked by his outburst. 'It's all right for you,' Quentin told him. 'It's not you who's going to get done over.'

He changed into clean jeans and a T-shirt, then sat on the sofa trying to collect his thoughts. Magpie came in, sprang onto his lap and purred. 'Oh, now you love me, eh?' Quentin said, fondling his ears. 'You fickle feline, you. Well, boy, we're in a tight spot, aren't we? What are we going to do?'

Chapter Twenty-five

Mid-morning the next day, Wanda came to see Quentin, looking worried. 'We're being watched,' she said. 'I keep seeing someone across the road. He's walked past at least four times in the last hour.'

Quentin went to the window and peered out. There were several people walking along, two women talking and a girl strapping a child into a pushchair. None were looking in his direction. 'I can't see anyone hanging about. What does he look like?'

Wanda screwed her face up. 'Tallish, and broad. I couldn't see his face that well. People kept walking in front of him, and he had a scarf pulled up over his mouth and one of those hats with a brim.'

'A brim? You mean a peak, like a baseball hat?'

'No. Like a trilby. It wasn't a kid, I'm sure of that.'

'Well, he's not there now.'

At that moment a figure appeared from a gap between the houses opposite, a narrow alleyway that gave access to the backs of the houses. Tall and broad, with a hat, and a scarf obscuring the lower half of his face. The man glanced over at Quentin's house, then turned and hurried along the street. He must have seen him at the window.

'What's the point of watching us now?' Wanda asked, uneasiness sounding in her voice. 'They haven't done since the note, so why now? Or do you think they have, and we haven't noticed?'

A chill came over Quentin. This confirmed his previous conviction that the criminals would have been keeping more than a casual eye on their movements. As yet he'd detected nothing suspicious, no one suddenly darting away when he'd looked in their direction. He shuddered. There was something very unsettling about the thought of someone watching your every move. Suppose they'd been followed over the last few days in the hope that they would lead their pursuer to the diamonds?

'No,' he murmured. 'I'm sure we would have realized if they'd been following us.'

'What?' Wanda spluttered. 'You think they've been following us as well as watching the house?'

'No. I'm sure we'd have realized.' Would they? Quentin wondered with a shudder. Whoever was after the diamonds was convinced John had left them in the house, but they might also think that he and Wanda had found them and taken them somewhere else. When he thought about it, it was quite likely that they'd been followed. Wanda's expression told him she thought so too, now the possibility had been mentioned.

'Still…' he muttered, pushing the thought from his mind.

'Still what?'

Quentin touched the mole by his ear. 'Well, you know, what you said yesterday.'

'What did I say?'

'About forcing their hand. Getting them to make a move before Saturday.'

Wanda sighed in frustration. 'All right, what have you come up with?'

Drawing back from the window, Quentin turned to her. 'Well, apart from seeing if we lead them to the diamonds, why would they be watching us? To be sure we don't come out with suitcases or overnight bags, that's why. They're afraid we might do a runner or go to the cops.'

Wanda nodded. 'If something doesn't give soon, we'll have to cut and run or go to the police. We can't stay here with nothing to hand over. We'll be sitting ducks.'

'Yeah,' grunted Quentin. 'Well, we don't have to leave, just make them think we are.'

'How? Go out with a couple of suitcases waving a rail ticket?'

'Better than that. Put a "For Sale" sign up.'

'What?' Wanda gasped. 'But it takes weeks to arrange a sale. They'd know that.'

'A "To Let" sign then. We'll whitewash the windows. Lots of people move out before disposing of their property. They'll think I've gone.'

Wanda stared at him as though letting this sink in. 'Right,' she said eventually. 'Then what? Won't they start trying to track us down?'

'I think they'll break in and have another attempt at finding the diamonds before they start trying to find us. This time we'll be ready for them.'

'But,' Wanda protested, 'you said they won't bother doing that again. They've tried and found nothing. That's why they've got us looking for them.'

'Maybe. But they'll want to be sure before they start tracking us down.'

Wanda shook her head. 'I don't think so. If they think we've legged it, they'll assume we've taken the diamonds with us.'

'A sign is bound to produce some sort of reaction,' Quentin reasoned, picturing the man he'd glimpsed across the street. He imagined him starting in surprise and reaching for his mobile phone to get further instructions, or hovering uncertainly wondering whether to risk crossing the road and peering through the window.

'He's not likely to break in in broad daylight, is he?' Wanda asked.

'He could,' Quentin countered, thinking of the previous break-in. 'It's been done before.'

'Yes, but the house was empty then. You were at work, weren't you? This bloke – what if he just walks away?'

'*I'll* follow him,' Quentin said, suddenly feeling decisive. 'At least I'll find out where he goes.'

'You've forgotten something, haven't you? Let's say we put a sign up and make them think you've gone. What about me? I don't live here.'

Quentin frowned. 'That's a point. We'll have to make you disappear too then, or they might try to get to me through you. Still, they don't know who you are – I mean they've got no reason to suspect you're Gerry's wife. The heavy that duffed me up just called you my friend.'

Wanda shook her head. 'No. Somehow I get the feeling they know who I am and why I moved here.'

Of course. That's why she'd been so scared on the night the brick had been thrown.

'It'll look odd, two adjacent houses up for let at the same time,' Wanda continued. 'Better if you move into mine for a few days, stay out of sight, then we can watch what's going on. Put the sign up, set your burglar alarm and if they break in, we can catch them in the act.'

'Hmm. I'm not so sure about that. I'm not putting you in danger.'

'That's sweet of you, but it's no more dangerous than before. Anyway, how are we supposed to make him think you've actually left if he's watching us all the time?'

Quentin sighed and gazed through the window again. 'He's not there all the time, is he? It would be too obvious. He could easily miss me going. I don't have to move everything out – I could be letting the place furnished. Even if they don't think I've gone, if our friend sees me putting the sign up, it'll be enough. They'll be panicked into doing something.'

He let the net curtains fall back into place. They badly needed a wash, he realized. He should get vertical blinds like Wanda. Shaking himself, he turned back to face her. 'Well, what do you think?'

'I think it's a stupid idea. Who's going to write this sign, you or me?'

* * *

'That looks OK,' Wanda said as Quentin held up the square of cardboard an hour later. 'It would be better if we had an estate agent's sign, but this will do. Lots of people advertise privately.'

Quentin stood back and surveyed his handiwork. "To Let, two-bedroom house, fully furnished", read the sign, followed by his mobile phone number.

'You'll be inundated with calls,' Wanda laughed nervously. 'What will you say to genuine enquiries?'

'Just that it's already been let.'

'And if *they* ring, you'll tell them we've found the diamonds like you said?'

'Uh-huh. Unless you want to go to the police before we put the sign up, just to be safe.'

'No point without the goods. We couldn't prove anything.'

Quentin stared at her. He could see she was anxious, and becoming more so as the deadline drew nearer. Yet still she was reluctant to involve the police.

'It could save us from having our heads bashed in, even if they didn't get done for handling stolen goods,' he pointed out.

He saw Wanda shiver and look away. 'Do you really think…?'

'Yes, I do, and so do you.' He continued to stare at her. Why, at this stage in their relationship, did he suddenly feel she was keeping something from him?

'You're right,' she breathed. 'Perhaps we should call them, tell them what's going on. But they said no police.'

Quentin rolled his eyes. 'You think the police not being there will stop them bashing our heads in when they don't get what they want? They'd probably do us over even if they did get what they wanted.'

'Why should they? We don't know who they are. I'm sure the brains behind all this won't let himself be seen. We can't identify them, and if we could they'd get a much longer sentence for murdering us than smuggling.'

'Only if they're caught.'

Fresh tension filled the air as the significance of his words settled. Wanda shivered again, but her head tilted up defiantly. 'Let's do it ourselves,' she said, 'but we might need some help.'

'Help? Who are we going to call? Superman?'

'Colin.'

'Colin!' Quentin almost choked on the word.

'You asked if you could call on him if we needed to, remember?'

'That was before I hit him over the head,' he reminded her. 'He's hardly likely to want someone else to bash it as well.'

'He'll do it for me, and he's all right now. Come on, Quentin, I don't suppose there'll be more than two of them, maybe only one. As long as we're prepared, we should be all right if Colin's with us.'

Quentin was silent. He didn't like the idea of sharing his secrets with Colin any more than he liked the idea of sharing Wanda with him. He pulled himself up sharply. This was no time to be worrying about petty jealousies, and any extra help they could get would be useful. In fact, it was fast becoming essential.

'Are you sure we can trust him?'

Wanda gave him a withering look. 'We've been through this. Yes, I'd trust him with my life.'

Your life, yes, Quentin thought, but what about mine?

'All right,' he said grudgingly. 'But if this doesn't work, we'll have to go to the police.'

'Yes,' Wanda agreed. 'We will. We won't put the sign up till Colin gets here in case something happens straight away. I'm sure he'll help. I'll call him now.'

Chapter Twenty-six

When Wanda returned to her own house, Quentin packed some essentials into a holdall. True, he was only going next door, but he didn't want to keep coming back if he didn't have to. He wondered what to do about Magpie. He wouldn't take kindly to staying with a dog, and Quentin doubted that Mozart would welcome having his domain invaded. He should have had a cat flap put in. No, that wouldn't work at the moment. He didn't want the criminals to detect any sort of movement in the house when it was supposed to be empty, and he recalled the vicious kick Magpie had suffered during the attempted burglary. Magpie would have to go with him. After all, he'd lived in Wanda's house before the previous owner had moved, and Wanda wouldn't mind.

Having made his decision, he went to the cupboard to get some cat food. The shelves were nearly empty, and he cursed. Before he could bend down and look thoroughly there came a knock on the door.

Was Colin here already? Through the frosted glass panel in the door he could see the outline of a figure, tallish and broad, but hatless. Pulling out his mobile, he keyed in Wanda's number.

'There's someone at my door,' he told her when she answered. 'It might just be someone selling something but I thought I'd warn you. It could be the person we saw watching the house.'

'All right. Colin should be there any minute, but I'll look out when you open the door. If there's a problem I'll–' her words were lost beneath another loud knocking.

Pocketing his phone Quentin stepped into the hallway. As he reached the door, he could see that the figure definitely resembled the man he'd seen across the road. He grabbed a golf umbrella from the stand, then pulled the door open a fraction and peered through the gap, ready to slam it shut again if necessary. A shock ran through him as he saw a scarf around the man's neck and a checked trilby hat in his hands. Instead of slamming the door, his fingers slid off the doorknob and he stepped back, gasping as recognition swept over him.

'F-Father! What are you doing here?'

* * *

Herbert Cadbury glared at Quentin, his face red with anger. 'What am I doing? What are you doing, that's what I want to know. You're supposed to be at work.'

Quentin gazed at him, unable to believe his eyes. It was *him* who'd been watching the house, and not very discreetly at that.

'I thought you were in Chelmsford,' he said, standing aside as his father pushed impatiently past him. 'Come in, why don't you,' he added, pushing the door shut and following him into the lounge. The sarcasm was wasted on the older man.

'Wanted to tell you we couldn't see you till next Monday,' Herbert Cadbury blustered. 'Phoned that law firm you said you worked for. They said you left months ago. Thought I'd find out where you went when we arrived here, if you weren't going to work as you said you were, before I upset your mother and told her what a lazy, good-for-nothing son she raised.'

Rage swept through Quentin. 'You had nothing to do with raising me then?'

'Pah! I was away with the army a lot of the time. Always knew Rosemary was too soft with you. So, what *are* you doing with yourself all day, and what are you living on?'

'It's none of your business,' Quentin replied sullenly.

'No one in our family's ever been on the dole!'

The words were spoken contemptuously, and Quentin's hackles rose even further. He drew himself up and they stood facing each other, the atmosphere growing thicker with every second.

'I've never claimed dole,' Quentin snapped. 'I saved when I was working and I'm living off my savings.'

'And how long is that going to last, eh? What will you do when the money's run out?'

'Actually, Quentin's working for me.'

The two of them swung round to see Wanda. She stood, head high and with an air of confidence, looking steadily at them. She held a gun in her hand.

'What the—' Quentin heard his father mutter and saw him grow pale. His own eyes widened when he realized that Wanda had managed to get in and creep up the hall without them hearing. And with a gun.

'It's all right, Wanda,' he said, eyeing the gun uncertainly. 'This is my father.'

'So I gather.' She stood there, not moving, still pointing the gun at his father.

'Which means you can put the gun away,' Quentin said.

He watched as Wanda lowered her hand, and breathed a sigh of relief. For a wild moment he'd thought she was going to turn the gun on him. Where on earth had she got it, and why didn't he know about it?

His father, recovering slightly, gazed at the gun before Wanda dropped it into a bag that swung from her free arm. 'It's not real,' he barked. 'It's a replica.'

'Burglars don't know that,' Wanda said, sending him a sweet smile. Quentin saw his father's expression soften a little.

'Perhaps not,' he growled, 'but I bloody well do. Wasn't in the army for over thirty years for nothing. I could tell from the way it dropped in the bag – the weight was wrong.'

'It fooled you at first though, didn't it?' Quentin jibed, pleased to be able to better his father for once.

'Not for long. Just the shock of it.'

Quentin couldn't counter that. He'd been shocked, more than shocked, to see Wanda standing there calmly wielding a gun.

'It belongs to my nephew,' Wanda explained. 'We've had a spate of burglaries in the area. I wanted some protection.'

'That's right,' Quentin said, quick to endorse her story. '*I've* been burgled.'

With a suspicious look in his direction, his father said, 'Have you? Your mother never mentioned it.'

'I didn't tell her. She'd only worry, and she couldn't do anything from ten thousand miles away.'

'Did you report it?'

'I did, but they haven't caught anyone yet.'

'Hmm. So what do you mean, Quentin is working for you?'

Quentin held his breath as his father turned to Wanda. What would she say?

'I've got my own business,' Wanda said smoothly. 'Quentin's helping me and if I make a go of it, I'm thinking of taking him in as a partner.'

'What sort of business?'

'A detective agency,' Wanda replied, her face deadpan.

'Detective agency! That's not a business, it's a lot of tomfoolery.'

'Tell that to CID and Scotland Yard,' Quentin put in.

'That's different, they're professionals. What can you possibly hope to achieve by going around snooping on people?'

'Like you were snooping on me, you mean?' Quentin said sourly. His father looked as though he would explode.

'We'd like to catch these burglars, for a start,' Wanda interrupted. 'But there's plenty of other work.'

'You mean trying to catch people out in adultery – divorce cases, and all that?'

'Some are domestic cases, yes, so Quentin's knowledge of the law is a great asset.'

Quentin eyed Wanda in amazement. At that moment he thought she was the most wonderful person in the world. He had no idea how she had weaved such a story out of thin air, and he didn't care. Thanks to her, he had saved face in front of his father.

'I see,' his father said. 'Perhaps I've been a bit hasty then, my boy. But why did you say you were still working at the office?'

'I didn't think you would like the idea of my being a detective,' Quentin lied. 'I was going to get established then come over to see you, tell you then.'

'What, with this girlfriend you told your mother about?'

Quentin hesitated. 'Well,' he began.

He caught Wanda's eye and she gave a half-smile. 'What Quentin means is Louise had to move away with her job, didn't she, Quentin? Edinburgh, wasn't it?'

'Yes,' Quentin mumbled, marvelling again at the performance Wanda was giving. She was winning his father over with her seductive smiles and sophisticated talk, like she'd won *him* over when they'd first met.

His father harrumphed. 'Seems a bit airy fairy to me, but I can see you're a woman of the world, my dear. Sounds as though you know what you're doing, and if you can teach my boy a thing or two it'll be no bad thing.'

Quentin had to turn away. Wanda had taught him a thing or two, delightful things, but that wasn't what his father meant. In an effort to keep his temper under control he strode to the cabinet and poured himself a whisky.

His father turned. 'Whisky, eh? I wouldn't say no to one of those.'

After picking up two more glasses, Quentin poured a measure into each, then handed one to Wanda and one to his father. Downing his in one gulp, his father held out his glass. 'Not bad,' he said. 'I'll have another for the road.'

Another for the road. Did that mean he was leaving? Quentin refilled the glass, hoping fervently that he would. His hand shook as he handed the glass back. Why had he gone along with this charade? Why hadn't he stood up to his father, told him the truth? What did it matter what this bully of a man thought of him?

He knew the answer. He couldn't face the thought of his father being proved right, and he didn't want to let his mother down.

Herbert Cadbury put his empty glass on the table. 'What's this?' he asked, picking up the cardboard sign that lay there. 'You're letting out the house without so much as a by-your-leave?'

'What?' Quentin had completely forgotten about the sign. He looked imploringly at Wanda, but now she looked blank. 'Oh that,' he said. 'It's just a ruse to make the place look empty, to see if the burglars will try to break in again.'

'Why would they break into an empty house? Nothing to steal.'

'There's the TV and stuff. The sign says fully furnished, and if they think there's nobody here…'

'Well, watch your back, that's all I can say. Should let the police do their job. Better be off. I'll get your mother to ring you, make arrangements where to meet up.'

'All right,' said Quentin, relieved. 'Give her my love.'

'Huh. Don't know what she'll say about all this nonsense.'

Not as much as she'd say if she knew the truth, Quentin thought. 'We'll talk about it,' he said, desperate to be rid of him.

'Goodbye, Mr Cadbury,' Wanda purred, smiling a farewell. 'It was so nice to meet you. I'm sorry I thought you were a burglar.'

Drawn by Wanda's tone Quentin looked at her, noticing the way her blouse hugged her figure. He could see that his father had noticed it too. He waited for his father's usual response to being called mister – It's Major Cadbury, actually – but it didn't come. Instead, his father looked uncomfortable and said, 'Yes, well, no harm done, but you shouldn't go waving that toy gun around. Could get you into trouble. Goodbye, my dear. Goodbye, Quentin. I'll see myself out.'

And with a rush of air and a slamming of the door, he was gone.

Chapter Twenty-seven

Colin arrived twenty minutes later.

'Sorry I took so long,' he said when Quentin let him in. 'The traffic was awful. Hello, Wanda love.'

'Have you found anything on the bloke on that list?' Quentin asked.

'Richard Simpson? Well, James wasn't happy, but he came through. Simpson only came to Britain from Spain with his parents not long before he was caught for handling stolen goods. He's only twenty and since his release he's been in a rehabilitation centre. James wouldn't say where, but nowhere near London.'

Deflated, Quentin exchanged looks with Wanda.

'Can't be connected to our case then,' Wanda said. 'Still, it was worth a try.'

Colin nodded towards the sign on the table. 'You've had enough then, Quentin?'

'I'm not really going,' Quentin said, and explained his idea.

Colin sat rubbing his chin thoughtfully. 'You're saying they still think the goods they're after are in this house? And you've no idea what it is they're looking for?'

He looked at Wanda as if he knew she was keeping something from him. 'If you know, tell me. I know you're trying to protect Gerry's name but you can't expect me to help you unless I know what I'm dealing with.'

Quentin exchanged an anxious glance with Wanda. He saw the uncertainty in her eyes and held his breath. Then, as if coming to a decision, she nodded. 'That's fair enough. Agreed, Quentin?'

Quentin shrugged, but he knew she was right. The time for procrastination was over. 'Agreed,' he said reluctantly.

Drawing a deep breath Wanda turned to Colin. 'It's diamonds.'

'Diamonds!' Colin stared at her, disbelief showing on his face. 'Gerry was handling diamonds? Are you sure?'

'That's what he told me before he died.'

'I always thought... you know, dodgy gear, antiques and things, but diamonds...' He gave a low whistle before he asked, 'Why didn't you tell me before? Don't you trust me, Wanda?'

Her face crimson, Wanda said, 'Of course I do. It's just – you thought so much of Gerry. I mean he saved your life, and you were friends – I know you guessed he had something going on, but he never wanted you to know what, and he never told me until he felt he had to. I... I didn't want to demean him in your eyes.'

Quentin watched Colin during this exchange. He seemed genuinely amazed. If he did know anything about Gerry's goings-on, or was involved himself, he was covering it up pretty well.

'Well,' Colin was saying, 'as far as I'm concerned, he was a good man. Still, I must admit, diamonds... This thing's worse than you made out. People get killed over diamonds.'

'Yes,' Wanda said, 'that's why we need your help, Colin. If that sign forces their hand and they turn up here, will you help us to catch them? Unless you can think of a better idea?'

'Not offhand, but I'll see what I can come up with. That sign – you're putting it up because someone's watching the house?'

'We thought there was,' Quentin said. 'Wanda saw someone, but it turned out to be my father. So if no one *is* watching us, the sign's a waste of time, isn't it?'

'Not necessarily,' Wanda said. 'Even if they don't see it until the time is up, when they do come they'll think no one's here, break in and we'll be waiting for them.'

'And then what?' Colin demanded. 'I can't believe the top brass of a smuggling ring would just wait around in the hope that you'll find these diamonds and meekly hand them over.'

'Not the top brass, no,' Quentin agreed, 'but whoever they've told to get them might.'

'But even if it is someone lower down the chain, they'd have been watching you. They wouldn't have wanted you running off with the goods. I mean, they want them enough to threaten you, both of you, so they must be pretty desperate. My guess is they're being threatened themselves by someone higher in the ring, you know, pay up or else.'

Quentin eyed Colin. 'How do you know it's a ring?'

Colin rolled his eyes. 'It can't be just one or two people, can it? The stones have to be brought into the country, and we know Gerry fenced them, so he must have handed them to someone who knew what to do with them. I mean, what would *you* do with hundreds of thousands of pounds worth of diamonds? You couldn't sell them without arousing suspicion. They don't take diamonds for cash in Tesco's–'

'All right,' Wanda interrupted. 'I think we've got the message, Colin. Anyway, it's no good speculating. Let's concentrate on what we're going to do.'

This seemed to render them all speechless. They sat looking at each other as if hoping one of them would jump up and shout Eureka! Colin lifted the hem of his shirt and rubbed at the lenses in his glasses. Wanda chewed her lip and Quentin fingered the mole by his ear.

'Well,' Wanda said after a while, 'all we've got at the moment is Quentin's idea, so let's carry on with that. If you're right, Colin, and we are being watched, it might work. We'll whitewash the windows; Quentin can move into mine and keep out of sight. If anything happens, we'll hear.'

Colin started. 'Quentin moved in with you? You didn't mention that. When you rang you just said you needed my help.'

'It's only for a few days, until this is all over,' Wanda told him. 'His house has to look empty.'

'But if you whitewash the windows, it will look empty. He can keep out of sight here just as easily as he can at yours.'

'No I can't,' Quentin snapped. 'The burglar alarm has internal sensors. If they pick any movement up, the alarm will go off. We'll have to set it even if I'm here. I have to sleep sometimes.'

'OK, but they could break in while you're asleep next door,' Colin pointed out. 'I'll move in with you too, Wanda, then one of us can keep guard. We'll sleep in shifts.'

Irritation swept over Quentin. Colin didn't like the thought of him sleeping under the same roof as Wanda so he was going to play chaperone. Or gooseberry. He wanted to reject the suggestion, but had to admit it made sense. He looked questioningly at Wanda.

'It would be better if he were on hand,' Wanda said. 'Yes, Colin, good idea.'

'Right then,' Quentin conceded. 'I'll get my things.'

* * *

In response to the sign that Quentin had fastened to the outside wall, his mobile rang twice during that evening with enquiries about the house. One woman got quite irate when he told her it was let already. 'Why don't you take the sign down then?' she asked, and Quentin wittered on about keeping it up until everything was finalized.

After blanking out the windows, he had left his home and walked around the block. When he was sure he wasn't being followed he'd doubled back, cut through the alley and climbed over Wanda's rear wall, praying no one would see him and mistake him for a burglar. Colin had gone the back way, over the wall between the two gardens, so anyone watching the front wouldn't know there were two men in the house with Wanda.

Wanda cooked pasta, and after they'd eaten, she sat next to Colin on the chaise longue. Despite the tension that hung in the air, and jumping at every little noise outside the room, she chatted to Colin amiably and laughed at the jokes he reeled off. Quentin's resentment grew. Damn the wretched man. *He* should be sitting next to Wanda, not Colin. Shouldn't he? Wanda had given him no commitment, no sign that she considered him a contender for her affections. At her own admission, she'd befriended him solely to get at the diamonds. That didn't apply now though. She'd said she'd genuinely grown to like him. But perhaps she didn't like him as much as she liked Colin. Ridiculous, he told himself, he's fifty if he's a day. But then Wanda's nearer his age than mine.

He was relieved when Wanda stood up and stretched. 'I think I'll turn in now. The single bed in the little bedroom's made up. I'll leave it to you to fight over who's going to take the first watch. Wake me up when it's my turn.'

'I'll go first,' Quentin said when she'd gone. 'All right if I wake you about three, Colin?'

'OK. I'll do the rest of the night – save waking Wanda.' Colin went upstairs and came down with a pillow and a blanket. 'You might as well be comfortable,' he said. Quentin took the blanket for warmth but refused the pillow – he knew if he lay down, he'd fall asleep.

When Colin had gone back upstairs there was a bark from the kitchen. Quentin went to see what was wrong and chuckled when he saw Mozart with his nose in his basket trying to push Magpie out. Magpie, ignoring his own blanket, raised a paw and biffed the dog on the nose. Mozart barked again and Magpie biffed him again. Defeated, Mozart backed away and looked pathetically at Quentin.

'Out of there, Magpie,' Quentin ordered. With a haughty toss of his head Magpie turned round three times, then curled into a ball, keeping a defiant eye on Quentin.

'Come on then, Mozart, you can keep me company on the sofa.' He found a dog treat and lured the terrier into the lounge. Mozart followed obediently and settled down by his feet. He looked uncertain when Quentin patted the seat next to him and encouraged him to jump up.

'It's all right,' he murmured, knowing that Wanda didn't let him on the furniture. 'I won't tell if you don't.'

Chapter Twenty-eight

The night was uneventful, and when Quentin awoke after sleeping from three to eight o'clock the smell of frying bacon floated up the stairs. Anxious not to miss out, he sprang out of bed and immediately stubbed his toe on the base of Wanda's computer desk. Pain shot through him, and he hobbled downstairs to the bathroom. Afterwards, he joined Wanda and Colin at the table.

'What's wrong?' Wanda asked as he limped in.

'Stubbed my toe. Forgot I wasn't in my own bed.'

Colin sniggered and tried to cover it up by saying, 'Bacon, Quentin?'

After he'd eaten, Quentin felt better. He located his mobile, only to realize the battery was flat.

'I've left my charger at home,' he confessed. 'I'll have to go back and get it in case they try to contact us.'

'I hadn't thought of that,' said Wanda, 'they might use your number now it's on the sign outside.'

'Exactly. I'll have to go.'

'Won't one of ours fit?' Colin asked.

They compared cables with a negative result.

'I'll go the back way,' Quentin said.

With that he left through the kitchen door, vaulted the garden wall and entered his own house, followed by Magpie. 'It's no good you coming in,' he told the cat. 'We're not staying.'

Magpie padded past him and disappeared upstairs. Turning off the burglar alarm, Quentin tried to think where he'd left the charger. Had he used the socket in the lounge next to Aunt Josie's chair? Yes, that was it. Going to the back of the lounge, he saw that the throw covering the knife slashes had slipped off the old chair and the charger lay on the seat. Bending to pick it up, he noticed the cord had disappeared into the gap between the seat and the arm. He tugged at it, but it didn't budge. Kneeling down, he slid his hand down the side of the chair. The cord was wrapped around one of the coiled springs, which scratched Quentin's hand as he fought to pull it free. Something else touched the back of his hand, something wider and rougher than a spring. Letting go of the cord, he turned his hand, grasped the object and eased it up through the horsehair padding between the springs. He blinked as it emerged into the daylight, its brightness dazzling him. It was a bracelet, gold, and set with sparkling stones. It must have been Aunt Josie's. What was it his mother had said? She had Josie's necklace and earrings but she'd never found the matching bracelet.

He pushed his hand into the chair again, locating the phone charger lead and yanking it up. The whole thing flew upwards, nearly causing him to hit himself in the eye. He put it aside, then turned his attention back to the bracelet. 'Lovely,' he said aloud. 'Mum will be pleased.'

He could see how it would have escaped the burglar's search – although the chair had been ripped open, the bracelet was well enmeshed in the horsehair filling and easy to miss. They couldn't have been after this anyway, or they wouldn't have torn open the picture frames. Wrapping it in a piece of kitchen roll, he pushed it into his pocket. He replaced the throw, picked up the charger, reset the alarm and went back to Wanda's.

* * *

'Perhaps we're wasting our time sitting round waiting for something to happen,' Wanda said that afternoon. 'Perhaps–'

A loud, continuous, clanging sound drowned out her words. It took Quentin a few seconds to register what it was. An alarm. *His* alarm. He jumped up, treading on Mozart's paw and making him yelp.

Too apprehensive even to acknowledge the dog, he exchanged glances with Colin. 'Go in the front,' he barked. 'I'll take the back. Wanda, give me that toy gun and stand by to call the police.'

For the second time that day he vaulted the wall and opened his own back door. He crept in, gun in hand, pausing to pick up a saucepan from the kitchen before carrying on. Double armed, he moved forward, peering round the lounge door expecting to see the same balaclava-clad figure as before. There was no one. Stepping back into the hallway, he saw the front door open and Colin appeared. At the same time, he heard a noise from upstairs. Signalling Colin to be quiet and pointing upwards, he started up the stairs. Someone was there – he was sure. He waited until he felt Colin come up behind him, then leapt up the last few stairs and into his bedroom, the gun pointing ahead of him.

Heart hammering, he glanced round the room. Empty. Except for a black and white cat, cowering on the bed as if afraid of the shrill noise that filled the air.

'Magpie!' Lowering the gun, Quentin leaned against the wall.

Colin burst in, a heavy-looking candlestick in his hand. He stopped dead when he saw Magpie. 'A cat!' he exploded. 'Your bloody cat!'

'I hadn't even missed him,' Quentin groaned. 'He followed me in when I came to get my charger. He must have triggered the alarm.'

Quentin squirmed under Colin's look. All this fuss because you forgot your stupid cat, it said.

'Turn that bloody noise off, before the neighbours call the police,' Colin shouted.

Hurrying to the control panel, Quentin switched off the alarm, then went outside and looked around. The curtain of the adjoining house twitched, then was drawn aside. Quentin recognized his neighbour, Carol, the wife of the man who had chatted to him when he'd been turning out the garden pots. The window opened and Carol leaned out.

'Is everything all right?' she called.

'Yes, thanks,' Quentin called back. 'My cat set the alarm off.'

'Oh. Sorry to see you're leaving,' she said, gesturing towards the sign. 'Had any interest yet?'

'No.'

'That's a surprise. I thought it would be snapped up. Where are you going?'

'I don't know yet. I'm staying with friends for a bit.'

'Oh well, as long as everything's all right.'

Carol withdrew and Quentin breathed a relieved sigh. He saw someone else gazing curiously from a doorway across the street. 'False alarm,' he shouted. No one else seemed worried. The street wasn't far from the main road where alarms went off accidentally all the time.

If we're being watched now our cover's blown, he thought grimly. They'll know I'm still here, sign or no sign. He saw Wanda peek through her window, and seconds later her door opened and she joined him on the pavement. They went into his house just as Colin was coming out.

After they'd explained what had happened, she said, 'I hadn't missed Magpie either. Are you coming back to mine?'

'In a minute,' he said, thinking the whole charade was futile. 'You and Colin go on.'

When they'd gone, he shut the door and went into the lounge. He slumped onto the settee, the anti-climax of the last half hour leaving him deflated. Magpie came in and rubbed against his legs.

'What a ruckus you caused, boy,' he said, stroking him. 'Still, it was my fault. I should have made sure you came back with me.'

He sat for a while, staring into space. This is silly, he thought gloomily. How much longer can we go on like this, clutching at straws and getting nowhere? Shifting position, his hand brushed against the package in his pocket and he remembered the bracelet. If jewellery could be lost in an armchair, why not diamonds? The criminals had obviously thought of that – that's why they'd slashed the chair, the sofa and his mattress.

After a frantic forty minutes of feeling and poking around inside the slashes, down the sides and along the backs of the sofa and the chair, all he got was a broken pen and sore fingers. He collapsed on to the sofa again, deflated, wishing the diamonds would just miraculously turn up.

Magpie mewed, disturbing his thoughts. 'Hungry, eh?' he said, stroking the cat behind the ear. 'I think you ate the last lot yesterday.'

He looked in the cupboard for any tins of cat food. He'd been so tied up with the diamond mystery he hadn't done any shopping, and he knew Wanda didn't have cat food.

Magpie gazed up at him expectantly. 'Sorry, boy, the cupboard is bare, unless you want soup or baked beans. Hold on, I'll see if there's any sardines at the back.' He pulled out the front tins and felt behind them for the flat sardine cans, but all he found was the two old packets of porridge. 'Bloody things,' he said, pulling them out. 'I might as well throw them out – I'll never use them. What's this–'

Pushing the first packet aside he stared at the second. 'Cat food,' he murmured, picking it up. 'Dried cat food. How on earth did I miss this before?'

He frowned, trying to recall if he had handled the packets. When he'd moved in, they'd already been in the cupboard, unopened. The porridge box must have been in front of the cat food, so he hadn't noticed it. After the break-in, he'd shoved the boxes to the back of the shelf without really looking at them – they were similar in colour and size and he'd just assumed they were both porridge. Well, he reasoned, Magpie had been Aunt Josie's cat, so it wasn't really surprising there was cat food here.

'You're in luck,' he chuckled, waving the packet in front of Magpie. The cat mewed, and walked to where his food bowl should have been. Realizing he'd taken it next door, Quentin took a metal butter dish and set it down on the worktop. Sliding his finger under the flap, he opened the box and tipped it up over the steel dish. 'Looks awful. Still, it's better than porridge, eh boy, and it's got a free scoop, according to the packet – oh!'

Something fell from the packet and hit the dish, making a metallic clink. Funny looking scoop, Quentin thought, reaching out to pick it up. His hand hovered over it, and his breath stopped. They didn't put free scoops in cloth bags. He froze, his mind in turmoil. It couldn't be. Could it?

Chapter Twenty-nine

His hand was pushed away by an impatient Magpie, who jumped up and started nibbling at the biscuit-like food. 'Wait!' Quentin shouted, causing Magpie to shrink back. Snatching up the bag, he felt heat spread over his body while blood thundered in his ears. His fingers felt the contents through the material. It felt like pea shingle – small, hard stones, and lots of them. 'Please,' he whispered. 'Please let it be them.'

Fetching a cereal bowl, he held the bag over it. Gingerly, he pulled open the drawstring and turned it upside down. A cascade of brilliance poured out like a waterfall. 'Yes!' yelled Quentin, jumping in the air and almost knocking the bowl over. He gazed in awe at the glittering gems as they shone up at him, treasure and tawdry bowl merging into one. He picked up a few of the stones and laid them in his palm, taking in their varying shapes and sizes. Most were small, a few were bigger, some as big as frozen peas; all sparkled like the sun on the sea on a summer's day.

'Wow!' Quentin couldn't stop staring at his find. Even with his limited knowledge he was pretty sure he was looking at a fortune.

He must tell Wanda. She should know straight away, but now he'd found them he was afraid to let them out of his sight. He couldn't leave them in the house – after all, the sign was practically inviting the criminals in with open arms. No, he would have to keep them on him, and he'd have to go back to Wanda's. Go back and show her.

But he stood motionless, wondering whether he should. Perhaps he should delay telling her. Why?

Pouring the diamonds back into the bag, he noticed several larger than the others and thought they must be the most valuable of them all. He pulled the drawstring tight, went back to the lounge and sat down, nursing the bag in his lap. He no longer thought Wanda was involved with the gang or knew anything about the diamond smuggling, yet still he hesitated. Wanda wanted to hand over the goods and get the criminals off her back. Well, that was understandable, but why should they get away with it? Why should she want them to? 'No police,' they'd said. All very well in theory, but suppose handing over the diamonds wasn't the end of it? Once they'd given them up, they would be criminals themselves. Quentin didn't like the sound of that. Lying, avoiding work, treating the money he'd found as a free handout, yes. Not exactly admirable qualities, but knowingly handing over stolen gems – it didn't feel right, somehow.

But still, he should tell her. Her and Colin. That was another thing. It had been Wanda's suggestion to bring Colin in, and he'd seen them kissing, hadn't he, through the window? Suppose... No. They couldn't be working together. Wanda had been adamant that Colin wasn't involved. She was definitely on his side, and Colin was only interested in protecting Wanda. Or was that a ruse to get at the diamonds? Had he really not known what Gerry was dealing in?

Perplexed, Quentin shook his head. His hand closed round the bag in his lap and he smiled. Despite his quandary he couldn't help a little beat of victory. All through his childhood and teenage years his father had told him what a disappointment he was. He'd never been good enough, never done as well as his contemporaries with their high-flying jobs, expensive cars and social life to match. He was the one not tied to a job, not saddled with a mortgage or extortionate rent, not striving to do better, yet he was the one sitting with a stash of gems worth thousands, possibly more. It was incredible.

Magpie came in, bits of biscuit clinging to his whiskers. 'I'm beginning to think you're my lucky cat.' Quentin grinned. 'I found the money because of you, and now I've found this lot. I don't suppose you could turn into a genie and find the people behind all this, could you?'

Licking his paw and using it to clean the food from his whiskers, Magpie ignored him.

'Oh well, it was worth a try.' Striding to the cabinet Quentin found the whisky bottle and poured himself a measure. 'Cheers,' he said, raising the glass towards Magpie. 'Don't look at me like that. I know it's early, but if you were me you'd need a drink too. The point is, what am I going to do now?'

Two whiskies later, he'd made up his mind.

* * *

'I was just about to come and see what was keeping you,' Wanda said when he got back to hers. 'What have you been doing all this time?'

'Thinking about what to do,' Quentin said. 'And I've come to a decision.'

'Well?' said Colin.

'We're going to the police. *I'm* going to the police. You two don't need to be involved – they don't need to know everything, just that I've been threatened and that the person who's after the diamonds is coming for me. I'll work something out with them.'

Colin looked bemused. 'Really? And how do you intend to do that?'

'Well, we had a plan, didn't we, Wanda? We said we'd wait for them to contact us, arrange to meet them then nab them. Only we'll get the police to nab them instead.'

'Sounds sensible to me,' Colin admitted. 'But what if they don't believe you?'

'Yes,' Wanda put in. 'We've already agreed that they wouldn't do anything without proof.'

Thinking of the diamonds nestling in his jacket pocket, Quentin felt a pang of guilt. Involuntarily he stole a glance at the jacket laid over the back of a vacant chair, folded so as the bulge in the pocket didn't show. 'Well, we have tried doing things ourselves and we've got nowhere. I agreed to wait, but now I'm having second thoughts. I've got no right to put you in danger, Wanda.'

'That's the most reasonable thing I've heard you say so far,' Colin grunted. 'I told you to go to the police in the first place.'

That was true, Quentin realized. Was he being over cautious? Should he tell them?

'They threatened me too,' Wanda reminded him, 'before they even knew about you living in that house. I'll have to come with you if we're going to convince the police to take any action. I still think we'll be wasting our time. They'll probably think we're a couple of cranks.'

Quentin looked at her, his mind clouded by doubt. He could see she was still reluctant to resort to the police. 'I'm sorry, Wanda, but I really don't want to end up in hospital. I know I said we could handle it with Colin's help, but... No. I think we've gone far enough.'

'But if we go to the police now and the criminals find out we *will* end up in hospital, or worse,' Wanda said. 'And what about Gerry? It will all come out.'

'That's why you shouldn't come with me,' Quentin said, glad she hadn't mentioned his uncle. 'There's no need to tell them about Gerry, at this stage anyway. The police don't need to know your connection – I'll just say I've been broken into – they should have the first report on record – and that someone's threatened to kill me if I don't produce the diamonds. I'll take the note that came with the brick – they'll have to take me seriously then.'

'But it mentions me in the note,' Wanda said.

'Only as a neighbour. There're no names.' He pulled the note from his pocket. 'Just as well I kept it. Look.'

Colin took it. 'Quentin's right,' he said when he'd read it. 'A delectable neighbour could just be a neighbour who happened to be there when they broke in the second time.'

'Yes,' said Quentin. 'I'll say you're away at the moment. That'll cover you if they ask why you didn't come forward with me. I'll say they mentioned diamonds that day I was attacked and I didn't report it because I was scared and didn't know what to do. That's the truth, anyway.'

Wanda looked at Colin. 'Do you think I should go with him?'

'No, and I don't think you should stay here either. Come home with me, out of harm's way. If we need to back up Quentin's story, we can do it after he's seen them.'

Beating back the jealousy that invaded him, Quentin said, 'Good idea, Colin. If I need you, I'll ring you.'

'All right,' Wanda said. 'I don't relish the thought of going to the police I must admit, but I feel like I'm running away.'

'That's the best thing you can do,' Colin said. 'You'll be safe with me.'

He put an arm around Wanda's shoulders and gave what looked to Quentin like a triumphant smile. A vision floated before Quentin's eyes – Colin, luring Wanda to his lair with the sole intention of seducing her. Stupid, he realized. There was no chance of Wanda being seduced unless she wanted to be.

Colin took off his glasses and used the bottom of his shirt to clean them. It was a habit more than the need to remove any smears, Quentin had decided after witnessing this action several times, and wondered if this was the sole reason Colin usually wore shirts hanging over his trousers rather than T-shirts.

'Right, Wanda,' Colin said. 'I think we should go straight away. No point hanging around. Once Quentin's been to the police it will be out of our hands.'

White-faced, Wanda nodded then rose and went upstairs.

'When are you going then, Quentin?' Colin asked while he waited.

'No time like the present,' Quentin snapped. 'I'll just go home and get some ID. They'll want something to prove who I am.'

Colin rolled his eyes. 'You might as well take that sign down. You've been in and out so many times since yesterday, the whole neighbourhood must know you haven't left.'

'I've only been seen once, when the alarm went off.'

'Oh yes, I forgot, the *cat* burglar!' Colin smirked, and Quentin had a sudden urge to hit him.

'Sorry,' Colin said, as if sensing Quentin's indignation. 'Look, it was an OK idea originally, but it hasn't done much good, has it? Seems odd. I really thought they'd be watching the place. Still, I daresay they've got their reasons for handling it the way they are.'

Quentin thought it seemed odd too, but he wasn't about to agree with anything Colin said. He let out a long breath when Wanda reappeared, looking drawn and tense. Why is she so uptight about me going to the police? he mused as she scooped up Mozart and attached his lead. It occurred to him that she might not be worried about Gerry's posthumous reputation at all – perhaps she was the one with a criminal record. He gave it up, assured her he would call her, and went the back way to his house. 'Just in case somebody is watching and missed the escapade earlier,' he said. 'You never know, the police might want to put someone in there tonight.'

From his upstairs window he saw them leave, Mozart trotting beside them. He was glad of these few minutes to himself, glad that Wanda and Colin had seen him come back here. It was easier to go to the police alone, before Wanda knew he'd found the diamonds and without the hassle of her wondering whether they should or shouldn't hand them over to the criminals. Now he'd made up his mind he knew he was doing the right thing.

He would tell the others he'd found the diamonds after they'd left to go to Colin's and before he'd gone to the police. It wouldn't make any difference to them.

There was something he wanted to do before he left. Locating the telephone handset, he settled himself on his bed in anticipation of a lengthy call. It was no good turning up at the local nick with a bag of diamonds. Officers on duty there wouldn't know their value any more than he did, and surely a valuable amount of stolen gemstones should warrant a higher authority than the local police force. He wanted to see someone quickly, someone who could take action without him being pushed from one department to another. No need to mention smuggling – stolen would do, for now at least.

At the last minute he decided to call from his mobile in case the criminals had somehow tapped his landline, and after much rerouting his call was eventually put through to a Detective Inspector Philmore. After giving a brief outline of why he wanted to see him, Philmore agreed to meet him at his office in two hours' time, with a gemstones expert to examine the diamonds.

Pleased with his foresight, he went downstairs. He checked his pocket for his wallet and his passport for ID, then picked up his phone and keys. He was about to set the alarm when his mobile trilled.

'Hello,' he said, impatient to be gone.

A chill settled over him when a well-modulated male voice said, 'Hello, Mr Cadbury. I hope you're not planning on going anywhere.'

Chapter Thirty

Quentin gasped.

The voice continued. 'Because if you are, you might want to look out of your upstairs front window.'

Panic swept over him. They had phoned his mobile, presumably gaining the number from the sign outside. But how did they know he was in the house? He could have been anywhere.

Suddenly coming to life, he raced upstairs and looked down into the street. Parked just outside his gate was a black car, a Ford Focus, he guessed from the shape. The windows were tinted and he couldn't see the driver. The nearside back window began to wind down, and Quentin gave a cry as he saw Wanda's face in profile. A gloved hand pushed her head round to reveal the strip of black tape that covered her mouth. She gazed upwards, her eyes meeting his for a fleeting moment. Then the window went up and the car sped away. Quentin was just able to glimpse part of the number plate before it was out of sight.

His mobile crackled and with a shaking hand Quentin raised it to his ear.

'I hope that's enough to convince you not to go to the police,' the voice drawled. 'This little lady's very attractive. I should hate to have to spoil her beauty.'

'Don't you touch her!' Quentin gabbled. 'Don't you bloody touch her!'

'Or you'll do what, exactly?'

'Listen, it's me you want,' Quentin said, forcing himself to be calm. 'She's got nothing to do with it.'

This brought a laugh from the caller. 'Come now, Mr Cadbury, I think we both know better than that. Anyway, it's immaterial. We've only had a quick chat, but she swears she doesn't know where my goods are, and she says you don't know either. There's loyalty for you.'

'She doesn't know.'

There was a perceptible change in the man's tone. '*She* doesn't know? But you do?'

Realizing his mistake, Quentin said, 'No, why should I?'

'Well, that's a pity. Mr Cadbury. I assumed you thought more of your friend than that. I'll call back in an hour. Perhaps you'll have come to your senses by then.'

Unable to believe what he'd heard, Quentin stared at his phone. They had Wanda. How? They must have been watching and seen her leave with Colin.

Quentin punched the window frame with his free hand. It was Colin. It had to be. He had lured her away just as he'd feared, not to win her heart but to get the diamonds. He felt dazed, winded, as though someone had hit him in the stomach. His head swam with possibilities, of all the ways Colin could have planned to get to the diamonds through Wanda, all the things he would do to Colin if he was connected to the kidnappers. But, he reasoned when the turmoil in his mind quietened, Wanda had known Colin for years. Surely he wouldn't really hurt her? Colin didn't strike him as a strong-arm man.

His thoughts still in chaos, he went downstairs and threw off his jacket. If he went to the police now, Wanda would suffer. She might even be killed. Quentin shivered. He couldn't let that happen. Why hadn't he just said he had the diamonds and arranged to hand them over? He dredged up the same reasons he'd given Wanda before – they were just as likely to be hurt or killed whether they handed over the goods or not.

His mobile rang again, and he tensed. They'd said an hour. It had only been five minutes. 'Hello?' he said tentatively.

'Quentin, they've got Wanda.' Colin's voice sounded croaky, like he'd just woken up. 'They must have followed us. I didn't see anyone. We were walking from my car, and the next thing I knew two blokes ran out from an alley and pushed Wanda into a car. The other one tried to get me in, but I struggled and he dragged me into the alley and coshed me on the head.'

Stunned, Quentin didn't answer. Not Colin then.

'Quentin? Did you hear what I said? They've got Wanda.'

'I heard you, Colin.'

'The thing is, before he hit me the bloke said no police. "No police, or she cops it", so for God's sake don't go to them. Or are you at the police station now?'

'No. The people who took Wanda have already called and said they'll hurt her if I go to the police.'

Colin exploded. 'You should have gone to them when I said. They might have caught the bastards by now. If anything happens to Wanda because of you–'

'What happened to "Come home to mine, Wanda, you'll be safe with me?"' Quentin snapped irritably. 'Anyway, that's not the point. The point is getting Wanda back and getting these people off our backs. Where are you, Colin?'

'Home now. The lady who found me said I should go and get my head stitched. That'd look good, wouldn't it? At casualty for head injuries twice in a week?'

'Do you need your head stitched?' Quentin asked, glancing at his watch. Fifty minutes.

'I don't think so. So, what are we going to do?'

'I don't know. What happened to Mozart?'

'What?'

'Mozart. What happened to him?'

Colin coughed in his ear. 'Don't know. Didn't see him when I came round. He must have run off, or perhaps they took him. Come to think of it, I bet they did, so they can threaten to hurt him to get Wanda to talk.'

Quentin groaned. Using Mozart to threaten Wanda. Using Wanda to threaten him. What else were they capable of? And was Colin telling the truth? How did he know Colin was at home nursing a sore head? It could be an elaborate ploy to add weight to the kidnapper's demand of not calling the police.

'We've got to do something,' Colin bleated. 'I feel so useless. I've never been in a situation like this before.'

He sounds really sorry for himself, Quentin thought, his mind darting back and forth. And he's right. We've got to do something. He sighed. He had to trust someone, and Colin was all he had.

He looked at his watch again. Forty-five minutes. 'Right, Colin, here's what we're going to do. They're going to call me back, and I'm going to tell them I've found the diamonds. When we know what the arrangements are you're going to tell the police what's going on and get them to come with you for the hand-over.'

'But Wanda—'

'I'll insist they bring Wanda with them. If I don't see her, then no deal.'

'But when they find out you haven't got the diamonds, they could kill you both.'

'Not if there's police back-up, and diamonds or no diamonds we can get them on kidnapping now.'

There was a silence, as though Colin was digesting this. 'Come on, man, for Christ's sake,' Quentin urged. 'We haven't got all day.'

'It could work, I suppose,' Colin conceded. 'All right, let me know as soon as you know the location of the hand-over.'

Quentin couldn't help a wry smile. This was becoming more like a detective novel than ever. He'd always thought their plots were over complicated, but now he realized why so many different plans and places were used – to avoid detection. And this explained why the criminals hadn't taken immediate action when he'd put the sign up. They had been watching the house, enough to see Wanda with him many times. No need to break in again. Far more certain of getting a result by kidnapping her.

'Quentin?'

'Just thinking, Colin.' He hesitated.

'Well?' It was Colin's turn to sound impatient. 'Come on, Quentin, think of something.'

'I'm trying. You could think of something. Why do you think *I* can conjure something out of thin air?'

'Because you're not the one who was jumped on and coshed.'

'Right.' Despite his earlier desire to take a swipe at Colin, Quentin felt a measure of empathy. It had taken him days to get over *his* unexpected attack. 'Did you get a look at them?'

'No. They came from behind. The one that tackled me was big, I can tell you that much.'

'What did he sound like?'

'What do you mean?' Colin said, his tone filled with exasperation. 'He didn't tell me to have a nice day.'

'When he said no police – what was his voice like?'

'Common, I suppose – typical East End.'

That fitted with Quentin's recollection of the man who had attacked him.

'Did you see the car?' he asked, wondering if Colin could confirm that it was a Ford Focus.

'I didn't notice,' Colin admitted. It was black, that's all I can say.'

'OK, Colin, if I think of anything else we can do, I'll call you back. If I don't, I'll ring you after they've contacted me again and tell you what they said.'

'All right,' Colin sighed. 'But for God's sake make it soon. I can't just sit here while Wanda's in danger.'

My feelings exactly, Quentin thought.

After he'd rung off, another thought occurred to him. That phone call – *the* phone call – surely it could be traced? He looked at the recent calls, but the penultimate call showed as number withheld. He began pacing the room, seeing Wanda's face as she'd looked up at him from the car. Whatever else happened, he had to make sure she was safe. But how?

In the past he'd fooled so many people with his credible lies, so why couldn't he come up with something now, something that would guarantee Wanda's release?

'It's no good,' he said aloud. 'We'll have to go with the original plan – tell them I've got the diamonds, arrange the hand-over and hope they let Wanda go.' He stared down at the floor. It should work. After all, he had Colin as back-up. Why didn't that reassure him?

He wondered what the detective, Philmore, would do when he didn't go to his office. Would he work on the information he had and make investigations, or would he dismiss Quentin's call as a hoax?

I'm being stupid, he thought. The police have people trained in this sort of thing. I'll get back to them myself and tell them what's happened. He glanced at his watch. Thirty-five minutes. He recalled the chilling, cultured tone of the man who had threatened him. Suppose he rang early? If he rang and his mobile was engaged, he would wonder whom he was calling. He stood for a moment, racked by indecision. Then he snatched up the house phone handset and punched in the detective's number.

Chapter Thirty-one

Fifteen minutes later he used the house phone again, this time to call Colin.

'I've called the police, Colin,' he told him, wishing he could see his expression. He listened intently for Colin's reaction, half expecting recriminations for going against the kidnapper's instructions.

'Oh?' Colin sounded uncertain. 'But… OK, what did they say?'

'Just to let them know what arrangements we make to hand the diamonds over, and they will make sure they're there.'

'Never mind the diamonds – did you tell them about Wanda?'

Never mind the diamonds. He wondered if Colin's attitude would change if he knew he'd found them. His suspicion of Colin, however, had lifted. He was genuinely concerned for Wanda. Quentin could hear it in his voice.

'Yes,' he said, 'of course I told them about Wanda. They said they'll make sure she comes to no harm. They're getting a negotiator just in case, you know, someone who knows how to talk to kidnappers–'

'I know what a negotiator is. What about me?'

'What about you?'

'Did you tell them about me, and what can I do to help?'

'I didn't mention you, no.'

'Thanks a bunch. I'm in danger too, you know. They've already assaulted me.'

Quentin jumped as his mobile rang. 'That's them. Get back to you, Colin.'

'Let me know!' Colin yelled as he hung up.

Hand trembling, Quentin picked up his mobile.

'Hello, Mr Cadbury. I trust you've had enough time to consider your position. It would really be most unfortunate if you haven't.'

'Where's Wanda? What have you done with her?'

'She's perfectly safe, Mr Cadbury.'

'How do I know that?'

There was a rustling noise, and Quentin heard Wanda's voice, shaky but unmistakeable. 'I'm all right, Quentin.'

'And she'll stay safe if you cooperate, Mr Cadbury. Now, where are my goods? Please don't tell me you don't know.'

Reeling from the relief of hearing Wanda's voice, Quentin tried to marshal his thoughts. What had DI Philmore said? Say the diamonds aren't in the house but you know where they are and you'll deliver them to wherever they say, as long as Wanda is at the drop-off point and free to walk away. That would give the police time to get the officers and back-up they needed.

'I don't have them here,' he said cautiously, 'but I know where they are.'

'Excellent. And of course you're going to tell me.'

'I'm not doing anything until Wanda's released.'

'Come now, Mr Cadbury, I can hardly take such a risk without insurance, can I?'

'I'll get them and bring them to you. You bring Wanda to me.'

There was a pause. 'That sounds reasonable, as far as it goes.'

Sweat began to trickle down Quentin's face. 'What do you mean?'

'I'd need to see the goods first. You could be handing me a load of marbles for all I know. May I ask how you found them?'

Quentin was prepared for that. 'I found them in the lock-up garage where my uncle kept his car.' It was the same story he'd told the police. He didn't want to admit to the diamonds being in the house. If they were in the garage anyone could have put them there, but if they were in the house his uncle would be implicated, and he wasn't comfortable with that.

'I didn't know what to do with them,' he continued, 'so I put them in a safety deposit box at the bank. That was before you sent your thug round to kick my cat and cave my ribs in.'

'Tut, tut, Mr Cadbury, no need for unpleasantness. Why don't you tell me the truth? You came across a nice little nest egg and decided to keep it for yourself.'

Heat crept up Quentin's neck. That's exactly what he'd done with the money, after all.

The voice carried on. 'It's a pity we've had to take such extreme measures to persuade you to give it up. Which bank?'

Quentin gave the information.

'If you'd told me this at the beginning,' the caller said, 'we could have settled the matter right away. As it is, I don't think you'll get to the bank before they close, so it looks as though your friend will have to spend the night with us. I'll try to make sure she's comfortable, but unfortunately my associates aren't as fastidious as I am.'

'If you hurt her—'

'You're not listening, Mr Cadbury. *I* won't be doing anything to her. Go to the bank first thing in the morning, then wait for my call. And don't bother trying to trace this phone. I never use the same one twice.'

The line went dead. The man's patronising tone made Quentin feel like his father often did – inferior. He wished now he'd ignored the police advice and said he had the diamonds with him. Perhaps then a deal could have been done at once – a straight swap, Wanda for the diamonds.

He rang Colin. 'Nothing doing till tomorrow,' he said. 'They're going to call me then.'

'Poor Wanda,' Colin said on a sigh. 'What can we do in the meantime?'

'I'll get in touch with the police again to update them. I don't think we can do anything else tonight, and you don't sound like you're up to much anyway.'

'I've been better,' Colin admitted. 'Won't the police want to see you? I should be there.'

'Why? You can't tell them anything I can't. Get some rest – it could be a long day tomorrow.'

'True. All right, but let me know as soon as you hear anything.'

'I will. Colin—'

'Yes?'

'Er, nothing, just take it easy. Bye.'

Quentin shook his head as he hung up. He'd been on the verge of admitting to finding the diamonds. Why hadn't he? He was convinced now that Colin wasn't involved with the criminals, so why not tell him?

Dismissing thoughts of Colin, he went upstairs and looked through the window. He saw nothing untoward, no one hanging about or looking suspicious. Why would they need to watch him now? He had shown concern for Wanda. They knew he wouldn't go anywhere, or do anything to jeopardise her safety. Nevertheless, he felt uneasy.

He needed to ring DI Philmore, but now he was afraid to use his mobile in case he missed a call from the criminals, or his landline in case they had tapped it. Wanda's landline would be safer – after a spate of wrong calls she'd recently had the number changed. Taking Wanda's key, he let himself into her house and called from there.

'Right,' Philmore said after Quentin had assured him that he wasn't on his own phone, 'I think we should meet, Mr Cadbury.'

'I'm not coming to you,' Quentin said at once. 'They might be watching me. You can't come here either.'

'Of course not. Is there a restaurant or a pub near you? Somewhere busy, where you would normally go?'

'There's the Cutty Sark, on the embankment.'

'Good. I'll meet you there. Say, seven o'clock?'

'Seven? OK. How will I know you?'

'Just go in and order – act normally. I'll find you.'

'He'll find me,' Quentin mumbled when he'd hung up. 'He must think I've got idiot tattooed on my forehead. But then again, perhaps I should have.'

Chapter Thirty-two

DI Philmore was a slim man with greying hair and intelligent brown eyes. 'Is this seat taken?' he asked, setting down a pint of beer on Quentin's table.

'Actually,' Quentin replied, 'I'm waiting for someone.'

'That's all right then, we'll sit here till they come.' Gesturing to a second man, he sat down opposite Quentin. His companion was younger but with the beginnings of a paunch showing beneath his jacket.

'Nice evening,' Philmore went on. 'I know you from somewhere, don't I? Quentin, isn't it?'

When Quentin nodded, he continued, 'You remember me – Steve Philmore. This is my colleague, Mick Harris.'

Keeping up the pretence, Quentin said, 'Yes, I remember.'

'Good. Can I get you a drink?'

'Whisky please, no ice.'

'Right. Harris, get our friend a whisky. It's so warm in here – why don't we find a table outside?'

While Harris battled his way to the bar, Quentin and Philmore made their way outside. There were no free tables so they moved along and claimed an area of the wall that separated the pavement from the Thames, which gleamed below them in the evening sun. People were sitting or standing around the area overlooking the river, clustered in pairs or groups, drinking and smoking. The late summer air hummed with their chatter and the appetizing aroma of food escaped from the open doors of the pub, mingling with the smell of tobacco and alcohol.

'So,' Philmore said when he seemed satisfied that they couldn't be overheard. 'All this must be a bit scary for you.'

'You could say that.'

'Don't worry, we'll work something out.'

When Harris returned with the drinks Philmore got straight down to business.

'Now then, Quentin – can I call you Quentin? Good. I know what you told me on the phone, but tell me again.'

Carefully, Quentin related all the relevant details, omitting his discovery of the money, the place he'd found the diamonds, any mention of Colin and that Wanda was more than just a neighbour. From the policeman's face he couldn't tell if he believed him; his expression remained impassive, whilst his sergeant's showed clear signs of disbelief. When he'd finished, he produced the note that had been tied round the brick.

'We'll keep it,' Philmore said, 'though it would have been much more use if you'd given it to us when you first received it.'

'Sorry, but… I was scared, and I didn't know what to do.'

Quentin saw Philmore and Harris exchange glances.

'I'm not making this up, you know,' Quentin said. 'I didn't write that note myself, I have found the diamonds and my neighbour has been kidnapped.'

'Keep your voice down,' Harris growled, glancing around. 'Where are these diamonds anyway?'

Quentin moistened his lips, thinking of the pouch with its precious contents nestled in the cavity behind the fridge plug socket. 'Em, I didn't know whether to bring them or not. I've brought one. You said you had someone who could authenticate them.'

'Yes,' Philmore agreed, 'but he couldn't make it tonight. Let's have what you've got, and he'll look at it in the morning.'

'It's taped up in here,' Quentin said, pulling an envelope from his inside pocket. 'But I'm more worried about Wanda than anything else.'

'Well, try not to worry too much. They're not likely to hurt her while they need her to bargain with. About the phone call – was there any background noise, anything you can remember that might help us figure out where he was calling from?'

Quentin racked his memory. He'd been so intent on what the cultured voice had been saying, nothing else had registered.

'All right,' Philmore went on. 'Tell me again what he said, word for word.'

Repeating the conversation as best he could, Quentin waited while Philmore thought it over.

'He said *he* wouldn't be doing anything to her? Only his associates? Sounds like he's not with them then, only directing operations from somewhere else.'

'He must have been in the car when I saw Wanda,' said Quentin. 'He knew I'd seen her, and he was there when he put Wanda on the phone to say she was all right.'

'Maybe, but that doesn't mean he's with them now. You didn't get the full registration number? Never mind. Probably false plates anyway. At least we've got time to get a team together. Go home and get some sleep, Quentin, and go out first thing and buy a pay-as-you-go phone. Call me from it to let me know the number, and tell me what instructions they give you. I daresay it'll be late morning before you hear anything. They'll give you time to get to the bank.'

'Do you think I should go to the bank, pretend I'm picking up the diamonds, in case they're watching?'

'Yes,' Philmore said. 'Better safe than sorry.'

Quentin thanked them and walked home. As he let himself in, guilt swamped him. He was going to sleep in his own bed tonight, while Wanda…

He thought of all the girls he'd been out with, all the lines he'd spun to get out of doing things he didn't want to do, making sure he raised enough money to get by without having to work if he didn't want to. And he'd succeeded. What was to stop him taking off now, with the money and the diamonds? Going abroad, South America perhaps, like Ronnie Biggs, living a life of luxury? Leaving everything and everyone behind, like his sister and parents had left him behind? There was nothing to stop him, except his conscience. And Wanda. And the fact that apart from the criminals, the police now knew he had the diamonds.

A mewing outside jolted him back to the moment. Opening the back door, he watched as Magpie stalked past, head and tail high.

'Don't look so pleased to see me,' Quentin muttered. On auto pilot, he shook some of the dried cat food into a bowl and set it on the floor, then went to the cabinet to pour himself a whisky. He changed his mind and made tea instead – he would need a clear head tomorrow.

Thoughts swirling around in his head, he took the tea up to bed. When Magpie followed him and took up a forbidden position on the bed, Quentin merely fondled his ears. 'What a mess, eh boy? What a bloody mess.'

Chapter Thirty-three

The next morning Quentin was outside a mobile phone store when they opened. He bought a basic model, with the numbers on the front and no cover to open. To save time he got it set up and loaded with extra credit in the shop. He'd noticed no one hanging around or following him, but he went to the bank and stayed what he thought was a credible amount of time inside. Once home, he put the phone on charge and selected a new ring tone. He'd only use this phone to make and receive calls from DI Philmore. That way there was no chance of calls clashing.

While he waited for the expected call, he busied himself with unimportant tasks – tidying his room and the smaller front bedroom, all the time thinking of the black car and Wanda's fearful face staring up from it. How should he handle this? Could he handle it? Was he up to it?

As he turned away, he caught his foot on a pile of books stacked in the corner. Law books, thick and dusty, along with notes he'd made at university. He'd left them in a box when he'd moved in, but the box had been ripped open and the contents rifled through during the break-in. Somehow, he hadn't had the heart to throw them away. Seeing them always made him think of Nathan, and he stabbed at them now with his toe, angry with himself for leaving them there. Nathan was dead. He hadn't been able to save him. Had he done enough? He didn't know, but one thing he did know – he would do anything it took to save Wanda.

* * *

It was eleven-thirty when his everyday mobile trilled. Stomach churning, he snatched it up.

'Hello?'

'Good morning, Mr Cadbury. Have you got my goods?'

'Yes.'

'Excellent. This is what you're going to do. Drive to the service station on the A2 going south, just before Bexley. Pull in there and wait until I call you again. Got that?'

'Yes, but if Wanda's not there–'

'She'll be there, Mr Cadbury, but not with you until our deal's completed. Come alone or she'll be history. One-thirty, Mr Cadbury.'

The call ended, the instructions from the cultured voice ringing in Quentin's ears. One-thirty. Could he get to the service station by then? He'd have to get to the lock-up, get the car out and fill up with fuel before he went anywhere. 'Sod it,' he muttered, reaching for his coat. He felt in his pocket for his keys as an idea came to him. Wanda had gone in Colin's car – hers was still in the allocated parking space on the road. That would be much quicker. There was a spare set of keys in her kitchen, he was sure.

After retrieving the diamonds from their hiding place, he rushed out and let himself into Wanda's. He located her car keys and was about to leave when he realized he hadn't called the detective or Colin. Using the new mobile, he got through to DI Philmore and gabbled out the kidnapper's instructions.

'Slow down, Quentin. What car do you drive?'

'I'm using Wanda's. It's a blue Toyota.'

'Registration number?'

'Don't know. I'll ring you when I'm in it.'

'Let me know the next lot of instructions, if you can do it without arousing suspicion. If we know where you're headed, we won't have to follow you so closely and risk being spotted. If at any time you can't talk, text my mobile. It never leaves me when I'm out of the office. Take the number.'

Quentin gulped, overcome by doubt. Would they really back him up? After all, they only had his word that Wanda had been kidnapped. 'You will come? Wanda really is in danger.'

'It's all right, Quentin. We've run a background check on her. We know all about her late husband's activities.'

Alarmed, Quentin replied, 'She knew nothing about it!'

'Don't worry about that. Let's just make sure she's safe, shall we? We've had the diamond checked too. It's the real McCoy.'

'Wow! OK. Anything else?'

'Stay calm. We'll be right behind you, but don't keep looking round for us or they'll suss us out.'

Stay calm, Quentin mused as the call ended. I bet he wouldn't bloody well be calm if he was in my shoes. He entered the detective's number into the frequently called facility then slipped the new phone into his jacket pocket, comforted by its promise of protection. Putting his other phone into his right-hand pocket, he felt the roughness of the pouch and the reassuring chink of the diamonds. With the phone nestled beside it, the pouch filled his pocket. As he took Wanda's keys he was filled with misgivings. Had he put Wanda in more danger by calling the police? Suppose it all went wrong? 'Too late now,' he muttered as he left the house and walked to her car. When it came in sight, he texted the registration number to Philmore's mobile.

"On our way," came the return message as he unlocked the car.

He'd just opened the door when he saw a woman coming towards him, a small white dog padding along beside her. The dog barked as it approached, then bounded up to him, making the woman break into a run.

'Mozart!'

'I found him wandering in the street late last night,' the woman explained. 'His address was on his collar, so I brought him back.'

'Thanks so much. I'm really grateful. Here.' He reached for his wallet and brought out a twenty-pound note. 'Sorry to be rude, but I'm in a tearing hurry.'

He reached for Mozart's lead, but the dog pulled free, leapt into the car, squeezed through the gap between the front seats and settled down in the back. As the woman walked away, Quentin lowered himself into the driver's seat. There was no time to take Mozart home. He'd have to take him along.

He was speeding down the road when he remembered that he hadn't spoken to Colin. What was the point? Colin couldn't do anything, and he had back-up now. He grimaced at what DI Philmore had said. They had checked up on Wanda and knew about Gerry, so why hadn't they questioned Wanda about his dodgy dealings?

He cursed as he ground to a halt in the lunchtime traffic, and groaned as his knee hit the steering wheel. His long legs were cramped, and he adjusted the seat while Mozart whined.

'It's all right, we'll see your mistress soon,' Quentin said, wishing he felt as confident as he sounded. 'Lie down.'

The dog obeyed, and Quentin eased the car forward as the line of traffic started moving. Approaching a crossroads, he stared at the signpost for direction. Having lived in Oxford until he moved to Greenwich, and not having driven much since, he was still unsure of the roads.

'Let me over, you moron,' he murmured when a van blocked his access to the outside lane.

He swung in behind it, cutting in front of a white Honda and earning a toot from its driver. Get lost, he thought, not bothering to raise a conciliatory hand. He had forty minutes to get to the services. He hadn't bargained on the heavy traffic, and the kidnappers couldn't have either, or they would have given him more time.

He jumped as his old mobile sang out and it vibrated against his hip. Glancing at the dashboard, his gaze fell on the clock: 12.50. Why were they calling again? His hand slid into his pocket and he pulled the phone out. A bike wobbled into view and he swerved, dropping the phone down the side of the seat. 'Bugger it!' he shouted, steadying the car and pushing his hand down to retrieve the phone. He heard it slide when he braked at traffic lights. In the momentary respite he bent and rummaged under the seat until his fingers closed round the familiar shape. A series of hoots sounded behind him, and he saw that the lights had changed.

'All right, all right,' he muttered, and caught his breath when he saw a white Honda in the rear-view mirror. The driver's face was a blur, but something about the shape seemed vaguely familiar.

Not knowing whether to look at the Honda or his phone, he did neither as the next crossroads loomed and he sought direction. As well as the keys he should have grabbed Wanda's sat nav, he realized. A pity she didn't leave it in the car.

Taking a left turn, he straightened and glanced at his phone. A missed call from Colin. No time to think about Colin now. He'd have to stay home and nurse his broken head. The Honda showed in the mirror again, and Quentin swerved as the driver waved frantically at him.

'Bloody hell!' he groaned as he realized who his pursuant was. Colin! The wretched man was haunting him. He sped up and so did Colin, who pulled out and tried to overtake him. As he drew level, Colin opened his window and shouted something Quentin couldn't hear. Evidently recognizing the voice, Mozart jumped up at the side window and barked excitedly.

'Hush!' hollered Quentin accelerating away. If the kidnappers saw him with Colin, who knew what would happen. Come alone, they'd said. Glancing in the mirror again, a grin spread over his face. A motorbike cop was pulling Colin over. Well, he had been driving erratically.

He drove on and realized he'd nearly reached his destination. He knew roughly where the service station was, although he'd never used it. Pulse racing, he saw the rendezvous ahead. Deliberately passing the entrance, he turned into a side road. There was still eight minutes before the deadline. He didn't want to draw attention to himself by sitting on the forecourt too long. Stopping on a single yellow line, he turned off the engine and waited, trying to think of how he should act and what he should do when the kidnappers appeared. He couldn't believe the exchange would happen here. It was too public, and they would want to be sure he hadn't been followed. Had he been followed? He hadn't noticed a particular car except Colin's. He shivered. Suppose the police didn't turn up?

Mozart climbed up, licked his ear and pawed at his shoulder. 'Scared, eh Mote? Me and you both. Now listen, you've got to behave. Just stay in the back quietly if you want to see your mistress again. OK?'

I'm going doolally, he thought, talking to a dog as though he understands. Whether he understood or not, Mozart obediently returned to his previous position and laid his head on his front paws. Quentin checked his watch, then started the engine. Here we go, he thought, turning the car round and going back the way he'd come.

When he drove onto the service station forecourt, he pulled over by the air pump and waited. Grasping his mobile ready for the expected call, he glanced around. There were two cars at the pumps, both with women filling up their tanks, and a small van attended by a middle-aged man. Further along by the shop, a grey Vauxhall stood empty. Quentin assumed the driver had gone to pay for fuel. No black Ford, and no sign of any police. His phone rang and his hand shook as he raised it to his ear.

'Glad to see you made it, Mr Cadbury. I hope you're insured to use your neighbour's car.'

Quentin's gaze flickered round the forecourt. The only cars were the ones he'd already seen and none of their occupants were on their phones.

'Where's Wanda?'

'She's safe, Mr Cadbury. Where are my goods?'

'They're safe too.'

'Don't let's play games. Have you got them?'

'Yes.'

'Good. Keep going on the A2, and just before the Dartford crossing turn onto the B258 towards Wilmington. You know it?'

'I'll find it.'

'A few miles down there's a filling station on the left-hand side, and just after is a disused motel. Drive round to the car park at the back. Shall we say three quarters of an hour?'

'If Wanda's not there—'

'She'll be there. And I wouldn't try using your phone to call anyone else. We don't want to see your hand anywhere near your head.'

The line went dead and Quentin stared around him. How could they see him? Stumped, he started the engine. He couldn't ring DI Philmore. Text, he'd said, if necessary. How could he text and drive without it being obvious? Making a show of fiddling with his seat belt, he brought up the DI's number on the new phone. Then he placed it in the dip by the gear stick where he could reach it before easing the car forward.

As he turned off the forecourt, he took a last look in the mirror. Emerging from the car wash was a black Ford Focus.

Chapter Thirty-four

Quentin cursed. The car wash! Why hadn't he thought of that? He'd noticed it, but it had looked empty. Perhaps they hadn't been *in* the car wash. Perhaps they'd been hidden behind it.

He drove on, constantly checking his mirror for the Focus. There was no sign of it, so when he reached a quiet stretch, he slowed and reached for the new phone. Keeping it on his lap while glancing alternately from it to the road, he managed to press the call button. When he heard Philmore answer, he yelled, 'Disused motel past garage on B258!' Gathering speed, he carried on, expecting the Ford to overtake him at any moment. Were sending him on a fool's errand? Did they want him to arrive first, or had they taken a different route?

He kept going, praying that Philmore had made sense of his scant information.

A shadow passed over him and he looked sideways as a large white van cruised by. 'He's in a hurry,' he murmured. Mozart barked, his ears pricking up. 'It's all right, Mozart. We're nearly there.'

Keeping up a steady speed, Quentin drove on. The filling station the cultured voice had mentioned was in sight when the Toyota's engine suddenly died. Momentum carried it forward a few yards, allowing Quentin to steer into the side of the road. Alarm swamping him, he stared at the dashboard.

'Bloody hell,' he murmured in disbelief. 'It's out of petrol!'

Getting out and winding down the window he managed to steer while he pushed the car onto the filling station forecourt. At the pump the nozzle refused to go into the petrol tank.

'Go in, damn you,' he muttered, forcing the nozzle in.

He pressed the trigger, then immediately released it, hot and cold flushes engulfing him as he realized what he was doing – putting diesel into a petrol driven car. 'Sod it!' He groaned, yanking the nozzle out. Only a dribble had gone in – surely that couldn't do any damage? He switched to petrol and hoped for the best.

After he'd paid and was heading back to the car, a grey Vauxhall pulled onto the forecourt. Quentin started. A grey Vauxhall. Hadn't he seen that before? Yes, at the previous service station. Had the criminals changed cars? Surely not. He'd seen the black Focus in his mirror.

From where he was, Quentin couldn't see the driver clearly. Was it DI Philmore? It must be, he decided, relief sweeping over him. Why else would the same car be in the same places as him at the same time?

Remembering Philmore's instructions and keeping his gaze away from the Vauxhall, he drove out. The engine coughed a little but kept going. A few hundred yards on he saw the motel.

As he approached, he noticed how seedy it looked, with most of the windows boarded over. A prime site for redevelopment, Quentin realized, and a good choice for the hand-over; no one to peer through windows or come seeking accommodation. Heart racing, he turned into the weed-strewn driveway and stopped, suddenly aware of the importance of what he was about to do, the risk he was taking. Tapping his fingers on the steering wheel, he tried to think how he should act. How do you talk to kidnappers? Were they even here yet? Were the police here?

The clock on the dashboard showed 2.10 p.m. Easing the car forward, he drove on towards the rear car park. There he saw a wide parking area fringed with high, bushy shrubs, a frail-looking wooden fence showing between the greenery. His gaze swept around and his pulse quickened. In the shadow of the motel was the black Ford Focus.

For a panicky moment he thought of snatching up the phone and calling Philmore, but didn't dare put it to his ear. Instead he glanced down, brought up Philmore's number and pressed it. When the ring tone stopped he yelled, 'Bloody hell, Philmore, I'm here and so are they. Where the hell are you?'

As he came to a halt, his attention was riveted on the other car and what he had to do. He pulled up the hand brake but left the engine running. And sat. Should he get out, or wait for them to make the first move? The door of the Focus opened and a man got out. Quentin got out too, leaving the door open, and the two of them eyed each other from where they stood. There was something odd about the man's face. It was brown and undefined, with the nose squashed almost flat. The stocking did a good job of masking the man's features.

'OK, let's have them,' he called. 'Bring them over.'
Quentin shook his head. 'Not until I see Wanda.'
'The goods first.'

'Let me see her.'

The masked man didn't move.

'Let her out so I can see she's all right.'

Nothing. Quentin cursed the vehicle's darkened windows – he couldn't see if there was anyone else inside.

At that moment the passenger door opened and Quentin watched expectantly. Instead of Wanda, a second man got out, stocky and solid-looking, his features also obscured by a stocking pulled taut over his head.

Bloody mop-heads, Quentin thought, for a fleeting moment remembering the dolls his mother used to make for charity bazaars. He gazed at the men, trying to draw his thoughts together. He pressed his hand over his pocket, feeling the bulge where the diamonds nestled in their pouch. Damned if he was going to surrender them without getting Wanda back. Where were the police? Had they really left him to face the criminals alone? The purr of a car engine from the other side of the building renewed his confidence. They were here. Quentin's hopes soared. These criminals would be caught, but Wanda's safety was more important.

Drawing himself up, he said, 'Let her out, or no deal.'

When there was no response, alarm filled him. They had no intention of releasing their captive. They were going to grab the goods and run, take Wanda with them as a hostage until they were safely away, or…

He blanched, and nodded towards the black car. 'She's not in there, is she?'

'Of course not, Mr Cadbury. She's here.'

The cultured voice came from behind. Quentin swivelled round and gasped. A thin man of medium height was stepping out of a grey Vauxhall. Quentin swayed, confused. This wasn't DI Philmore. He should have known better than to think it was. For a start, he wouldn't have come alone, and he wouldn't have let himself be seen. This man wasn't letting himself be seen, either. His expression was fixed, his features moulded into the rubberised mask he wore. They were taking no chances,

Quentin realized, and felt marginally relieved. If he couldn't identify them there was no reason not to let him go after they'd got what they'd come for.

His gaze strayed to the Vauxhall. Without its driver it looked empty.

'Don't worry, Mr Cadbury, she's here. I couldn't risk putting her in with my friends, could I? I've been watching them to make sure they weren't followed. You saw that car in Greenwich. How do I know you didn't tell someone the registration number? No, they're just here as back-up.'

Which is more than I've got, Quentin thought. If the police were anywhere nearby, they were doing a good job of keeping hidden. And they weren't likely to make a move until they could see that either Wanda or the diamonds were in the criminals' possession.

Cultured Voice opened the Vauxhall's rear door and pulled at something – a blanket, Quentin saw.

'You can come out now, my dear.'

Quentin held his breath as a shapely ankle appeared, then another, and Wanda unfolded herself, slowly and with apparent difficulty, from the back seat. As she stepped clear of the car, Quentin could see that her hands were tied behind her. Hope came over her face when she saw Quentin.

Cultured Voice held her arm with a gloved hand. 'Now we need to examine the goods, Mr Cadbury, and if we're satisfied, we'll make the exchange. My man will come forward and you will show him what you've got. He knows genuine articles from fakes, believe me.'

Fakes? Quentin baulked. As if he'd had time to substitute the diamonds for fakes. Or the know-how.

The driver of the Focus walked forward. Quentin's stomach clenched. When the man reached him, Quentin turned sideways so he could see both his opponents.

'Well?' said the Focus man.

Quentin reached into his pocket and took out the pouch. When he'd loosened the drawstring he felt inside, drew out two stones and placed them in the upturned palm. The man rolled them between his fingers, then extracted an eyeglass from his pocket and gazed through it intently. At length he looked over at the man by the Vauxhall and nodded.

'Good,' said Cultured Voice. 'I'm glad you've been sensible, Mr Cadbury. Now, hand the rest to my friend.'

Pushing the pouch back into his pocket, Quentin said, 'Let Wanda go first.'

'Patience, Mr Cadbury. All right, here's what we'll do. Turn off your engine and give the keys to my friend, then the lady will walk over and get in your car. You hand the diamonds to my friend and he'll give you back your keys. Then we'll be away with no harm done. Unless of course you try something foolish, in which case my other friend over there might take offence and be obliged to put you in your place.'

Quentin glanced at the thickset man by the Focus and something stirred in his memory. Could he be the man who'd attacked him?

'Agreed?' asked Cultured Voice.

'Agreed.' Quentin reached in, took out the keys and handed them to Focus Man.

With faltering steps Wanda made her way towards him, her progress impeded by the blanket that had somehow got tangled in the rope around her hands. Quentin took out the pouch in preparation. It was useless to resist handing it over.

Wanda had almost reached him when she tripped on the blanket and cried out, 'Quentin!'

He lurched forward to catch her, and at the same time, Focus Man sprang into action and snatched the pouch from his grip. Just as he was straightening up, something white flew past Quentin and launched itself at Focus Man. It took a few disorientating moments for Quentin to realize that Mozart, having heard his mistress's voice, had jumped through the open car door straight onto his adversary.

'Arrgh!' yelled Focus Man as Mozart's teeth sunk into his hand. 'Get him off me!'

Mozart hung on tenaciously, growling as he bit deeper. Focus Man loosened his grip on the pouch and it dropped to the ground.

In the chaos that followed, Quentin wasn't sure what happened first. From the corner of his eye, he saw a flash of dark blue, then another, as several policemen appeared as though from nowhere. Two of them grabbed Focus Man, who swore and kicked out at Mozart. At the same time, he heard Wanda call out 'Mozart!', and the dog let go of his prey and jumped at her, barking.

The thickset man ran round to the driver's side of the Focus, and the engine roared. Quentin saw the car move, the passenger door still open. A policeman, who had been heading towards the black car, tried to hurl himself into the passenger seat, missed, caught hold of the door and was dragged a few feet before falling heavily on the tarmac. Convinced that the driver was the thug who had beaten him up, Quentin was desperate to stop his escape. Without thinking, he snatched at the blanket, pulling it free of Wanda's bonds and flinging it at the Focus's windscreen. Then he seized the driver's door handle and clung on, his feet scraping the ground as the vehicle gathered speed. The driver, his vision momentarily obscured and distracted by Quentin's action, swerved then lost control, driving headlong into the perimeter fence with a resounding crunch.

For a few seconds all was quiet. Quentin, having been forced to relinquish his grasp on the door whilst being bumped across the tarmac, struggled to his feet in time to see the thug climb out of the car. He saw a policeman pounce on him as he began to run. In a tussle of entwined arms and legs Quentin caught the glint of a blade, and something snapped in his head. Oblivious to everything around him, he launched himself forward, catching the thug's arm as it broke free of the police officer's grip and was swinging in a deadly arc towards the cop's chest. Forcing the thug's arm wide,

Quentin squeezed it hard, digging his fingers into his flesh and causing the knife to fall from his grasp. In a desperate attempt to break free, the thug gave a mighty shove, sending Quentin stumbling sideways. Immediately the thug started running towards the exit.

'Oh, no you don't,' Quentin muttered, recovering his balance and catching the fleeing man in two easy strides. Hurling himself at his legs he brought him down. The man kicked out viciously, freed himself and was halfway to his knees before two more uniformed officers hauled him up by his arms.

'That's enough, mate,' one of them said. 'You've had it.'

'So have we,' said a male voice. 'All right, Sergeant, take him away.'

Quentin turned to see DI Philmore looking at him with an exasperated expression.

'Philmore! You took your time.'

'You should have taken yours, Quentin. Nice show of heroics, but quite unnecessary. We had the exit covered – had being the operative word. Thanks to that bloody dog and your epic shenanigans, our people at the front were lured round here and the one we wanted got clean away.'

Quentin stared at him, uncomprehending. Then he realized what was missing from the scene.

The grey Vauxhall had gone.

Chapter Thirty-five

The next morning Quentin abandoned his usual shower and opted for a long soak in the bath. His hips and calves were bruised and scratched, his nails on one hand were torn and bleeding and his whole body ached. After spending four hours with the police the night before, making statements and trying to recall the events of the day, he and Wanda had eventually been allowed to go home.

On the way he'd given Wanda brief details about finding the diamonds, giving the time of their discovery as after she'd left with Colin. Mentally exhausted and too tired to talk any more, they had gone to their respective homes for a good night's sleep. Colin had been called to substantiate their story, and he was due to give a statement later that day.

A knock came at the door. I'm not moving, Quentin thought savagely. Whoever it is can come back. Then he heard the grating of a key in the lock and Wanda's voice calling, 'Quentin?'

He'd been so tired last night he hadn't put the bolt across.

'Won't be long,' he answered.

Getting up gingerly from the tepid water, he dried and dressed himself. The smell of freshly brewed coffee assailed him as he emerged from the bathroom. Wanda, freshly bathed herself judging from the damp tendrils clinging to her forehead, smiled at him from behind the cafetière.

'My toy-boy hero,' she beamed.

Quentin didn't know which he resented more – toy boy or hero. Although he had deflected the knife from the police officer, his efforts to slow down the fleeing thug had been laughable and achieved nothing beyond causing enough disruption for the brains of the outfit to escape. And toy boy? They only went with older women for money, didn't they?

'I hope you don't think of me as your toy boy,' he huffed. 'You can get that idea right out of your head. Anyway, you're not rich enough to have a toy boy, unless there's something you're not telling me.'

Wanda's smile fled. 'I can see heroism doesn't suit you. It was a joke, Quentin, and you are a hero. You put yourself in danger for me and saved that copper – he could have been killed but for you.'

Quentin grunted, recalling the tussle which had resulted in the thickset man dropping the knife. He hadn't even thought about what he was doing. Pure adrenaline had pushed him on.

'I rang Colin to tell him that I was all right, and all about you finding the diamonds and what happened,' Wanda went on. 'Now, do you want some coffee or are you going to sulk all day?'

'Yes, please,' Quentin said sheepishly. 'Sorry. Feeling a bit delicate, that's all.'

Wanda poured the coffee and handed him a cup. 'I'm not surprised after the way Philmore went on. Telling us we should have gone to him sooner, and it was your fault the main culprit got away. How were you to know who he was and when the cops would show?'

How indeed, Quentin thought, though it was obvious even to him that Cultured Voice wasn't a run-of-the-mill gang member, or the organisation as Philmore called it.

Still, the young police officer had thanked him for preventing what could have been a fatal stabbing, and even Philmore had begrudgingly acknowledged that Quentin's quick action had probably saved his life.

He led the way into the lounge and lowered himself slowly onto the settee next to Magpie. His rest disturbed, the cat transferred himself to Quentin's lap and purred. 'Careful, boy,' he said, wincing as one of Magpie's paws brushed his bruises.

'Anyway,' Wanda continued as she sat opposite him, 'at least they agreed to keep Gerry out of it. I suppose that's a bonus.'

'He's not much good to them dead, is he? There's no point them naming him now, any more than naming my uncle. I suppose it might come out at the trial, but I shouldn't think it's of any interest to the papers. It's not as if they were famous or anything.'

'I suppose not, but I've been really worried about that.'

Quentin eyed her for a long moment. 'Is that why you didn't want to go to the police?' he asked. 'To protect Gerry's name?'

That's what she'd said all along, but did she have a hidden agenda? Even now, Quentin wasn't sure.

'Not only that, no,' Wanda admitted, colouring. 'I had this horrible feeling that Gerry knew a lot more than he told me, and that somehow I'd be implicated if I reported it. While he was in hospital, I had a visit from the police. They said they had reason to believe Gerry was involved in illegal trading. They searched the shop and the flat and demanded to see the accounts. They took them but found nothing, and they questioned me. I didn't know anything at the time and they believed me, or so they said. I never heard any more from them, and I didn't want to reopen a can of worms.'

This answered the question that had been nagging at Quentin since DI Philmore's admission that he knew about Gerry's dealings. 'Why didn't you tell me before, when you told me about Gerry being a fence?'

Wanda flinched. 'I didn't think it was important, and I didn't want you to think... you know, that I was involved in any way. You already thought I used you to get at the diamonds.'

'Well, you did.'

'Only at the beginning. Anyway, I didn't want to go to the police if I didn't have to, and admit they were right to suspect Gerry. It would be bad enough having to tell my family I'd married a dodgy dealer, without getting myself involved as well. My mother said he was bad news – I couldn't face having to tell her she was right.'

She looked stricken, and Quentin instinctively knew she was telling the truth. 'Sounds as though your mother and my father would make a good pair,' he consoled. 'Anyway, from what you say Gerry wasn't all bad news. He looked after you, didn't he?'

Smiling wanly, Wanda looked at him. 'Yes, of course he did. He loved me.' She stopped and shifted her gaze. 'Despite his goings-on Gerry was a good man. He picked me up when I was in a bad place and helped get me back on my feet.'

Quentin burned to know how and why Wanda had been in a bad place. He couldn't imagine her being anything except as she was now – confident, serene, with a dry wit and a natural charm. Curious as he was, something told him not to push this further.

The silence that fell between them was interrupted by the ringing of Quentin's mobile.

'Hello,' he said in answer to Philmore's greeting. Without giving Philmore time to speak, he asked, 'The bloke who got away – did you find him?'

He switched on the loudspeaker so that Wanda could hear.

'No.' Irritation sounded in Philmore's voice. 'He's like the bloody Scarlet Pimpernel. I can't believe we were so close and he's got away again.'

Wanda frowned. 'That's not our fault. Anyway, how do you know who he is? He had that mask on.'

'We're pretty sure we know,' Philmore replied. 'Whitelaw's the name he's been using in the UK, though he may have changed it by now.'

A thought came to Quentin. 'Wanda, you must have seen his face at some point, didn't you?'

'No. Like I told the police last night, I was only transferred to his car just before we got to the first service station. He wore the mask then. I don't know if he took it off when he was driving. I had to keep down under a blanket, and he said if I moved a muscle they'd kill me.'

'What about the others?' Quentin persisted. 'You didn't see them?'

'No. As soon as I was in the car, they put a hood over my head. They only took it off long enough for you to see me from your window. After we got to where I was held, I was locked in a room. Whenever I saw them, they had stockings over their faces.'

'Must have been awful,' said Quentin.

Philmore's voice came again. 'Listen, you two.'

'Sorry,' Quentin said. 'Why did you ring?'

'Just to tell you I've arranged for a couple of officers to watch your houses for a while.'

'Why?' Wanda sounded alarmed. 'This Whitelaw will know you've got the diamonds now so surely he'll leave us alone?'

'Yes, if he's got any sense, he'll be miles away keeping a low profile.' Quentin said this mainly to reassure Wanda. From the conversations he'd had with the man with the cultured voice he guessed that, if he wanted revenge for Quentin ruining his plans, he could easily send someone else to carry it out.

'Better safe than sorry,' Philmore said. 'You won't even know the officers are there. It's just a precaution.'

Wanda moved over to the window and stared out, as if trying to spot anyone watching the house.

'Quentin,' Philmore continued, 'what we talked about last night–'

With an anxious glance at Wanda, Quentin switched off the loudspeaker. 'I'll get back to you on that,' he said before Philmore had finished the sentence. 'Thanks for the protection.'

He ended the call abruptly. He had questions for Philmore, but he would go to see him alone.

Still preoccupied with the thought of police officers outside, Wanda hadn't seemed to notice the sudden ending of the call. Quentin went to where she stood and slipped his arms around her.

'Don't worry,' he said, 'I'm sure we'll be fine. Whitelaw's got better things to do than trouble himself with us. You've got to hand it to Philmore. He arranged that whole stake-out at short notice, and without being spotted. Very clever.'

'Hmm. How did he do that, exactly?'

'The motel backs onto an old warehouse. They were in a van on the other side of the fence. We couldn't see them behind the bushes.' Quentin remembered his chagrin when he eventually saw the van – it was the same one that had passed him on the way to the rendezvous – white, with black lettering advertising a non-existent building company.

Wanda swung round to face him. 'Philmore couldn't have done it without you, Quentin. You're the one who went to him, told him where to go.'

Quentin felt himself grow. Let Philmore say what he liked. Let anyone say what they liked. Wanda was safe, and she thought he'd done right by her. And surely they were in the clear? The heavies were off their backs, and the diamonds no longer made them a target.

Nevertheless he wanted to see DI Philmore, not just to get the answers he sought but to recap on what they'd agreed last night.

Chapter Thirty-six

Quentin had to wait over an hour to see Philmore, but he learned things that made everything fit together.

'You went without me!' Wanda complained as he sat in her house that evening.

'I thought you needed a break,' he told her. Ignoring her reproachful look, he relayed what he'd found out.

'The guy with the knife – the one who attacked me and broke in here – he's admitted everything, everything he knows, anyway. It took me a while to work it out when I heard his name. Robert Shoesmith.'

This earned him a blank look from Wanda. 'RS. The initials in Gerry's notebook with my uncle's,' he explained. 'He was the boss at the garage where my uncle worked; Mum said it was a common name like Smith. Apparently, he used the name Bob Smith as well as Robert Shoesmith.

I'm guessing he's the Bob who sent the wreath to John's funeral. Shoesmith didn't want the diamonds on the garage premises, so he got John to take the diamonds directly to Gerry. Gerry passed them on to a bent jeweller, who made them into exclusive jewellery for rich customers. They all got their cut. That way, if Gerry or my uncle were found in possession, Shoesmith could deny all knowledge.'

'OK, so Shoesmith didn't want illicit goods at the garage, but when the last lot weren't delivered to Gerry, he must have known they were in your uncle's house. Why didn't he try to get them himself at the time?'

'He got banged up for drink-driving – his third offence – and started his prison sentence a few days after John's funeral, so he didn't have time to recover the diamonds himself. He leaned on Gerry to do it, but when Gerry got sick, Shoesmith didn't trust anyone else while he was inside – too easy to get left high and dry, I guess. Someone in the hierarchy got wind of him creaming off some of the proceeds, and evidently the Inland Revenue were hounding him as well. Anyway, he served six months and when he got out, with no John, no Gerry and no diamonds readily available, he ran off to Spain in a hurry.'

There was silence while Wanda mulled this over. 'What made him come back?'

'He ran out of money. He'd been out of the country for years, so he thought it was safe to sneak back and try to get hold of John's last consignment. It was more valuable than usual, apparently. He was probably going to keep it for himself – he broke in and searched my place, but no luck. Whitelaw, the one with the cultured voice, heads up the operation. He has eyes and ears everywhere. Somehow, he knew Shoesmith was back and that's when things got nasty. Shoesmith was ordered to get the diamonds and hand them over or else.'

Wanda chewed at her bottom lip. Quentin could see she was trying to fit all the pieces together. 'So that's why this Whitelaw got involved now. To get the diamonds and make sure Shoesmith didn't help himself to them. And now Shoesmith's going away – for longer than six months this time, I bet.'

'Yep. He's going away, though Philmore said he's squealing like a pig to get a deal. All he knew was that John brought the goods in and gave them to Gerry. He told Philmore he had no idea where the goods came from, only where John had to pick up or drop off the car he was transporting. Everything else was arranged over his head.'

Wanda put her hand to her forehead. 'But how did John know where the diamonds were hidden?' she asked eventually.

'Don't know,' Quentin admitted, trying to imagine his uncle brazening his way through international borders. 'I suppose they had standard hiding places, or there was some clue left in the car for him to find.'

'Why did Shoesmith take so long to try getting at the goods after the first attempt back in April?'

'Who knows? He spun Philmore some sob story about a sister in Scotland who's at death's door, so maybe that had something to do with it.'

'Hmm. Possible, I suppose. Even criminals have relatives. But how did he know where the cars had to be collected from and how did any proceeds get back to Whitelaw?'

'You'll never believe this – it was so simple. After the jeweller paid for the diamonds, Shoesmith took out John and Gerry's cut as well as his own. He left the rest of the money in a designated locker at the train station. Each time he dropped off the cash there were sealed instructions for the next job.'

'God!' Wanda had turned pale. 'Real professionals, then. I didn't realize what Gerry had got himself into. I don't think he did either.'

Don't be stupid, Quentin wanted to say. Wanda would be naïve if she thought diamond smuggling was for amateurs. And Wanda wasn't naïve.

'All right, perhaps he did know,' Wanda conceded, as if reading his mind. 'But he didn't mean to hurt anyone, especially me.'

This Quentin did believe. In which case it was Gerry who'd been naïve, thinking his shady activities wouldn't affect his wife at some time or other.

'OK, let's see if I've got this right,' Wanda said. 'The bloke Gerry told me about, the one who threatened him and went to prison, that was Shoesmith, your uncle's boss at the garage. His job was to tell your uncle where to collect and deliver the cars, and then collect the money and drop it off. But the diamonds – why didn't Whitelaw send someone else to get them?'

'I asked Philmore about that,' Quentin said. 'Evidently only Shoesmith and Gerry knew that John was the driver. After Gerry died, that just left Shoesmith, but he didn't let on. Probably thought he was safe in prison and planned to get the goods himself after he got out.'

Wanda looked bemused. 'Sounds complicated to me.'

'It's not really, Wanda. A huge organisation, but only a few people knowing each other, at the lower end at least. They couldn't play it much safer than that.'

A rap at the door prevented Wanda from answering. 'It's Colin,' she said jumping up.

Quentin's mouth tightened. His resentment subsided when he recalled the last time he'd seen Colin – being pulled over by traffic police as he'd followed him along the road.

A black look showed on Colin's face when he saw Quentin. 'Thanks a bunch, Quentin. You were supposed to let me know the arrangements. Instead you left me wondering what was going on, so I drove down here and there you were, going off in Wanda's car! Then you didn't answer my call and ignored me when I tried to flag you down. Not enough that I got coshed. Thanks to you, I nearly got done for dangerous driving.'

Resisting the urge to laugh, Quentin said, 'Sorry, Colin. I was so stressed I didn't think to ring you back while I was still at home, and I couldn't stop when I was on the road. I was on the way to the rendezvous, and they said to go alone.'

'Yes, well,' Colin spluttered. 'You ask for my help, then you leave me out of the action. And now you're taking all the credit.' Taking a newspaper from under his arm, he flung it at Quentin.

It was folded so that the headline showed: "Hoard of stolen diamonds recovered by police."

Quentin unfolded it and read the accompanying paragraph:

> *A Greenwich man, Mr Quentin Cadbury, 24, a former solicitor's clerk, helped police to recover a hoard of stolen diamonds. Mr Cadbury discovered the gems, believed to have been smuggled into the country over three years ago, accidentally. When members of the smuggling ring learned of the diamonds' discovery, Mr Cadbury was threatened and his partner was kidnapped. However, Mr Cadbury went to the police and led them to where his partner was being held. Her release was secured, the diamonds recovered, and the thieves apprehended. In an interview earlier today, Mr Cadbury said he was delighted to have helped the police in this case. The detective leading the investigation, DI Philmore of the Metropolitan Police, said Mr Cadbury had shown good judgement and personal courage in helping to track down the kidnappers.*

'You didn't say anything about an interview!' Wanda sounded shocked. 'Why not?'

'It's all about him, that's why,' Colin bleated. 'Good judgement and personal courage! Where did that come from?'

'This story's not even accurate,' Wanda said, wrinkling her nose. 'What are people supposed to make of "when the smugglers learned of the discovery"? How were they supposed to have found out? And I'm your partner now, am I?'

'Sorry, Wanda. I thought if it was worded like that it wouldn't give anything away, and I didn't think you'd want your name in the paper.'

'Worded like that?' Colin snorted. 'Since when have you had any influence over what the papers print?'

Quentin sighed. 'It was Philmore's idea – he's got a contact on the paper. He rang them last night and they agreed to get it into today's editions. I'm sorry I didn't get back to you, Colin. I was too worried about Wanda to think of anything else.'

Colin glared at him. 'So was I, believe it or not.'

'Quentin, why don't you tell Colin what you told me before he got here,' Wanda said.

Her voice had a calming effect, and Quentin shot her a grateful look before repeating what he'd learned. Colin listened, looking surprised in places but not interrupting. When he'd finished, Colin stared at him suspiciously.

'How come you know all this? Suddenly you're Philmore's confidante?'

Quentin shrugged and looked away. 'I asked.'

'He did get a good result and save a policeman's life, Colin,' Wanda said. Then, as if sensing the rising tension between them, she continued, 'You said you *nearly* got done for dangerous driving.'

'Well, I did get done, but after I gave my statement, and as it was my first offence, they said I wouldn't hear any more about it.'

'Good,' said Wanda. 'Now I think we all deserve a drink.'

'Brilliant idea,' Quentin said, pleased that he hadn't had to admit to his uncle being the smuggler, or that Wanda hadn't mentioned that John had lived next door. Time enough to explain if it came out later.

'Did Philmore know why they gave you ten days in that note?' Colin asked, polishing his glasses with the hem of his shirt.

'Well, we thought at the time that Shoesmith didn't write that note himself. When he didn't get the diamonds, someone – Philmore thinks it was Whitelaw – wrote or dictated it. Our cultured friend was getting impatient, and he didn't trust Shoesmith. He wanted to be there to take delivery of the diamonds, but Philmore reckons he was either out of the country or tied up with another job, so he gave ten days. He didn't wait that long though. When he found out about the sign and thought I might be doing a runner with the diamonds, that's when he felt he had no choice but to get personally involved.'

'Well,' Wanda said, 'I don't care why or when they did anything, as long as they don't do it anymore. I'm going to get that drink.'

She swung round and went to the kitchen, returning a few minutes later with a bottle of brandy.

'There's no whisky left, Quentin, so you'll have to put up with brandy,' she said, pouring a measure for each of them. 'A toast, to the end of this horrible business.'

'The end,' Quentin repeated. 'Maybe.'

'What do you mean, maybe?' Wanda demanded.

Silence.

'Come on, man,' barked Colin. 'What *do* you mean?'

Quentin felt the heat rise to his cheeks. Fingering the mole by his ear he said, 'Em, well, DI Philmore said, well, actually asked, that if he could think of a way to catch Whitelaw, would we, I mean, would *I* be willing to help.'

'You, help catch an international criminal?' Colin asked, incredulous. 'How?'

'Well, he thinks the newspaper story... he thinks it might trigger a response from this guy. I mean, it makes it look as though I thwarted all his plans, and it could annoy the bloke enough to do something to give himself away.'

'You mean they're appealing to his ego? A sort of psychological ploy?' Wanda sounded amazed.

'That's the idea. Philmore said if he contacted me, we could work something out if we, I mean *I*, was willing to help.'

'Do their job for them?' Colin snapped. 'Bloody cheek. I hope you said no.'

Putting down her glass, Wanda gave him a knowing look. 'Oh no, I think he said yes, otherwise the newspaper story wouldn't be focused on him. Did you say yes, Quentin?'

'Em, sort of.'

'Sort of? What does that mean?'

'Colin. Let him speak.'

Aware of their gaze on him, Quentin drew a long breath and said, 'I said I would help if I could. Well, why not? It's not as if I've got anything else to do.'

Nobody spoke. Quentin could guess at their thoughts – how on earth did a detective inspector in The Metropolitan Police think an unemployed, inexperienced twenty-four-year-old could help?

'So that's why you got all this information from Philmore,' Colin said after a while. 'In exchange for agreeing to work with him? You mean you'll be set up as bait somehow? A sprat to catch a mackerel.'

'Something like that I should think,' Quentin said.

Wanda looked astounded. 'They can't do that, can they? Put a member of the public in danger? Surely they have people specially trained for that sort of thing.'

'Yes, but Whitelaw knows me now. We might be able to draw him out – set a trap.'

'It won't work,' declared Colin. 'And I can't believe Philmore asked you to help. The other way round, more like.'

Quentin felt Wanda's accusing stare on him. 'Is that it, Quentin? Was it you who said you'd like to help, suggested setting a trap? Is that why he's got people watching our houses?'

Colin looked startled. 'Has he? I didn't notice anyone.'

Without answering Colin, Quentin reddened. 'I just asked him what I should do if the guy contacted me, that's all. He said I should let him know and it sort of went from there.'

'Told you,' Colin said, casting a triumphant look at Wanda.

'I don't see what difference it makes.' Quentin's temper was shortening. 'He's agreed to it provided he gets the go-ahead from the powers that be.'

Colin's contempt was obvious. 'Why should this Whitelaw contact you?' Colin persisted. 'You haven't even seen his face.'

'True. But I'd know that voice anywhere.'

The look on Colin's face left Quentin in no doubt as to what Colin thought of this. Shaking his head Colin said, 'Ridiculous. He'll have more sense than to put himself at risk. It'll never happen.'

Wanda shot Quentin a speculative glance. 'I'm not so sure,' she said. 'Philmore wouldn't have agreed if he thought it wasn't possible, and they've been after this guy for years.'

'But Quentin stumbled into the whole thing by accident, that's all,' Colin spluttered. 'Just because he happens to live in a house where the diamonds were hidden.'

'Accident or not, this bloke's had his ego dented,' Wanda pointed out. 'He was nearly caught. He might want some sort of retribution.'

'Well, you can count me out,' Colin said. 'My head's been bashed enough for one year.' He glugged his brandy, refilled the glass and glugged again.

Wanda put a hand on his arm. 'Steady on, Colin.'

With his hand halfway to his mouth, Colin jerked away, the remaining brandy splashing up onto his glasses. For once though, he didn't bother cleaning them. 'I think I've had enough of this talk. I'm off.'

'Colin—'

'Don't try and sweet-talk me, Wanda. Save it for lover boy here.'

Quentin gasped and swallowed at the same time, brandy burning his throat. 'Running out on us, Colin?' he sneered when he recovered. 'I thought you said you wanted some action.'

Colin banged his glass down on the table. 'Since you came on the scene the only action I get is having my head stitched up.' With that he pushed past Quentin and stalked out.

In the ensuing silence, Quentin could feel Wanda's hostility. 'Oh dear,' he murmured into his brandy.

'Oh dear? You upset my long-standing friend, hit him with a TV aerial, forget to tell him what's going on, then insult him when he's tried to help us and all you can say is "oh dear"?'

Pausing, Wanda took a long, deliberate gulp of her drink, then looked into Quentin's eyes. 'Honestly, you two. If you ask me, you're both as bad as each other. Goodnight, Quentin.'

'But Wanda—'

'Go home, Quentin.'

Seeing that it was useless to protest, Quentin went.

Chapter Thirty-seven

The events of the last few days were still uppermost in Quentin's mind when his landline rang early the next morning.

'Hello, Quentin dear,' said his mother when he answered.

'Mum! How are you? Is Uncle Rupert looking after you?'

'Yes, thank you, but I really want to see you, Quentin. Are you free later today?'

Quentin thought how he would love to meet his mother, have a proper conversation with her, boast about his exploits, preferably without his father who was bound to find some reason to belittle him.

'Er… Did Father tell you about…'

'He said you'd left the office and were working for the woman next door. Some sort of detective work, isn't it? I must say I'm surprised. I thought you were doing well at the solicitors.'

'I was. I know it sounds daft, Mum, giving up a proper job, but I'll be all right, honestly.'

'Your father said you've been broken into. Is that what you're working on, or have you got a client?'

A client. Oh yes, he thought, I'm a right Philip Marlowe. His mother obviously hadn't seen the newspaper article. 'It's a bit complicated, Mum—'

'Oh well, if you're too busy…'

Sensing her disappointment, Quentin made a snap decision. 'Can you come on your own, Mum?'

'Yes, dear. Rupert's taking your father to his club this afternoon and your aunt Winifred's got her WI meeting.

It's your father's reunion tonight but I've decided not to go. I won't know anyone and he'll be too busy to miss me.'

Quentin tried to remember when he'd last seen his mother's sister-in-law. Long before his parents had emigrated, he was sure.

'In that case, please come. I'd love to see you. I'll introduce you to Wanda.'

'Wanda? Is she your boss?'

Quentin grimaced. 'You could call her that, I suppose. More of a partner, really. We're... sort of working together.' Or we were, he added silently.

'All right, dear, if it won't put you out. I've looked up the train times. I could be with you by eleven.'

'Great, Mum. I'll see you then.' Pleased with this outcome, Quentin rang off.

His mind went back to what Philmore had said when they'd discussed any future contact with the man Quentin now thought of as Cultured Voice. He'd agreed to contact Quentin if he came up with a feasible plan.

'He'll probably lie low for a while,' he'd said. 'You may not hear from him until he thinks it's safe to contact you, or you may never hear from him. Perhaps we won't need to do anything more; the news coverage could be enough to trigger him into action, or it might be enough to scare him into lying low permanently. Unlikely though. His type never likes relinquishing power, or money. Let me know if you hear from him, or if you're suspicious about anything. Don't take any risks or do anything without checking with me first.'

Quentin had consented readily. He understood everything Colin had pointed out the previous day and took DI Philmore's warning seriously; but he knew he'd agree to any plan to catch this infamous criminal who'd evaded justice for so long.

Since this whole thing had started, Quentin had been frightened, frustrated, threatened and beaten up. But, he realized now, nothing had taxed his senses more. He'd never felt more exhilarated, more satisfied with the results of his efforts; he'd never felt more alive. Perhaps that was how soldiers felt when they went into battle – the adrenaline rush, the sense of purpose. For the first time he understood that, in spite of the hard time he'd endured, he had enjoyed the challenge.

With his mother's visit imminent, Quentin swept up any clothes that were lying about and bundled them into the wash basket. Grabbing a duster he ran it over the furniture, straightened the throws and moved the picture of Shelagh's wedding to a more prominent position. When he'd finished, he tidied up the kitchen and laid a tray with the Spode teacups. Then he rang Wanda.

'Good morning,' he said tentatively, praying that she'd forgotten, or at least forgiven, his treatment of Colin the day before.

'Is it? I thought it was good yesterday, until you ruined it. There I was, thinking I could have a nice quiet life, and you calmly tell me you've set things up so we might never sleep peacefully in our beds again. Not to mention you upsetting Colin.'

'No hard feelings then?' he said, and was relieved to hear her laugh.

'I'm not sure a quiet life suits me,' she confessed, 'but I wouldn't want to be kidnapped again.'

'Of course you wouldn't, and I'm sure you won't be. I'm sorry if I was rude to Colin, but let's face it, we seem to rub each other up the wrong way, for some reason.' Quentin paused. Wanda knew very well why he and Colin didn't get on, and he wondered if she would acknowledge it.

'I've told you before, you've got no need to be jealous of Colin. He's a friend, a good friend, and that's what he'll stay.'

Reassured, Quentin continued, 'Right. I'll try to be nicer to him in future. Listen, my mother's coming over for the day. Can I bring her to meet you? She thinks we're working together.'

'Yes, or I'll come to yours. Play it by ear.'

'OK. Thanks, Wanda. You're a star.'

* * *

It was just gone eleven when Rosemary Cadbury arrived. Quentin opened the door expecting to see her smiling and eager to see him. Instead, she stood on the doorstep, an accusing look on her face. His gaze dropped to the newspaper that protruded from the canvas bag hanging from her arm.

'I'm so glad you've come,' he said, gesturing her in.

'Are you?' she asked, gazing at him. 'Are you sure you're not too busy helping the police? I thought I was seeing things when I read about it on the train. Why didn't you tell me you were on a big case?'

So they'd run the story again, though it was no longer front-page news, from what Quentin could see of the paper. Probably an update from the previous day. Taking her arm, Quentin led her into the lounge.

'Sorry, Mum. I couldn't say anything before.'

'I understand, Quentin dear. It was just such a shock, seeing it like that and realizing the danger you must have been in.'

Quentin tried to appear modest. 'Well, that's another reason I didn't tell you. I didn't want you to worry.'

'Oh Quentin! I'm so proud of you.' She reached up and flung her arms around his neck. He'd forgotten how small and slight she was. When she drew back, she went on, 'Wait till your father reads this. He'll be proud too.'

'Will he? You mean he won't find fault with me for once?'

There was a heavy silence. 'Let's not talk about him now – tell me how you found these diamonds, Quentin.'

Quentin floundered. He didn't want to admit to finding the diamonds in the house. She was Aunt Josie's sister and

John's sister-in-law – he didn't want to cast aspersions on their characters, even by suggestion.

'I found them in the lock-up,' he said, sticking to the story he'd given the police. 'You know, the garage Uncle John rented, where you left the car for me. They're not very secure, those garages. Anyone could have got in and hidden them.'

'Really? Fancy Josie being so close to a fortune and not even knowing! And your partner was kidnapped – what a fright for her. Is she all right?'

'Yes, she's fine. You'll meet her later.'

His mother gave him a shrewd look. 'Does "partner" mean business partner, or something else?'

Quentin reddened. 'Well,' he began, then stopped, uncertain what to say.

'Something else then, obviously, or if it's not, you'd like it to be. Is there a problem?'

'Not exactly. She's a bit older than me, that's all.'

'Oh yes, your father said something about that.'

'She's a widow,' Quentin told her. 'Her husband died two years ago.'

'Well, age doesn't matter as long as you get on. So, you've been working together to catch this gang. That's why she was kidnapped?'

'Yes,' replied Quentin, pleased that she had made her own assumptions and relieved him of explanations. It didn't matter if she didn't know all the details. 'Let me make you some tea. Sit down, Mum. I won't be long.'

When he returned bearing the tea tray, his mother was examining the seat of the sofa, with part of the throw gathered in her hand.

'What's happened to this?' she asked, fingering a long slash in the material. 'It looks as though it's been cut deliberately.'

'It has. That's what the burglars did during the break-in.'

'Oh yes, your father told me about that. Wretched hooligans, causing damage like this. Why couldn't they just take what they wanted without making a mess of everything!'

Quentin shrugged, praying she wouldn't make a connection between the break-in and the diamonds. She seemed not to as she carried on, 'Anyway, you can't sit on a settee full of holes. Get another one. I'll pay for it.'

Before he could protest, she continued, 'It's nice that you've got a few family photos on show, Quentin. It was a lovely day, wasn't it, Shelagh's wedding? I don't think I've worn that suit and hat since. And you've still got that one of your friend that died. I only met him that once when he stayed with us, but he seemed very nice – so polite and intelligent. Such a waste of a young life.'

Quentin saw her look of concern as her tone changed. 'I know it affected you deeply, Quentin. Things happen, things that can make a difference to the rest of your life. You can't forget them. You just have to learn from them, and learn to live with them.'

For a moment her face had a haunted look, and a rush of affection filled Quentin. He wanted to hug her, tell her how grateful he was for her understanding. He was prevented by a knock at the door. When he answered it, Wanda smiled up at him.

'Hello,' she whispered. 'I thought I'd knock as your mother's here.'

'She only knows what's in the paper,' he whispered back. 'I said I found the diamonds in the lock-up.'

Speaking normally, Wanda said, 'Good morning, Quentin. I thought I'd pop in this morning, as I'm going to the hairdresser's after lunch.'

Seeing his mother's look of surprise when she saw her, he said, 'This is Wanda, Mum.'

Wanda took his mother's hand in both of hers and squeezed it. 'Hello, Mrs Cadbury. It's so nice to meet you at last. Quentin's always talking about you.'

215

'Is he? That's nice. I thought, you know, with us being so far away—'

'I don't think it would matter if you went to the moon, Mrs Cadbury. Quentin would still think the world of you.'

Once again Quentin was amazed by Wanda. From anyone else the words would sound glib, ingratiating, but Wanda had a way of making them seem sincere.

His mother, obviously pleased with this, glanced at Quentin and raised her eyebrows. 'Well,' she said, 'I can see this lady is just what you need, Quentin.' Turning back to Wanda, she continued, 'Thank you, Wanda. How are you feeling? It must have been awful being kidnapped.'

'I wasn't very comfortable, but they didn't hurt me. I was lucky. I was freed quite quickly, thanks to Quentin.'

Quentin glowed as his mother looked at him with adoring eyes. 'I knew I was right to have faith in you, Quentin. I told your father it didn't matter two hoots what job you did, and obviously detective work suits you, and you, Wanda.'

'Thank you, Mrs Cadbury.'

'Please, call me Rosemary. Where do you go to get your hair done? Mine could do with a good cut.'

'I could ring them, if you like, see if they can fit you in?'

'Would you? I'd like that, except I don't want to leave Quentin in the lurch after inviting myself over.'

'That's all right, Mum. We'll have lunch together, then you can go with Wanda and come back for tea. What time do you need to be back at Uncle Rupert's? You can stay the night if you like.'

'Thanks, but I'll have to go back. Your aunt Winifred's arranged a day out for us tomorrow, and we'll need to be up early.'

Just as well, Quentin thought, remembering he didn't have a spare bed, though he would happily have slept on the sofa to accommodate his mother.

'Oh, hello, Magpie,' his mother said as the cat rubbed against her legs. 'I'd forgotten all about you. I see Quentin's looking after you all right.'

Quentin grinned. 'He's my lucky cat. I'm glad he decided to come back here.'

'I'll be off then, Quentin,' Wanda said. 'I'll knock for you about two, Rosemary.'

'Wait a minute, Wanda. Quentin, have you got anything in for lunch?'

Quentin looked sheepish. 'Er, no actually.'

'Don't worry, dear, you weren't expecting me after all. Why don't we all go out to lunch, my treat.'

'That's nice of you, Rosemary,' Wanda said, 'but you and Quentin must have a lot of catching up to do.'

'We'll have time over tea, and I'm sure Quentin would much rather you were with us. That's settled then. Lunch is on me.'

* * *

While his mother and Wanda were at the hairdresser's, Quentin went shopping.

'Special treats for a special cat,' he said when he came back and unpacked the bags.

Magpie sniffed at the pouches, then gave him a look that said they were no more than he deserved. Quentin had just put the last of the shopping away when his landline rang.

'Hello?' he said, wondering if it was DI Philmore with an exciting idea. A groan came to his lips when he heard his father's voice.

'Quentin? Just seen the paper. What's all this then?'

'Hello, Father. It's exactly what it says. That's the case I was working on, but I couldn't say anything.'

'It says your partner was kidnapped.'

'That's right.'

'That nice woman you work for?'

'Yep.'

'And she's all right now?'

'Yes, she's fine.'

Quentin heard his father grunt. 'It says you helped recover some diamonds.'

'I did, yes.'

'So, it's all true then, this story?'

'It is.'

There was a pause, as though his father was trying to think of what to say next. Quentin imagined him, red-faced and disbelieving, frowning as he grasped the receiver.

'I see,' he said eventually. 'Well, that's good, my boy, very good. Looks like you haven't let the family name down after all.'

Quentin felt the rage boil up inside him. He opened his mouth, then flung the handset down before he could say something he knew he would regret. If he sounded off at him, as he'd longed to for years, his mother would bear the brunt of his anger. It wouldn't be long before his father was ten thousand miles away. It wasn't worth rocking the boat.

He decided to ignore the phone if his father rang back. He'd say there was a fault on the line. By the time he and his father met again his anger would have cooled. Or perhaps not. Perhaps when he saw his father, he wouldn't be able to hold back any longer.

'The family name! I'd do anything not to be a bloody Cadbury! Chocky bloody Cadbury!' he fumed to Magpie, remembering his schoolboy nickname. 'If he comes here again, perhaps you'd do me the honour of scratching his eyes out! Better still, bite his tongue off, then we'd all have some peace.'

His mobile rang, and Quentin cursed. His father couldn't get through on the home phone so he was ringing his mobile. His father hardly ever rang mobiles. He glanced at the display but the number was withheld.

'Hello,' he snapped, still irritated by the previous call. All thoughts of his father fled when the caller spoke.

'I hope you don't think you've heard the last of me, Mr Cadbury.'

Chapter Thirty-eight

Quentin held his breath, wondering what to say. Before he could answer, the cultured voice went on, 'I don't take kindly to having my plans disrupted. You've deprived me of an awful lot of money, Mr Cadbury, and got some of my friends arrested. They can be replaced, of course, but it's very inconvenient.'

'You should be with them.' It was out before he could stop it. Not upsetting a bungling fool like his father was one thing, but a cold, calculating criminal, and a kidnapper? 'You should be behind bars where you belong.'

'Now, now, Mr Cadbury. I think you've done enough damage without insulting me. My friends can't expose me because they don't know who I am, not who I *really* am. I'm not worried about that, but I'm very annoyed with you.'

'You won't get away with this, you know. You'll get caught sooner or later.'

A snigger sounded in Quentin's ear. 'You think so? And who's going to do that, you? I wouldn't count on it. You're smart, Mr Cadbury, and possibly quite brave, but I'm smarter. I've been getting away with it, as you call it, for years, and I intend to continue doing so.'

Quentin gasped at the man's brazenness.

'You seem surprised, Mr Cadbury. You can tell your policeman friend not to waste his time trying to track me down. Thanks to you, I'm going to have to disappear for a while, but I'll be back, and when I am, you can expect to hear from me.'

The underlying threat filled the short silence that followed, hitting Quentin's ears and echoing like a drumbeat. He heard the controlled anger in the cultured tones, felt the vibrations of simmering fury that promised to erupt and turn the conversation into a tirade.

'Goodbye, Mr Cadbury, and give my regards to your delectable neighbour.'

The line went dead. Quentin stood staring into space, unable to believe what he'd heard. Head swimming, he went to the cabinet, poured himself a whisky and downed it. Feeling marginally better, he rang DI Philmore.

'Thanks for letting me know,' Philmore said after Quentin had recounted the call. 'If he slips off the radar, we'll just have to wait it out. We've got nothing else to go on at the moment, and I've been told to leave it as it stands. Still, it looks as though the news story did its job. He intends to contact you again at some point. We'll leave the surveillance in place for a few days just in case, and we'll need you and Mrs Merrydrew at the trial when the kidnapping case goes to court, but otherwise that's it for now.'

Philmore cleared his throat before carrying on. 'Our arrangement doesn't give you carte blanche to take the law into your own hands. If you hear from him, contact me before you do anything. Clear?'

'Clear,' Quentin said, and rang off.

* * *

By the time Wanda and his mother returned, Quentin was feeling calmer. When he heard them at the front door he flicked the switch on the kettle, then went to let them in.

'Wow! Look at you two. You look great, Mum.'

Rosemary patted her hair. 'Wanda talked me into having it coloured.'

'Well, it suits you. Yours looks good too, Wanda.'

'Thanks,' Wanda said. 'They do a good job in that salon. Anyway, I'll leave you to have some time together. I need to take Mozart for a walk. See you tomorrow, Quentin. Bye, Rosemary.'

'Goodbye, Wanda. Thank you so much for taking me with you.'

Wanda left them and Quentin stood aside to let his mother pass.

'She's quite a woman, Quentin. I can see why you like her so much.'

Quentin felt the blood rush to his face. *Quite a woman.* Yes, Wanda was that all right. But then, so was his mother. Had she really wanted her hair done, or was it just a ploy to get to know Wanda?

'She reminds me of that film star in some of those old films you used to watch, Mum, you know, the ones with Humphrey what's-his-name.'

'Lauren Bacall? Yes, now you mention it she is like her. It's the voice, mainly. What did you do with yourself this afternoon, dear?'

'I went shopping, Mum, that's all.'

Quentin paused. He had no intention of telling her about the phone call, and he'd decided not to tell Wanda either. Time enough for that if he ever did hear from Cultured Voice again.

'Quentin?'

Bringing his thoughts back to the present, Quentin said, 'I bought some of those nice scones for tea, Mum, with clotted cream like we used to have on Sundays.'

'Oh, Quentin, how lovely that you remember that.'

'Of course I remember. We had some good times together, didn't we?' You, me and Shelagh, he thought, especially when the old man was away.

An hour later, over their cream tea, Quentin sat gazing at his mother. Now she'd recovered from her jet lag and had a new hairstyle she looked better, younger. Her caramel-coloured eyes, the only feature Quentin had inherited from her, looked brighter too. Her unannounced arrival from Australia had been ill-timed, but now the case was solved and he'd had time to spend with her he realized how much he'd missed her.

'I wanted to ask you something, Quentin,' she said, putting her cup aside. 'Are you going to carry on with the detective agency?'

'Em, well, I'd hardly call it an agency yet. We've only just started, and the case we've just worked on – well, it came about accidentally really. But yes, it's what I want to do.'

'An accidental detective, eh? Somehow that suits you, Quentin. Still… I know you've solved one case, a big one, but I should think most cases are pretty mundane. You can't expect to have excitement all the time.'

Quentin laughed. 'I know that, Mum, but working in an office is mundane too. I'll be all right. I've got some money saved until I get on my feet.'

Rosemary looked at her plate. 'But if you spend that, you won't have enough to come over and see us.'

Quentin thought before he answered. 'Don't worry, I'll come. We just need to get more established. It won't take much – a cheap room to rent, some advertising and a computer. If I go in with Wanda, she'll put something in.' He wished he felt as confident as he hoped he sounded. As yet he had no idea whether Wanda would agree to his suggestion. 'Did she say anything about it to you?'

'About what she told your father – taking you in as a partner? No, she didn't talk about her work at all really. But Wanda's got a bit of experience of the world. I should think that's a good thing – you'll be dealing with all sorts of people after all. You'll need someone a bit worldly-wise.'

Quentin smiled. Dear Mum. She still thought he was her innocent little boy.

'Mind you,' Rosemary went on, 'I'm not sure your father will see it that way.'

'He can see it any way he likes. He can't tell me what to do any more,' Quentin said, his mouth set in a determined line.

'No. It's just… you know what he's like.'

'I do, but it's time he accepted that we can't all be like our parents. I mean, I'm like you in some ways, Mum, but I'm nothing like him.'

Holding her gaze, Quentin saw her flush before she looked away. 'Of course you're not.'

Taking her hand, Quentin searched her face. There was something there he couldn't fathom. 'Are you happy, Mum? In Australia? I know you've got Shelagh, Howard and Michael, but… You can always stay here with me, if Dad insists on going back and you don't want to.'

Tears filled her eyes and she blinked. 'I love it there, as a place, and I love being with Shelagh and little Michael. But I miss England, and I worry about you.'

'No need to worry about me. I miss you too, but I'm getting on fine now, really. And I promise I'll come over and see you soon. And' – jumping up, he went to the bureau – 'I've just remembered. I thought you might like this. Now where is it – here we are.'

He held the photo out for her to see.

She seemed to stop breathing. Her face paled and her eyes widened. Snatching the photograph from his grasp, she stared at it. 'Where did you get this?' Her voice was barely audible.

'I found it in the loft.'

'Did you? I thought…' She stopped, as though she couldn't find any words.

Quentin felt uneasy. He'd expected her to be pleased to have a picture of her sister and brother-in-law. 'It's John and Josie, isn't it? It must be. She looks just like you–'

Taking the photo back, Quentin looked at it again. The woman's face radiated love, just as he'd noticed when he'd first discovered it. Shifting his gaze to his mother, his mind went numb. Then thunder echoed round in his head, and when it faded, lightning flooded his thoughts.

'It is you,' he said, amazed. 'It's you and Uncle John.'

'Yes.'

Turning the photo over, Quentin read the words on the back.

Summer, 1979.

The year before he was born.

'S-so?' He gazed at his mother, unable to believe the idea that was taking root. She sat staring straight ahead, as if she was afraid to look at him.

'Yes.'

Quentin sat down. Yes? Did she really mean... 'Y-y-you and... him?'

'Yes. I'm sorry. I didn't want you to find out this way.'

This way? Had she meant him to find out at all? She could have denied it, made something up. She wasn't just telling him she and John had been lovers – why would she admit to that without a reason? There could only be one reason.

'Mum?'

He heard her sigh, saw her fingers clenching and unclenching.

'Your father and I'd been married nearly five years. I thought I loved him. He was forceful even then, but I thought he'd be all right once we'd settled down. My parents said he was a good catch, good career prospects, reasonably well-off, not bad-looking when he was younger. I had Shelagh in the first year. If I hadn't, things might have been different.' She paused, as if wondering whether to carry on. 'I wouldn't have stayed with him after I met John. He asked me to leave Herbert and marry him.'

Quentin gulped. 'So why didn't you?'

'I told you, I had Shelagh to think of, and your father – Herbert I mean. It would have broken him. He doesn't take defeat easily, and he worships Shelagh.'

Chaotic thoughts chased themselves round Quentin's head. He still couldn't say the words that were uppermost in his mind.

'So how did Josie end up being married to John?'

Rosemary's eyes clouded. 'Herbert was away – abroad, with the army. I was due to meet John, but Herbert came home unexpectedly. I asked Josie to meet John, to explain why I wasn't there. She… she fell for him.'

The tremor in her voice told Quentin how painful this was for her. He waited until she went on.

'Before I knew what was happening, they were engaged. Then I found out I was pregnant.'

Quentin held his breath. 'With… me?' he choked.

'Yes. I'd already told her and John I wouldn't leave Herbert, so there was no reason for them not to get together.' She sniffed, and Quentin saw tears gathering again.

'I never told John you were his. I think he guessed, but he never mentioned it, not in words anyway. I caught him looking at you sometimes though. I think Josie may have suspected, but she never said anything. Pretty good of her really, considering they never had any children of their own.'

Quentin flopped back in his chair, letting this sink in. His father wasn't the bullish, blustering dictator he'd suffered all his childhood, not the bigoted, snobbish man who'd marched around the house laying down the law. That person was Herbert Cadbury. And Herbert Cadbury wasn't his father.

He didn't understand the lightness of heart that crept over him. Shouldn't he be shocked, upset that the man he'd thought of as his father for twenty-four years, wasn't? Shocked, yes. Upset? No. All he felt now was confusion tinged with relief.

'I hope you don't think too badly of me, Quentin. It wasn't just a sordid affair. I loved John very much. I've never stopped loving him.'

Quentin wanted to laugh. She'd just given him the best present he'd had in his life so far. 'I don't think badly of you, Mum. I... I'm glad you loved someone, well, someone normal.'

He saw her smile, and she seemed relieved. 'Thank goodness. Actually, when you kept asking all those questions about John, I thought you'd found out somehow. That thing about the family tree didn't ring true.'

Quentin reddened. Unless he poured out the whole story, including finding the money, he would have to keep up the family tree pretence. 'No, I didn't know, but I've given up the family tree idea now. I didn't realize it was so time consuming. Anyway–' he hesitated before carrying on '–it doesn't seem so important now.'

'Doesn't it?'

'No, not now I know who I really am.'

'You don't mind that your father was just a car mechanic?'

Just a car mechanic. Quentin suppressed a grin. 'No, Mum, I told you, I'm pleased.'

His mother's anxiety seemed to lessen. 'Well, I didn't think you'd be pleased exactly, I hoped you'd understand. Herbert doesn't know and I could never tell Shelagh. She wouldn't take it the same way as you. She's like Herbert in some ways.'

'Don't worry, she won't hear it from me. Is that why we didn't see much of John and Josie?'

The harrowed look returned to Rosemary's face. 'Yes. It killed me, seeing him with Josie all those years, but I learned to accept it in the end.'

'And that's why John was hardly ever at family dos? To avoid embarrassment?'

'Yes. It's funny, I thought I'd never tell you, but now you know I feel liberated somehow. I suppose all I've got to worry about is Herbert and Shelagh finding out.'

'Why should they? We'll keep it between us. After all, John and Josie are gone. There's only you and me.'

The words echoed in Quentin's head. Only you and me. But only I know what Uncle John – my father – really was. A charmer, obviously, capable of deception. A car mechanic turned smuggler. A criminal mind perhaps, but a warm-hearted man with faults, and *feelings*, he thought. A man much more like himself than the one he had called Father all his life.

He stared at his mother. She knew nothing of John's dealings, that was obvious. Why would she? As far as he could make out the smuggling business hadn't started until long after they'd stopped seeing each other. And there was no need for her to know, not now, not ever. The news reports had only mentioned the people currently involved with the case, so John's name should never be associated with it, at least not in the papers.

'I can't believe I've told you,' Rosemary was saying, 'but when I saw that photo… I couldn't bear it if anything came between us, Quentin. It was one of the hardest things I've ever done, going away without you. You mean so much to me.'

Quentin swallowed, and he hugged her to him. *You mean so much to me.* Those words would stay with him. Of course she loved him because she had loved John, his father. She loved him still. Instead of the anger he should have felt, the dismay at discovering his family wasn't what he'd been led to believe, he felt enlightened, elated even. It answered so many questions. And it brought him closer to his mother.

When he drew back, he looked into her eyes. 'It's our secret, Mum. It won't come between us. It'll bind us together.'

It was another hour before Quentin remembered the present he'd been keeping for her. Going back to the cabinet, he took out the package.

'I found this down the side of Aunt Josie's chair,' he said, unwrapping the bracelet to show her. 'I thought it might be the one that matches the necklace you told me about.'

His mother's face lightened at the sight of it. 'Yes,' she murmured, taking it and holding it up to catch the light. 'Beautiful, isn't it?' She gazed at it for a moment, then lowered her hands. 'Why don't you keep it, Quentin?'

'What for? It's yours, Mum. Aunt Josie would want you to have it.'

His mother nodded. 'When Herbert first mentioned coming over for this reunion, he wanted to come on his own. I think he was scared that if I came, I wouldn't want to go back. I was determined to come, even if I had to book the flight without him knowing. I didn't want to use our money – he would have found out about it then – so I had the necklace valued.'

Quentin swallowed, a premonition coming to him.

'It's worth a lot of money,' Rosemary went on. 'Real diamonds, apparently. I didn't have to sell it in the end, because Herbert relented and agreed I could come. So you see, Quentin, this probably means the bracelet is valuable too. You could sell it, and the money would help towards your business.'

'Oh, Mum, I don't know what to say.'

'There's no need to say anything. I want you to have it, to have a chance to get started in something you want to do. Mind you, I've no idea how John could afford such expensive gifts. I don't know, and I don't want to know. This house is Josie's legacy to me, but somehow I feel...'

'What?' Quentin prompted.

Averting her eyes, his mother whispered, 'I know the necklace was Josie's, but somehow I feel it's a legacy from John. Josie said he had it made especially, so... you know, it's something he might have given me if we'd been together. Anyway,' she cleared her throat, 'I've had it insured, in my name, just in case.'

In case of what, Quentin wondered. For some reason he couldn't define, he didn't think she meant only in case it was lost or stolen. It was sentimental, a reminder of the man she'd secretly loved as well. But was it also a safety net, a source of independent income if she needed it?

'I… haven't mentioned it to your father,' she said, bringing her gaze back to Quentin.

Quentin felt a little thrill. Of course she hadn't. And now they were co-conspirators, sharing a secret that meant much more than her defending him against bad exam results and not working. She had her own defence, her own chance of escape if she needed it.

'I am happy with Herbert,' she said, as if reading his mind. 'As I said earlier, he's mellowed a bit lately, and my way of life suits me. It's just nice to have a back-up, in case I want to come and see you, or do anything he doesn't agree with, that's all.'

'I understand, Mum, and don't worry, I won't say anything.'

'Good. I'd better be going. As I said, we've got an early start tomorrow, then we're travelling up to see my friend in York for a few days.' She stood up, her gaze lingering on the photo, which lay face up on the table.

'Do you want to take it, Mum?' Quentin asked. Seeing her hesitation, he went on, 'Or I could keep it here if you like?'

'Would you like to keep it, Quentin?'

Quentin picked up the photo and looked at it closely. 'You look so happy together,' he said softly. 'Do I look like him, do you think?'

'A little, yes, not only in looks but in certain mannerisms… You keep it, Quentin. You found it, after all.'

Quentin thought of all the family photos he had seen. The few that included John didn't show him as clearly as this. Suddenly he wanted to keep it. It felt precious, like a gift.

'I don't need a reminder,' his mother said, putting her hand on his arm. 'I've got you.'

'OK,' Quentin croaked, blinking back the moisture that had collected in his eyes.

'That's settled then. Now I must go. We'll get together again before we go back, though. Now you won't forget what you promised, will you? You'll come over as soon as the business is up and running? I don't want to hear that you're too busy to leave it.'

Quentin managed a smile as he helped her with her coat. 'Don't worry, Mum. Business or no business, I'll be there.'

Chapter Thirty-nine

'I was wondering…' Quentin said when he was in Wanda's house the following evening.

The meal she'd cooked for him filled his stomach pleasantly, and the wine gave the room a rosy glow. Mozart lay curled up in the corner, and from where he sat on the floor, leaning against Wanda's chair, Quentin couldn't see the photo of Wanda with Gerry that stood on the sideboard. All of which made it easier to say what he had in mind.

Wanda stopped massaging his shoulders. 'Well?'

Quentin hesitated. 'Just, you know, now the excitement's all over, I was wondering what your plans are.'

'Plans?'

'Yes. Will you carry on living here? Now there's no one next door who's sitting on a fortune, that is.'

There was a pause. 'I don't plan to move. I like it here.'

Another pause. Now, shouted a voice in Quentin's head. Ask her now.

'Right. Only I was thinking I might really become a private investigator – nothing as dangerous as the trouble we've been through, but you know, other people's problems…'

'Other people's problems could be dangerous.'

'Maybe. At least it wouldn't be boring, and we could take the cases we fancy now we can afford to pick and choose.

'We?'

'Well, I'll need a partner.'

'Will you? And where do you intend to operate this business from?'

'We could work from home, but I thought we'd hire a room. What do you think?' He swivelled round to look at her and his breath caught in his throat. She was stunning in a sheer white top and well-cut, blue trousers, her fair hair falling to one side in ripples like a waterfall.

'I'm not sure,' she drawled, as though thinking about it was an effort. 'I think I've had enough excitement for a while. I'd need a break first.'

'We could have a break,' Quentin suggested, mesmerised. 'And– and–'

'And what?'

'You could move in with me if you like.'

Mistake. He knew as soon as he said it.

Wanda's expression was as cool as the day he'd first met her. 'Now why would I want to do that? It's a sweet offer, Quentin, but not practical, and not fair on you.'

Quentin shook his head. What could be fairer than having Wanda to himself?

'You're young, Quentin. If you shackle yourself to me, you'll never meet girls your own age. And you could do something sensible – like finish your degree. You never know – in a few years you really could be QC, QC.' She paused, then as if sensing his antipathy to this suggestion, she carried on, 'Look, we've got a good thing going – let's leave it at that. Keep it simple.'

Keep it simple. The words stung. Love wasn't always simple. Love? It shocked him that he'd even thought it. At least she wasn't ending their relationship, but his earlier diagnosis had been correct. She liked him and was happy to continue – continue what? To use him? No, he wouldn't have it. It would be all or nothing. He pulled away from her hands.

'I'm not good enough for you, is that it? Not so well set up as Gerry. Is that why you married him?'

There was a frosty silence.

'It was one of the reasons, yes,' Wanda said, calmly. 'I've already told you that. I knew he would always look after me, but the main reason was I knew he would never hurt me – emotionally, I mean. I'd been there, done that, and I wasn't prepared to go through it again. You see, Quentin, we're not as far apart as you think. You feel you've been let down by people you thought you could depend on and so do I. We're all products of our past.'

That was true, Quentin realized, but somehow the revelation of his parentage had made him think differently about his past.

Wanda paused, then went on. 'If you're serious about the business partnership though, it might be an idea. We do make a good team, don't we? It could be fun.'

Fun. A year ago, he would have given anything for the choices he had today. To be able to work as and when he wanted, a secure roof over his head, a thrilling sexual partner who made no demands. No responsibility. Fun.

No, he wanted to scream, I want you. Instead, he said, 'About that break you wanted. You could come to Australia with me. We don't have to stay with my parents all the time.'

Wanda smiled. 'Now that *is* an attractive offer. I've got a better idea though. Why don't you go and have a good time. I'll look after Magpie. You might not want to come back. If you do, we'll review the situation, and if you still want to set up the business, we'll take it from there.'

Quentin fell silent. Not coming back wasn't an option. London had been full of surprises and he was keen to stay and see what else it had to offer. It was the ideal place to be a private investigator. But without Wanda?

Perhaps she was right. Having a break didn't mean they were giving up on each other. Or did it? He might come back and find she'd disappeared without a trace. Despite everything they'd done together, she was still an enigma to him. Wasn't that one of the reasons he found her so attractive?

'On second thoughts, it would be daft going to Australia now,' he said. 'It would be better to go in a few months, give Mum something to look forward to. I think I'd like to get the business up and running first. We could still have a break though – shoot off somewhere if you'd like to.'

Wanda raised an immaculate eyebrow. 'I'll think about it.'

'You do that,' Quentin said, his mouth tightening. She was still playing games with him, still thought she could bounce him around like a ball.

He stood up. 'Bye, Wanda.'

'Going so soon?'

'Yes.'

'Don't go.'

He drew a long breath, his knees weak but his resolve holding. 'I'm going.'

Her coolness changed to warmth and she pouted seductively. 'I thought you might stay the night.'

'I don't think so.'

He felt the air between them pulsate. She stood up and snaked her arms around his neck, and he felt the warmth of her body against him.

'Stay,' she whispered, kissing his chin.

The hairs on his arms and the back of his neck seemed to quiver, as though they were being shot through with an electric current. He closed his eyes and felt himself slipping. Her hips pressed against him and her hair tickled his face. He breathed in the heady scent of her, the pure wonder of her, and all reason fled.

Oh, what the hell, he thought as his lips closed on hers.

What the bloody hell.

THE END

If you enjoyed this book, please let others know by leaving a quick review on Amazon. Also, if you spot anything untoward in the paperback, get in touch. We strive for the best quality and appreciate reader feedback.

editor@thebookfolks.com

www.thebookfolks.com

More fiction by the author

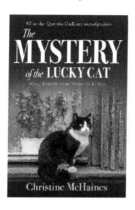

THE MYSTERY OF THE LUCKY CAT

Book #2 in the Quentin Cadbury Investigations

Private detective Quentin Cadbury has his neighbour's recently demised cat in a holdall. Quite why, will be explained. But when he tackles a mugger, his bag gets mixed up with another. This has different contents – some very suspicious goods. Seeing an opportunity to catch a criminal, he blunders into a dangerous situation.

FREE with Kindle Unlimited and available in paperback!

Other titles of interest

THE MISSING AMERICAN
by Julie Highmore

Private detective Edie Fox is more than a little suspicious when a wealthy American turns up to her cluttered backstreet office and hands her a bundle of cash to find his missing cousin. But not enough to turn down the deal. Yet she soon has more on her hands than she bargained for when an old flame enters her life, and the witnesses in her case start giving her the run-around.

FREE with Kindle Unlimited and available in paperback!

THE WIFE'S BOYFRIEND
by Robert McCracken

Charlie Geddis is thrown out by his wife but, determined to win her back, decides to prove that her new boyfriend, a property developer with a lot of assets, is in fact a lying crook. In the process, he becomes embroiled in a web of bribes, infidelities and possibly a murder.

FREE with Kindle Unlimited and available in paperback!

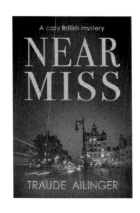

NEAR MISS
by Traude Ailinger

Almost hit by a car, fashion journalist Amy Thornton visits
the driver who ends up in hospital after evading her. She
soon becomes convinced she's unveiled a murder plot. But
it won't be easy to persuade grumpy Scottish detective DI
Russell McCord who is not happy about a young woman
telling him how to do his job. Even if she seems better at it!

FREE with Kindle Unlimited and available in paperback!

Sign up to our mailing list to find out about new releases and special offers!

www.thebookfolks.com

Printed in Great Britain
by Amazon

32380250R00139